# Hammer's THE WARRIOR Slammers

## DAVID DRAKE

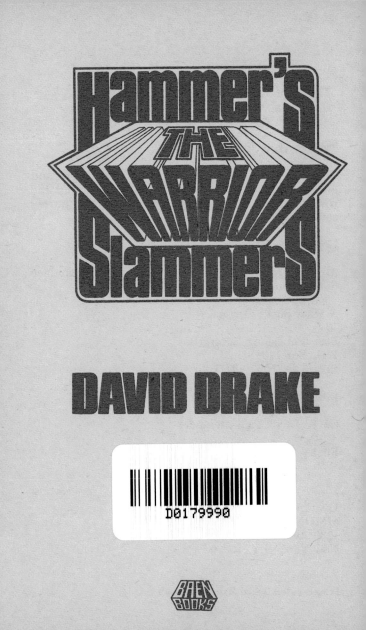

D0179990

BAEN
BOOKS

THE WARRIOR

This is a work of fiction. All the characters and events portrayed in this book are fictional, and any resemblance to real people or incidents is purely coincidental.

A Baen Books Original.

Baen Publishing Enterprises
P.O. Box 1403
Riverdale, N.Y. 10471

ISBN: 0-671-72058-9

Cover art by Paul Alexander

First printing, May 1991

Distributed by
SIMON & SCHUSTER
1230 Avenue of the Americas
New York, N.Y. 10020

Printed in the United States of America

A Slammers' tank was a slope-sided iridium hull whose turret, smooth to avoid shot traps, held a twenty-CM powergun. The three-barreled automatic weapon in the cupola could operate independently or be locked to the same point of aim as the main gun. Eight intake ducts pierced the upper surface of the hull, feeding air down to drive fans in armored nacelles below.

At rest, the tanks sat on their steel skirts. When the vehicles were under way, they floated on a cushion of air pressurized by the fans. At full throttle, the power required to drive a tank was enormous, and the fusion bottle which provided that power filled the rear third of the hull.

The tanks were hideously expensive. Their electronics were so complex and sensitive that at least a small portion of every tank's suite was deadlined at any one time. The hulls and running gear were rugged, but the vehicles' own size and weight imposed stresses which required constant maintenance.

When they worked, and to the extent they worked, the Slammers' tanks were the most effective weapons in the human universe. As *Warrior* was about to prove to two divisions of Republican infantry. . . .

# Baen Books from David Drake

**The Hammer's Slammers Series:**
*Hammer's Slammers*
*At Any Price*
*Counting the Cost*
*Rolling Hot*
*The Warrior*

*Ranks of Bronze*
*The General: Volume I, The Forge* (with S.M. Stirling)
*Old Nathan*
*Lacey and His Friends*
*Vettius and His Friends*
*The Sea Hag*

**The Crisis of Empire Series:**
*An Honorable Defense* (with Thomas T. Thomas)
*Cluster Command* (with W.C. Dietz)
*The War Machine* (with Roger MacBride Allen)

# THE WARRIOR

# PART I

The tribarrel in the cupola of *Warrior*, the tank guarding the northwest quadrant of Hill 541 North, snarled in automatic air defense mode. The four Slammers in Lieutenant Lindgren's bunker froze.

Sergeant Samuel "Slick" Des Grieux, *Warrior*'s commander, winced. He was twenty-one standard years old, and a hardened veteran of two years in Hammer's Slammers. He kneaded his broad, powerful hands together to control his anger at being half a kay away from where he ought to have been: aboard his vehicle and fighting.

The incoming shell thudded harmlessly, detonated in the air.

Sergeant Broglie had counted out the time between the tribarrel's burst and the explosion. "Three seconds," he murmured.

The shell had been a safe kilometer away when it went off. The howl of its passage to an intersection with *Warrior*'s bolts echoed faintly through the night.

"Every five minutes," said Hawes, the fourth man in the bunker and by far the greenest. This was the first time Hawes had been under prolonged bombardment. The way he twitched every time a gun fired indicated how little he liked the experience. "I wish they'd—"

Lieutenant Lindgren's tank, *Queen City*, fired a five-round burst. Cyan light shuddered through the bunker's dogleg entrance. A pair of shells, probably fired from the Republican batteries on Hill 661 to the northeast, crumped well short of their target.

"*Via*, Lieutenant!" Des Grieux said in a desperate voice. He stared at his hands, because he was afraid of what he might blurt if he looked straight at the young officer. "Look, I oughta be back on *Warrior*. Anything you gotta say, you can say over the commo, it's secure. And—"

He couldn't help it. His face came up. His voice grew as hard as his cold blue eyes, and he continued. "Besides, we're not here to talk. We oughta be kicking ass. That's what we're here for."

"We're here—" Lindgren began.

"We're the Federals' artillery defense, Slick," Broglie said, smiling at Des Grieux. Broglie didn't shout, but his voice flattened the lieutenant's words anyway. "*And* their backbone. We're doing our job, so no sweat, hey?"

"Our job . . ." said Des Grieux softly. *Warrior* fired three short bursts, blasting a salvo inbound from the Republicans on Hill 504. Des Grieux ignored the sound and its implications. ". . . is to fight. Not to hide in holes. Hey, Luke?"

Broglie was four centimeters shorter than Des Grieux and about that much broader across the shoulders. He wasn't afraid of Des Grieux . . . which interested Des Grieux because it was unusual, though it didn't bother him in the least.

Des Grieux wasn't afraid of anyone or anything.

"We're here to see that Hill 541 North holds out till the relieving force arrives," said Lindgren.

He'd taken Broglie's interruption as a chance to get his emotions under control. The lieutenant was almost as nervous as Hawes, but he was a Slammers officer and determined to act like one. "The AAD in the vehicles does that as well as we could sitting in the turrets, Slick," he continued, "and unit meetings are important to remind us that we're a platoon, not four separate tanks stuck off in West Bumfuck."

"North Bumfuck fiver-four-one," Broglie chuckled.

Broglie's face held its quizzical smile, but the low sound of his laughter was drowned by incoming shells and the tanks' response to them. This was a sustained pounding from all three Republican gun positions: Hills 504 and 661 to the north, and Hill 541 South ten kilometers southeast of the Federal base.

The Reps fired thirty or forty shells in less than a minute. Under the tribarrels' lash, the explosions merged into a drumming roar—punctuated by the sharp *crash* of the round that got through.

The bunker rocked. Dust drifted down from the sandbagged roof. Hawes rubbed his hollow eyes and pretended not to have heard the blast.

The sound of the salvoes died away. One of the Federal garrison screamed nearby. Des Grieux wasn't sure whether the man was wounded or simply broken by the constant hammering. The unanswered shelling got to him, too; but it made him want to go out and kill, not hide in a bunker and scream.

"Lieutenant," Des Grieux said in the same measured, deadly voice as before. "We oughta go out and nail the bastards. *That's* how we can save these Federal pussies."

"The relieving force—" Lindgren said.

"The relieving force hasn't gotten here in three weeks, so they aren't exactly burning up the road, now, are they?" Des Grieux said. "Look—"

"They'll get here," said Broglie. "They've got Major Howes and three of our companies with 'em, so they'll get here. And we'll wait it out, because that's what Colonel Hammer ordered us to do."

Lindgren opened his mouth to speak, but he closed it again and let the tank commanders argue the question. Des Grieux didn't even pretend to care what a newbie lieutenant thought. As for Broglie—

Sergeant Lucas Broglie was more polite, and Broglie appreciated the value of Lindgren's education from the Military Academy of Nieuw Friesland. But Broglie didn't much care what a newbie lieutenant thought, either.

"I didn't say we ought to bug out," Des Grieux said. His eyes were as open and empty as a cannon's bore. "I said we could *win* this instead of sitting on our butts."

Open and empty and deadly . . .

"Four tanks can't take on twenty thousand Reps," Broglie said. His smile was an equivalent of Des Grieux's blank stare: the way Broglie's face formed itself when the mind beneath was under stress.

He swept an arc with his thumb. The bunker was too strait to allow him to make a full-arm gesture. "That's what they got out there. Twenty thousand of them."

The ground shook from another shell that got through the tribarrels' defensive web. Des Grieux was so concentrated on Broglie that his mind had tuned out the ripping bursts that normally would have focused him utterly.

"It's not just us 'n them," Des Grieux said. Lindgren and Hawes, sitting on ammunition boxes on opposite sides of the bunker, swivelled their heads from one veteran to the other like spectators at a tennis match. "There's five, six thousand Federals on this crap pile with us, and they can't like it much better than I do."

"They're not—" Lieutenant Lindgren began.

Cyan light flickered through the bunker entrance. A Republican sniper, not one of the Slammers' weapons. The Reps had a few powerguns, and Hill 661 was high enough that a marksman could slant his bolts into the Federal position.

The *snap!* of the bolt impacting made Lindgren twitch. Des Grieux's lips drew back in a snarl, because if he'd been in his tank he just *might* have put paid to the bastard.

"Not line soldiers," the lieutenant concluded in an artificially calm tone.

"They'd fight if they had somebody to lead them," Des Grieux said. "Via, anything's better 'n being wrapped up here and used for Rep target practice."

"They've got a leader," Broglie replied, "and it's General Wycherly, not us. For what he's worth."

Des Grieux grimaced as though he'd been kicked. Even Hawes snorted.

"I don't believe you appreciate the constraints that General Wycherly operates under," Lindgren said in a thin voice.

Lindgren knew how little his authority was worth to the veterans. That, as well as a real awareness of the Federal commander's difficulties, injected a note of anger into his tone. "He's outnumbered three or four to one," he went on. "Ten to one, if you count just the real combat troops under his command. But he's holding his position as ordered. And that's *just* what we're going to help him do."

"We're pieces of a puzzle, Slick," said Broglie. He relaxed enough to rub his lips, massaging them out of the rictus into which the discussion had cramped them. "Wycherly's job is to keep from getting overrun; our job's to help him; and our people with the relieving force 're going to kick the cop outa the Reps if we just hold 'em a few days more."

Another incoming shell detonated a kilometer short of Hill 541 North. The Republicans knew they couldn't do serious physical damage so long as the position was guarded by the Slammers' tanks . . . but they knew as well the psychological effect the constant probing fire had on the defenders.

For an instant Broglie's hard smile was back. "Or not a puzzle," he added. "A gun. Every part has to do the right job, or the gun doesn't work."

"Okay, we had our unit meeting," Des Grieux said. He squeezed his hands together so fiercely that his fingers were dark with trapped blood between the first and second joints. "Now can I get back to my tank where I can maybe do some good?"

"The AAD does everything that can be done, Sergeant," Lindgren said. "That's what we need now. That and discipline."

Des Grieux stood up, though he had to bend forward to clear the bunker's low ceiling. "Having the computer fire my guns," he said with icy clarity, "is like jacking off. With respect."

Lindgren grimaced. "All right," he said. "You're all dismissed."

In an attempt to soften the previous exchange, he added, "There shouldn't be more than a few days of this."

But Des Grieux, ignoring the incoming fire, was already out of the bunker.

A howitzer fired from the center of the Federal position. The night outside the bunker glowed with the bottle-shaped yellow flash. There were fifteen tubes in the Federal batteries, but they were short of ammunition and rarely fired.

When they did, they invariably brought down a storm of Republican counterfire.

Des Grieux continued to walk steadily in the direction of *Warrior*; his tank, his home.

Not his reason for existence, though. Des Grieux existed to rip the enemy up one side and down the other. To do that he could use *Warrior*, or the pistol in his holster, or his teeth; whatever was available. Lieutenant Lindgren was robbing Des Grieux of his reason for existence. . . .

He heard the scream of the shell—one round, from the northwest. He waited for the sky-tearing sound of *Warrior*'s tribarrel firing a short burst of cyan plasma, copper nuclei stripped of their electron shells and ravening downrange to detonate or vaporize the shell.

*Warrior* didn't fire.

The Reps had launched a ground-hugging missile from the lower altitude of Hill 504. *Warrior* and the other Slammers' tanks couldn't engage the round because they were dug in behind the bunker line encircling the Federal positions. The incoming missile would not rise into the line-of-sight range of the powerguns until—

There was a scarlet streak from the horizon like a vector marker in the dark bowl of the sky. A titanic crash turned the sky orange and knocked Des Grieux down. Sandy red dust sucked up and rolled over, forming a doughnut that expanded across the barren hilltop.

Des Grieux got to his feet and resumed walking. The bastards couldn't make him run, and they couldn't make him bend over against the sleet of shell fragments which would rip him anyway—running or walking, cowering or standing upright like a man.

The Republicans fired a dozen ordinary rounds. Tank tribarrels splashed each of the shells a fraction of a second after they arched into view. The powerguns' snarling dazzle linked the Federal base for an instant to orange fireballs which faded into rags of smoke. There were no more ground-huggers.

An ordinary shell was no more complex than a hand grenade. Ground-hugging missiles required sophisticated electronics and a fairly complex propulsion system. There weren't many of them in the Rep stockpiles.

Ground-huggers would be as useless as ballistic projectiles *if* Lindgren used his platoon the way tanks should be used, as weapons that sought out the enemy instead of cowering turret-down in defilade.

*Blood and Martyrs!* What a way to fight a war.

The top of Hill 541 North was a barren moonscape. The bunkers were improvised by the troops themselves with shovels and sandbags. A month ago, the position had been merely the supply point for a string of Federal outposts. No one expected a siege.

But when the Republicans swept down in force, the outposts scrambled into their common center,

541N. Troops dug furiously as soon as they realized that there was no further retreat until Route 7 to the south was cleared from the outside.

*If* route 7 was cleared. Task Force Howes, named for the CO of the Slammers 2nd Battalion, had promised a link-up within three days.

Every day for the past two weeks.

A sniper on Hill 661, twelve kilometers away, fired his powergun. The bolt snapped fifty meters from Des Grieux, fusing the sandy soil into a disk of glass which shattered instantly as it cooled.

Kuykendall, *Warrior*'s driver, should be in the tank turret. If Des Grieux had been manning the guns, the sniper would have had a hot time of it . . . but Des Grieux was walking back from a dick-headed meeting, and Kuykendall wasn't going to disobey orders to leave the tribarrel on Automatic Air Defense and not, under any circumstances, to fire the 20 CM main gun since ammunition was scarce.

The garrison of Hill 541N, the Slammers included, had the supplies they started the siege with. Ground routes were blocked. Aerial resupply would be suicide because of the Rep air-defense arsenal on the encircling hills.

The sniper fired again. The bolt hit even farther away, but he was probably aiming at Des Grieux anyhow. Nothing else moved on this side of the encampment except swirls of wind-blown sand.

A shell fragment the size of a man's palm stuck up from the ground. It winked jaggedly in the blue light of the bolt.

*Warrior* was within a hundred meters. Des Grieux continued to walk deliberately.

The hilltop's soil blurred all the vehicles and installations into identical dinginess. The dirt was a

red without life, the hue of old blood that had dried
and flaked to powder.

The sniper gave up. A gun on 541S coughed a
shell which Broglie's *Honey Girl* blew from the sky
a moment later.

Every five minutes; but not regularly, and twice
the Reps had banged out more than a thousand
rounds in a day, some of which inevitably got
through. . . .

"That you, Slick?" Kuykendall called from the
*Warrior*'s cupola.

"Yeah, of course it's me," Des Grieux replied. He
stepped onto a sandbag lip, then hopped down to
*Warrior*'s back deck. His boots clanked.

The tanks were dug in along sloping ramps. Soil
from the trenches filled sandbag walls rising above
the vehicles' cupolas. Lieutenant Lindgren was afraid
that powerguns from 661—and the Reps had multi-
barreled calliopes to provide artillery defense—would
rake the Slammers' tanks if the latter were visible.

Des Grieux figured the answer to *that* threat was
to kick the Reps the hell off Hill 661. By now,
though, he'd learned that the other Slammers were
just going to sigh and look away when he made a
suggestion that didn't involve waiting for somebody
else to do the fighting.

Kuykendall slid down from the cupola into the
fighting compartment. She was a petite woman,
black-haired and a good enough driver. To Des
Grieux, Kuykendall was a low-key irritation that he
had to work around, like a burr in the mechanism
that controlled his turret's rotation.

A driver was a necessary evil, because Des Grieux
couldn't guide his tank and fight it at the same time.
Kuykendall took orders, but she had a personality of

her own. She wasn't a mere extension of Des Grieux's will, and that made her more of a problem than someone blander though less competent would have been.

Nothing he couldn't work around, though. There *was* nothing Des Grieux couldn't work around, if his superiors just gave him the chance to do his job.

"Anything new?" Kuykendall asked.

Des Grieux stood on his seat so that he could look out over the sandbags toward Hill 661. "What d' you think?" he said. He switched the visual display on his helmet visor to infra-red and cranked up the magnification.

The sniper had gone home. Nothing but ripples in the atmosphere and the cooler blue of trees transpiring water they sucked somehow from this Lord-blasted landscape.

Des Grieux climbed out of the hatch again. He shoved a sandbag off the top layer. *The bastard would be back, and when he was . . .*

He pushed away another sandbag. The bags were woven from a coarse synthetic that smelled like burning tar when it rubbed.

"We're not supposed to do that," Kuykendall said from the cupola. "A lucky shot could put the tribarrel out of action. That'd hurt us a lot worse than a hundred dead grunts does the Reps."

"They don't have a hundred powerguns," Des Grieux said without turning around. He pushed at the second-layer sandbag he'd uncovered but that layer was laid as headers. The bags to right and left resisted the friction on their long sides. "Anyway, it's worth something to me to give a few of those cocky bastards their lunch."

Hawes' *Susie Q* ripped the sky. Des Grieux

dropped into a crouch, then rose again with a feeling of embarrassment. He knew that Kuykendall had seen him jump.

It wasn't flinching. If *Warrior*'s AAD sensed incoming from Hill 661, Des Grieux would either duck instantly—or have his head shot off by the tribarrel of his own tank. The fire-direction computers didn't care if there was a man in the way when it needed to do its job.

Des Grieux liked the computer's attitude.

He lifted and pushed, raising his triceps muscles into stark ridges. Des Grieux was thin and from a distance looked frail. Close up, no one noticed anything but his eyes; and there was no weakness in them.

The sandbag slid away. The slot in *Warrior*'s protection gave Des Grieux a keyhole through which to rake Hill 661 with his tribarrel. He got back into the turret. Kuykendall dropped out of the way without further comment.

"You know . . ." Des Grieux said as he viewed the enemy positions in the tribarrel's holographic sight. *Warrior*'s sensors were several orders of magnitude better than those of the tankers' unaided helmets. "The Reps aren't much better at this than these Federal pussies we gotta nursemaid."

"How d'ye mean?" Kuykendall asked.

Her voice came over the intercom channel. She'd slipped back into the driver's compartment. Most drivers found the internal hatch too tight for use in anything less than a full buttoned-up emergency.

"They've got calliopes up there," Des Grieux explained as he scanned the bleak silence of Hill 661. The Republican positions were in defilade. Easy enough to arrange from their greater height.

"If it was me," Des Grieux continued, "I'd pick my time and roll 'em up to direct-fire positions. They'd kick the cop outa this place."

"They're not going to bet three-CM calliopes against tank main guns, Sarge," Kuykendall said carefully.

"They would if they had any balls," Des Grieux said. His voice was coldly judgmental, stating the only truth there was. He showed no anger toward those who were too stupid to see it. "Dug in like we are, they could blow away the cupolas and our sensor arrays before we even got the main guns to bear. A calliope's no joke, kid."

He laughed harshly. "Wish they'd try, though. I can hip-shoot a main gun if I have to."

"There's talk they're going to try t' overrun us before Task Force Howes relieves us," Kuykendall said with the guarded nonchalance she always assumed when talking to the tank commander.

Des Grieux's two years in the Slammers made him a veteran, but he was scarcely one of the longest-serving members of the regiment. His drive, his skill with weapons, and the phenomenal ruthlessness with which he accomplished any task set him gave Des Grieux a reputation beyond simple seniority.

"There's talk," Des Grieux said coldly. *Nothing moved on Hill 661.* "There's been talk. There's been talk Howes is going to get his thumbs out of his butt and relieve us, too."

The tribarrel roused, swung, and ignited the sky with a four-round burst of plasma. A shell from Hill 504 broke apart without detonating. The largest piece of casing was still a white glow when it tumbled out of sight in the valley below.

The sky flickered to the south as well, but at such

a distance that the sounds faded to a low rumble.
Task Force Howes still slugged it out with the
Republicans who defended Route 7. Maybe they
were going to get here within seventy-two hours.

And maybe Hell was going to freeze over.

Des Grieux scanned Hill 661, and nothing moved.

The only thing Des Grieux knew in the instant he
snapped awake from a sound sleep was that it was
time to earn his pay.

Kuykendall looked down into the fighting compartment from the commander's seat. "Sarge?" she
said. "I—" and broke off when she realized Des
Grieux was already alert.

"Get up front 'n drive," Des Grieux ordered
curtly. "It's happening."

"It's maybe nothing," the driver said, but she
knew Des Grieux. As Kuykendall spoke, she swung
her legs out of the cupola. Hopping from the cupola
and past the main gun was the fastest way to the
driver's hatch in the bow. The tank commander
blocked the internal passage anyway as he climbed
up to his seat.

The Automatic Air Defense plate on *Warrior's*
control panel switched from yellow, standby, to red.
The tribarrel rotated and fired. Des Grieux flicked
the plate with his boot toe as he went past, discon-
necting the computer-controlled defensive fire. He
needed *Warrior's* weapons under his personal direction now that things were real.

When the siege began, Lieutenant Lindgren
ordered that one member of each two-man tank crew
be on watch in the cupola at every moment. What
the tankers did off-duty, and where they slept, was
their own business.

Most of the off-duty troops slept beneath their vehicles, entering the plenum chamber through the access plate in the steel skirts. The chambers were roomy and better protection than anything cobbled together by shovels and sandbags could be. The only problem was the awareness before sleep came that the tank above you weighed 170 tonnes . . . but tankers tended not to be people who thought in those terms.

Lindgren insisted on a bunker next to his vehicle. He was sure that he would go mad if his whole existence, on-duty and off, was bounded by the steel and iridium shell of his tank.

Des Grieux went the other way around. He slept in the fighting compartment while his driver kept watch in the cupola above. The deck was steel pressed with grip rosettes. He couldn't stretch out. His meter-ninety of height had to twist between the three-screen control console and the armored tube which fed ammunition to the autoloading twenty-CM main gun.

Nobody called the fighting compartment a comfortable place to sleep; but then, nobody called Des Grieux sane, either.

A storm of Republican artillery fire screamed toward Hill 541N. Some of the shells would have gotten through even if Des Grieux had left *Warrior* in the defensive net. That was somebody else's problem. The Reps didn't have terminally-guided munitions that would target the Slammers' tanks, so a shell that hit *Warrior* was the result of random chance.

You had to take chances in war; and anyway, *Warrior* oughta shrug off anything but a heavy-caliber armor-piercing round with no more than superficial damage.

Kuykendall switched her fans on and brought them up to speed fast with their blades cutting the airstream at minimum angle. *Warrior* trembled with what Des Grieux anthropomorphicized as eagerness, transferring his own emotions to the mindless machine he commanded.

A Slammers' tank was a slope-sided iridium hull whose turret, smooth to avoid shot traps, held a twenty-CM powergun. The three-barreled automatic weapon in the cupola could operate independently or be locked to the same point of aim as the main gun. Eight intake ducts pierced the upper surface of the hull, feeding air down to drive fans in armored nacelles below.

At rest, the tanks sat on their steel skirts. When the vehicles were under way, they floated on a cushion of air pressurized by the fans. At full throttle, the power required to drive a tank was enormous, and the fusion bottle which provided that power filled the rear third of the hull.

The tanks were hideously expensive. Their electronics were so complex and sensitive that at least a small portion of every tank's suite was deadlined at any one time. The hulls and running gear were rugged, but the vehicles' own size and weight imposed stresses which required constant maintenance.

When they worked, and to the extent they worked, the Slammers' tanks were the most effective weapons in the human universe. As *Warrior* was about to prove to two divisions of Republican infantry. . . .

"Back her out!" Des Grieux ordered. If he'd thought about it, he would have sounded a general alarm because he *knew* this was a major attack, but he had other things on his mind besides worrying about people he wasn't planning to kill.

"Booster," Des Grieux said, switching on the artificial intelligence which controlled the tank's systems. "Enemy activity, one kay, now!"

*Warrior* shuddered as Kuykendall increased the fan bite. Sandy soil mushroomed from the trench walls and upward as the hull lifted and air leaked beneath *Warrior*'s skirts. Des Grieux's direct vision blurred in a gritty curtain, but the data his AI assembled from remote sensors was sharp and clear in the upper half of his helmet visor.

The ground fell away from the top of Hill 541 North in a 1:3 slope, and the tank positions were set well back from the edge of the defenses. Even when *Warrior* backed from her trench, Des Grieux would not be able to see the wire and minefields which the garrison had laid at mid-slope to stop an enemy assault.

Ideally, the tanks would have access to the Slammers' own remote sensors. Conditions were rarely ideal, and on Hill 541N they never even came close. Still, the Federals had emplaced almost a hundred seismic and acoustic sensors before the Republicans tightened the siege. Most of the sensors were in the wire, but they'd dropped a few in the swales surrounding the hill, a kilometer or so out from the hilltop.

Acoustic sensors gathered the sound of voices and equipment, while seismic probes noted the vibration feet and vehicles made in the soil. The information, flawed by the sensors' relative lack of sophistication and the haphazard way the units were emplaced, was transmitted to the hilltop for processing.

Des Grieux didn't know what the Feds did with

the raw data, but *Warrior*'s AI turned it into a clear image of a major Republican attack.

There were two thrusts, directed against the east and the northwest quadrants of the Federal positions. The slope at those angles was slightly steeper than it was to the south, but the surface fell in a series of shallow steps that formed dead zones, out of the fire from hilltop bunkers.

A siren near the Federal command post wound up. Its wail was almost lost in the shriek of incoming.

The Reps had ten or a dozen shells in the air at any one time. The three tanks still working air defense slashed arcs across the sky. Powerguns detonated much of the incoming during its fifteen-second flight time, but every minute or so a round got through.

Most of the hits raised geysers of sand from the hilltop. Only occasionally did a bunker collapse or a shellburst scythe down troops running toward fighting positions in the forward trenches, but even misses shook the defenders' morale.

Booster thought the attack on the northwest quadrant was being made by a battalion of infantry, roughly 500 troops, behind a screen of sappers no more than a hundred strong. The eastern thrust was of comparable size, but even so it seemed a ludicrously small force to throw against a garrison of over 5,000 men.

That was only the initial assault; a larger force would get in its own way during the confusion of a night attack. Booster showed several additional battalions and a dozen light armored vehicles waiting in reserve among the yellow-brown scrub of the valleys where streams would run in the wet season.

As soon as the leading elements seized a segment

of the outer bunker line in a classic infiltration assault, the Republican support troops would advance in good order and sweep across the hilltop. There was no way in hell that the Federal infantry, demoralized by weeks of unanswerable shelling, was going to stop the attack.

They didn't have to. Not while Des Grieux was here.

"Clear visor," Des Grieux said. He'd seen what the sensors gave him, and he didn't need the display anymore. He tugged the crash bar, dropping his seat into the fighting compartment and buttoning the hatch shut above him. *Warrior's* three holographic screens cast their glow across conduits and the breech of the squat main gun.

"Driver, advance along marked vector."

Default on the left-hand screen was a topographic display. Des Grieux drew his finger across it in a curving arc, down from the hilltop in a roughly northwestward direction. The AI would echo the display in Kuykendall's compartment. A trackway, not precisely a road but good enough for the Rep vehicles and sure as *hell* good enough for *Warrior*, wound north from the swale in the direction of the Republican firebase on Hill 504.

"Gun it!" Des Grieux snarled. "Keep your foot on the throttle, bitch!"

It didn't occur to him that there was another way to give the order. All Des Grieux knew was that *Warrior* had to move as he desired, and the commander's will alone was not enough to direct the vehicle.

Kuykendall touched *Warrior* to the ground, rubbing off some of the backing inertia against the sand. She rotated the attitude control of the drive fans, angling the nacelles so that they thrust *Warrior* forward as well as lifting it again onto the air cushion.

The huge tank slid toward the edge of the encampment in front of a curling billow of dust. Size made the vehicle seem to accelerate slowly.

"Oyster Leader to Oyster Two," said Lieutenant Lindgren over the platoon's commo channel. "Hold your position. Break. Oyster four—" Hawes "—move up to support Oyster Two. Over."

The note of *Warrior*'s fans changed. Massive inertia would keep the vehicle gliding forward for a hundred meters, but the sound meant Kuykendall was obeying the platoon leader's orders.

"Driver!" Des Grieux shouted. "Roll it! *Now!*"

Kuykendall adjusted her nacelles obediently. *Warrior* slid on momentum between a pair of bunkers as the fans swung to resume their forward thrust.

The Federal positions were dugouts covered by transportation pallets supported by a single layer of sandbags. Three or four additional sandbag layers supplied overhead protection, though a direct hit would crumple the strongest of them. The firing slits were so low that muzzle blasts kicked up sand to shroud the red flashes of their machine guns.

*Warrior*'s sensors fed the main screen with a light-enhanced 120° arc to the front. The tank's AI added in a stereoscopic factor to aid depth perception which the human brain ordinarily supplied in part from variations in light intensity.

The screen provided Des Grieux with a clear window onto the Republican attack. A two-man buzz-bomb team rose into firing position at the inner edge of the wire. Instead of launching their unguided rockets into the nearest bunkers, they had waited for the tank they expected.

Des Grieux expected them also. He stunned the night with a bolt from *Warrior*'s main gun.

Des Grieux used his central display for gunnery. It had two orange pippers, a two-CM ring and a one-CM dot for the main gun and tribarrel respectively. The sensor array mounted around *Warrior*'s cupola gave Des Grieux the direction in which to swing his weapon. As soon as his tank rose into a hull-down position that cleared the twenty-CM powergun, he toggled the foot trip.

Because the tribarrel was mounted higher, Des Grieux could have killed the Reps a moment sooner with the automatic weapon; but he wanted the enemy's first awareness of *Warrior* to be the cataclysmic blast of the tank's main gun.

The cyan bolt struck one of the Rep team squarely and converted his body into a ball of vapor so hot that its glowing shockwave flung the other victim's torso and limbs away in separate trajectories. The secondary explosion of the anti-tank warheads was lost in the plasma charge's flash*crash*.

Honking through its intakes, *Warrior* thundered down on the Republican attack.

Guns in dozens of Federal bunkers fired white tracers toward the perimeter of mines and wire. Heavy automatic weapons among the Republican support battalions answered with chains of glowing red balls.

The Federal artillerymen in the center of Hill 541 North began slamming out their remaining ammunition in the reasonable view that unless this attack was stopped, there was no need for conservation. Because of their hilltop location, the guns could not bear on the sappers. To reach even the Republican support troops, they had to lob their shells in high, inaccurate arcs. The pair of calliopes on Hill 661 burst many of the Federal rounds at the top of their trajectory.

Instead of becoming involved in firefights, the Rep sappers did an excellent job of pathclearing for the main assault force. A few of the sappers fell, but their uniforms of light-absorbent fabric made them difficult targets even now that Federal starshells popped to throw wavering illumination over the scene.

A miniature rocket dragged its train of explosive across the perimeter defenses. The line exploded with a yellow flash and a sound like a door slamming. Sand and wire flew to either side. Overpressure set off a dozen anti-personnel mines to speckle the night.

There were already a dozen similar gaps in the perimeter. An infiltration team had wormed through the defenses before the alarm went off. One of its members hurled a satchel charge into a bunker, collapsing it with a flash and a roar.

*Warrior* drove into the wire. Bullets, some of them fired from the Federal bunkers, pinged harmlessly on the iridium armor. A buzzbomb trailing sparks and white smoke snarled toward the tank's right flank. Five meters out, the automatic defense system along the top edge of *Warrior's* skirts banged. Its spray of steel pellets ripped the buzzbomb and set off the warhead prematurely.

The tank rang like a bell when its defensive array fired, but the hollow *whoomp* of the shaped-charge warhead was lost in the battle's general clamor. Shards of buzzbomb casing knocked down a sapper. He thrashed through several spasms before he lay still.

*Warrior* passed the Federal minefield in a series of sprouting explosions and the spang of fragments which ricocheted from the skirts. The pressure of air within the tank's plenum chamber was high enough to detonate mines rigged to blow off a man's foot. They clanged harmlessly as a tocsin of the huge vehicle's passage.

The tank's bow slope snagged loops of concertina wire which stretched and writhed until it broke. Republican troops threw themselves down to avoid the unexpected whips of hooked steel. Men shouted curses, although the gap *Warrior* tore in the perimeter defenses was broad enough to pass a battalion in columns of sixteen.

Des Grieux ignored the sappers. They could cause confusion within the bunker line, but they were no threat to the ultimate existence of the Federal base. The assault battalion, and still more the thousands of Republican troops waiting in reserve, were another matter.

*Warrior* had two dual-capable gunnery joysticks. Most tank commanders used only one, selecting tribarrel or main gun with the thumbswitch. Des Grieux shot with both hands.

He'd pointed the main gun 30° to starboard in order to blast the team of tank killers. Now his left hand swung the cupola tribarrel a few degrees to port. He didn't change either setting again for the moment. Not even Des Grieux's degree of skill permitted him to aim two separate sights from a gun platform travelling at fifty KPH and still accelerating.

But he could fire them, alternately or together, whenever *Warrior*'s forward motion slid the pippers over targets.

The tribarrel caught a squad moving up at a trot

to exploit pathways the sappers had torn. The Republicans were so startled by the bellowing monster that they forgot to throw themselves down.

Three survivors turned and fired their rifles vainly as the tank roared past fifty meters away. The rest of the squad were dead, with the exception of the lieutenant leading them. He stood, shrilling insane parodies of signals on his whistle. The tribarrel had blown off both his arms.

Des Grieux's right thumb fired the main gun at another ragged line of Republican infantry. The twenty-CM bolt gouged the earth ten meters short, but its energy sprayed the sandy soil across the troops as a shower of molten glass. One of the victims continued to pirouette in agony until white tracers from a Federal machine gun tore most of his chest away.

Fires lighted by the cyan bolts flared across the arid landscape.

Hawes in *Susie Q* tried to follow. His tribarrel slashed out a long burst. Sappers jumped and ran. Two of them stumbled into mines and upended in sprays of soil.

*Susie Q* eased forward at a walking pace. Hawes' driver was proceeding cautiously under circumstances where speed was the only hope of survival. Halfway to the wire, a buzzbomb passed in front of the tank. It was so badly aimed that the automatic defense system didn't trip.

*Susie Q* braked and began to turn. Hawes sprayed the slope wildly with his tribarrel. A stray bolt blew a trench across *Warrior*'s back deck.

A Rep sapper ran toward *Susie Q*'s blind side with a satchel charge in his hands. The automatic defense system blasted him when he was five yards away, but two more buzzbombs arced over his crumpled body.

The section of the ADS which had killed the sapper was out of service until its strip charge could be replaced. The rockets hit, one in the hull and the other in the center of *Susie Q*'s turret. Iridium reflected the warheads' white glare.

The tank grounded violently. The thick skirt crumpled as it bulldozed a ripple of soil. *Susie Q*'s status entry on *Warrior*'s right-hand display winked from solid blue to cross-hatched, indicating that an electrical fault had depowered several major systems.

Des Grieux ignored the read-out. He had a battle to win.

Under other circumstances, Des Grieux would have turned to port or starboard to sweep up one flank of the assault wave, but the Republican reserves were too strong. Turning broadside to their fire was a quick way to die. Winning—surviving—required him to keep the enemy off-balance.

*Warrior* bucked over the irregular slope, but the guns were stabilized in both elevation and traverse. Des Grieux lowered the hollow pipper onto the swale half a kilometer away, where the Republican supports sheltered.

Several of the armored cars there raked the tank with their automatic cannon. Explosive bullets whanged loudly on the iridium.

Des Grieux set *Warrior*'s turret to rotate at 1° per second and stepped on the foot-trip. The main gun began to fire as quickly as the system could reload itself. Cyan hell broke loose among the packed reserves.

The energy liberated by a single twenty-CM bolt was so great that dry brush several meters away from

each impact burst into flames. Infantrymen leaped
to their feet, colliding in wild panic as they tried to
escape the sudden fires.

An armored car took a direct hit. Its diesel fuel
boomed outward in a huge fireball which engulfed
the vehicles to either side. Crewmen baled out of
one of the cars before it exploded. Their clothes
were alight, and they collapsed a few steps from
their vehicle.

The other car spouted plumes of multi-colored
smoke. Marking grenades had ignited inside the turret hatch, broiling the commander as he tried to
climb past them. Ammunition cooked off in a flurry
of sparks and red tracers.

While *Warrior*'s main gun cycled its twenty-round
ready magazine into part of the Republican reserves,
Des Grieux aimed his tribarrel at specific targets to
port. The tank's speed was seventy KPH and still
accelerating. When the bow slid over the slope's natural terracing, it spilled air from the plenum chamber. Each time, *Warrior*'s 170 tonnes slammed onto
the skirts with the inevitability of night following
day.

Though the tribarrel was stabilized, the crew was
not. The impacts jounced Des Grieux against his seat
restraints and blurred his vision.

It didn't matter. Under these circumstances, Des
Grieux scarcely needed the sights. He *knew* when
the pipper covered a clot of infantry or an armored
car reversing violently to escape what the crew suddenly realized was a kill zone.

Two-CM bolts lacked the authority of *Warrior*'s
main gun, but Des Grieux's short bursts cut with
surgical precision. Men flew apart in cyan flashes.
The thin steel hulls of armored cars blazed white

for an instant before the fuel and ammunition inside caught fire as well. Secondary explosions lit the night as tribarrel bolts detonated cases of rocket and mortar warheads.

*Warrior*'s drive fans howled triumphantly.

Behind the rampaging tank, Rep incoming flashed and thundered onto Hill 541 North. Only one tribarrel from the Federal encampment still engaged the shells.

Federal artillery continued to fire. A "friendly" round plunged down at a 70° angle and blew a ten-meter hole less than a tank's length ahead of *Warrior*. Kuykendall fought her controls, but the tank's speed was too high to dodge the obstacle completely. *Warrior* lurched heavily and rammed some of the crater's lip back to bury the swirling vapors of high explosive.

A score of Rep infantry lay flat with their hands pressing down their helmets as if to drive themselves deeper into the gritty soil. *Warrior* plowed through them. The tank's skirt was nowhere more than a centimeter off the ground. The victims smeared unnoticed beneath the tank's weight.

*Warrior* boomed out of the swale and proceeded up the curving track toward Hill 504.

The main gun had emptied its ready magazine. Despite the air conditioning, the air within *Warrior*'s fighting compartment was hot and bitter with the gray haze trembling from the thick twenty-CM disks which littered the turret basket. The disks were the plastic matrices that had held active atoms of the powergun charge in precise alignment. Despite the blast of liquid nitrogen that cleared the bore after each shot, the empties contained enormous residual heat.

Des Grieux jerked the charging lever, refilling the ready magazine from reserve storage deep in *Warrior's* hull. The swale was blazing havoc behind them. Silhouetted against the glare of burning brush, fuel, and ammunition, Republican troops scattered like chickens from a fox.

Ten kilometers ahead of the tank, the horizon quivered with the muzzle flashes of Republican artillery.

"Now we'll get those bastards on 504!" Des Grieux shouted—

And knew, even as he roared his triumph, that if he tried to smash his way into the Republican firebase, he would die as surely and as vainly as the Rep reserves had died when *Warrior* ripped through the center of them

So long as Des Grieux was in the middle of a firefight, his brain had disconnected the stream of orders and messages rattling over the commo net. Now the volume of angry sound overwhelmed him: *"Oyster Two, report! Break! Oyster four, are you—"*

The voice was Broglie's rather than that of Lieutenant Lindgren. The Lord himself had nothing to say just now that Des Grieux had time to hear. Des Grieux switched off the commo at the main console.

"Booster," he ordered the artificial intelligence, "enemy defenses in marked area."

Des Grieux's right index finger drew a rough circle bounded by Hill 504 and *Warrior's* present position on the topographic display. "Best esti—"

An all-terrain truck snorted into view on the main screen. Des Grieux twisted his left joystick violently but he couldn't swing the tribarrel to bear in the moment before the tank rushed by in a spray of sand. The truck's crew jumped from both sides of the cab, leaving their vehicle to careen through the night unattended.

"—mate!"

Booster had very little hard data, but the AI didn't waste time as a human intelligence officer might have done in decrying the accuracy of the assessment it was about to provide. The computer's best estimate was the same as Des Grieux's own: *Warrior* didn't have a snowball's chance in Hell of reaching the firebase.

Only one of Hill 504's flanks, the west/southwest octave, had a slope suitable for heavy equipment—including ammunition vans and artillery prime movers, and assuredly including *Warrior*. There were at this moment—best estimate—anywhere from five hundred to a thousand Rep soldiers scattered along the route the tank would have to traverse.

The Reps were artillerymen, headquarters guards, and stragglers, not the crack battalions *Warrior* had gutted in her charge out of the Federal lines—

But these troops were prepared. The exploding chaos had warned them. They would fire from cover: rifle bullets to peck out sensors; buzzbombs whose shaped-charge warheads could and eventually *would* penetrate heavy armor; cannon lowered to slam their heavy shells directly into the belly plates *Warrior* exposed as the tank lurched to the top of Hill 504 by the only possible access. . . .

"Driver," Des Grieux ordered. His fingertip traced a savage arc across the topo screen at ninety degrees to the initial course. "Follow the marked route."

"Sir, there's no road!" Kuykendall shrilled.

Even on the trail flattened by the feet of Republican assault battalions, the tank proceeded in a worm of sparks and dust as its skirts dragged. Booster's augmented night vision gave the driver an image almost as good as daytime view would have been, but nothing could be sufficient to provide a smooth ride at sixty-five KPH over unimproved wilderness.

"Screw the bloody road!" ordered Des Grieux. "Move!"

They couldn't go forward, but they couldn't go back, either. The survivors of the Republican attack were between *Warrior* and whatever safety the Federal bunker line could provide. If the tank turned and tried to make an uphill run through that gauntlet, satchel charges would rip vents in the skirts. Crippled, *Warrior* would be a stationary target for buzzbombs and artillery fire.

Des Grieux couldn't give the Reps time to set up. So long as the tank kept moving, it was safe. With her fusion powerplant and drive fans rated at 12,000 hours between major overhauls, *Warrior* could cruise all the way around the planet, dodging enemies.

For the moment, Des Grieux just wanted to get out of the immediate kill zone.

Kuykendall tilted the nacelles closer to vertical. Their attitude reduced the forward thrust, but it also increased the skirts' clearance by a centimeter or two. That was necessary insurance against a quartz outcrop tearing a hole in the skirts.

Trees twenty meters tall grew in the swales, where the water table was highest. Vegetation on the slopes and ridges was limited to low spike-leafed bushes. Kuykendall rode the slopes, where the brush was less of a problem but the tank wasn't outlined against the sky. Des Grieux didn't have to think about what Kuykendall was doing, which made her the best kind of driver. . . .

A tank running at full power was conspicuous

under almost any circumstances, but the middle of
a major battle was one of the exceptions. Neither
Des Grieux's instincts nor *Warrior*'s sensor array
caught any sign of close-in enemies.

By slanting northeast, Des Grieux put them in
the dead ground between the axes of the Republican
attack. He was well behind the immediately-engaged
forces and off the supply routes leading from the two
northern firebases. If he ordered Kuykendall to turn
due north now, *Warrior* would in ten minutes be in
position to circle Hill 661 and then head south to
link up with the relieving force.

It didn't occur to Des Grieux that they could run
from the battle. He just needed a little time.

The night raved and roared. Brushfires flung
sparks above the ridgelines where *Warrior* had gutted the right pincer of the attack. Ammunition
cooked off when flames reached the bandoliers of the
dead and screaming wounded.

Bullets and case fragments sang among the surviving Reps. Men shot back in panic, killing their fellows and drawing return fire from across the flame
curtains.

The hollow chunking sound within *Warrior*'s guts
stopped with a final clang. The green numeral 20
appeared on the lower right-hand corner of Des
Grieux's main screen, the display he was using for
gunnery. His ready magazine was full again. He
could pulse the night with another salvo of twenty-
CM bolts.

Soon.

When Des Grieux blasted the Rep supports with
rapid fire, he'd robbed *Warrior*'s main gun of half
the lifespan it would have had if the weapon were
fired with time for the bore to cool between shots.

If he cut loose with a similar burst, there was a real chance the eroded barrel would fail, perhaps venting into the fighting compartment with catastrophic results.

That possibility had no effect on Des Grieux's plans for the next ten minutes. He would do what he had to do; and by God! His tools, human and otherwise, had better be up to the job.

The sky in the direction of Hill 661 quivered white with the almost-constant muzzle flashes. Shells, friction-heated to a red glow by the end of their arc into the Federal encampment, then flashed orange. Artillery rockets moved too slowly for the atmosphere to light their course, but the Reps put flare pots in the rockets' tails so that the gunners could correct their aim.

"Sarge?" said Kuykendall tightly. "Where we going?"

Des Grieux's index finger drew a circle on the topographic display.

"Oh, lord . . ." the driver whispered.

But she didn't slow or deviate from the course Des Grieux had set her.

*Warrior* proceeded at approximately forty KPH; a little faster on downslopes, a little slower when the drive fans had to fight gravity, as they did most of the time now. That was fast running over rough, unfamiliar terrain. The tank's night-vision devices were excellent, but they couldn't see that the opposite side of a ridge dropped off instead of sloping, or the tank-sized gully beyond the bend in a swale.

Kuykendall was getting them to the objective surely, and that was soon enough for Des Grieux. Whether or not it would be in time for the Federals on Hill 541 North was somebody else's problem.

The Republicans' right-flank assault was in disarray, probably terminal disarray, but the units committed to the east slope of the Federal position were proceeding more or less as planned. At least one of the Slammers' tanks survived, because the night flared with three cyan blasts spaced a chronometer second apart.

Probably Broglie, who cut his turds to length. Everything perfect, everything *as ordered*, and who was just about as good a gunner as Slick Des Grieux.

*Just about* meant *second best*.

Shells crashed down unhindered on 541N. Some of them certainly fell among the Rep assault forces because the attack was succeeding. Federal guns slammed out rapid fire with the muzzles lowered, slashing the Reps with canister at point-blank range. A huge explosion rocked the hilltop as an ammo dump went off, struck by incoming or detonated by the defenders as the Reps overran it.

Des Grieux hadn't bothered to cancel his earlier command: *Booster, enemy defenses in marked area.* When his fingertip circled Hill 661 to direct Kuykendall, the artificial intelligence tabulated that target as well.

Twenty artillery pieces, ranging from ten CM to a single stub-barreled thirty-CM howitzer which flung 400-kilogram shells at fifteen-minute intervals.

At least a dozen rails to launch twenty-CM bombardment rockets.

A pair of calliopes, powerguns with eight two-CM barrels fixed on a carriage. They were designed to sweep artillery shells out of the sky, but their high-intensity charges could chew through the bow slope of a tank in less than a minute.

Approximately a thousand men: gunners, command staff, and a company or two of infantry for close-in security in case Federals sortied from their camp in a kamikaze attack.

All of them packed onto a quarter-kilometer mesa, and not a soul expecting *Warrior* to hit them from behind. The Republicans thought of tanks as guns and armor; but tanks meant mobility, too, and Des Grieux knew *every* way a tank could crush an enemy.

Reflected muzzle blasts silvered the plume of dust behind *Warrior*. The onrushing tank would be obvious to anyone in the firebase who looked north—

But the show was southwest among the Federal positions, where the artillerymen dropped their shells and toward which the infantry detachment stared—imagining a fight at knifepoint, and thinking of how much better off they were than their fellows in the assault waves.

*Warrior* thrust through a band of stunted brush and at a flat angle onto a stabilized road, the logistics route serving the Republican firebase.

"S—" Kuykendall said.

"Yes!" Des Grieux shouted. "Goose it!"

Kuykendall had started to adjust her nacelles even before she spoke, but vectored thrust wasn't sufficient to steer the tank onto a road twenty meters wide at the present speed. She deliberately let the skirts drop, using mechanical friction to brake *Warrior*'s violent side-slipping as the bow came around.

The tank tilted noticeably into the berm, its skirt plowed up on the high side of the turn. Rep engineers had treated the road surface with a plasticizer that cushioned the shock and even damped the blaze of sparks that Des Grieux had learned to expect when steel rubbed stone with the inertia of 170 tonnes behind it.

Kuykendall got her vehicle under control, adjusted fan bite and nacelle angle, and began accelerating up the 10° slope to the target. By the time *Warrior* reached the end of the straight, half-kilometer run, they were traveling at seventy-KPH.

Two Republican ammunition vans were parked just over the lip of Hill 661. There wasn't room for a tank to go between them.

Kuykendall went through anyway. The five-tonne vehicles flew in opposite directions. The ruptured fuel tank of one hurled a spray of blazing kerosene out at a 30° tangent to the tank's course.

The sound of impact would have been enormous, were it not lost in the greater crash of *Warrior*'s guns.

The tank's data banks stored the image of bolts from the calliopes. Booster gave Des Grieux a precise vector to where the weapons had been every time they fired. The Republican commander could have ordered the calliopes to move since Federal incoming disappeared as a threat, but that was a chance Des Grieux had to take.

He squeezed both tits as *Warrior* crested the mesa, firing along the preadjusted angles.

The night went cyan, then orange and cyan.

The calliopes were still in their calculated positions. The tribarrel raked the sheet-metal chassis of one. Ready ammunition ignited into a five-meter globe of plasma bright enough to burn out the retinas of anyone looking in the wrong direction without protective lenses.

There was a vehicle parked between the second calliope and the onrushing tank. It was the ammunition hauler feeding a battery of fifteen-CM howitzers. It exploded with a blast so violent that the tank's bow lifted and Des Grieux slammed back in his seat. Shells and burning debris flew in all directions, setting off a second vehicle hundreds of meters away.

The shockwave spilled the air cushion from *Warrior*'s plenum chamber. The tank grounded *hard*, dangerously hard, but the skirts managed to stand the impact. Power returned to *Warrior*'s screens after a brief flicker, but the topographic display faded to amber monochrome which blurred the fine detail.

"S'okay . . ." Des Grieux wheezed, because the seat restraints had bruised him over the ribs when they kept him from pulping himself against the main screen. And it *was* all right, because the guns were all right and the controls were in his hands.

Buttoned up, the tank was a sealed system whose thick armor protected the crew from the blast's worst effects. The Reps, even those in bunkers, were less fortunate. The calliope, which Des Grieux missed, lay on its side fifty meters from its original location. Strips of flesh and uniforms, the remains of its crew, swathed the breech mechanisms.

"Booster," Des Grieux said, "mark movement," and his tribarrel swept the firebase.

The Republicans' guns were dug into shallow emplacements. Incoming wasn't the problem for them that it had been for the Federals, pecked at constantly from three directions.

The gunners on Hill 541 North hadn't had enough ammunition to try to overwhelm the Rep defenses. Besides, calliopes were *designed* for the job of slapping shells out of the sky. In that one specialized role, they performed far better than tank tribarrels.

Previous freedom from danger left the Republican guns hopelessly exposed now that a threat appeared, but Des Grieux had more important targets than mere masses of steel aimed in the wrong direction. There were men.

The AI marked moving objects white against a background of gray shades on the gunnery screen. *Warrior* wallowed forward again, not fully under control because both Kuykendall and the skirts had taken a severe shock. Des Grieux used that motion and his cupola's high-speed rotation to slide the solid pipper across the display. Every time the orange bead covered white, his thumb stroked the firing tit.

The calliopes had been the primary danger. Their multiple bolts could cripple the tank if their crews were good enough—and only a fool bets that an unknown opponent doesn't know his job.

With the calliopes out of the way, the remaining threat came from the men who could swarm over *Warrior* like driver ants bringing down a leopard. The things that still moved on Hill 661 were men, stumbling in confusion and the shock of the massive secondary explosions.

Des Grieux's cyan bolts ripped across them and flung bodies down with their uniforms afire. Artillerymen fleeing toward cover, officers popping out of bunkers to take charge of the situation, would-be rescuers running to drag friends out of the exploding cataclysm—

All moving, all targets, all dead before anyone on the mesa realized that there was a Slammers' tank in their midst, meting out destruction with the contemptuous ease of a weasel in a hen coop.

Des Grieux didn't use his main gun; he didn't want to take time to replenish the ready magazine before he completed the final stage of his plan. Twice *Warrior*'s automatic defense system burped a sleet of steel balls into Reps who ran in the wrong direction, but there was no resistance.

Mobility, surprise, and overwhelming firepower. One tank, with a commander who knew that you didn't win battles by crouching in a hole while the other bastard shoots at you. . . .

A twenty-CM shell arced from an ammo dump. It clanged like the wrath of God on *Warrior*'s back deck. The projectile was unfuzed. It didn't explode.

Only *Warrior* and the flames now moved on top of Hill 661. Normally the Republican crews bunkered their ammunition supply carefully, but rapid fire in support of the attack meant ready rounds were stacked on flat ground or held in soft-skinned vehicles. A third munitions store went up, a bunker or a vehicle, you couldn't tell after the fireball mushroomed skyward.

The shockwave pushed *Warrior* sideways into a sandbagged command post. The walls collapsed at the impact. An arm stuck out of the doorway, but the tribarrel had severed the limb from the body moments before.

The tank steadied. Des Grieux pumped deliberate bursts into a pair of vans. One held thirty-CM ammunition, the other was packed with bombardment rockets. A white flash sent shells tumbling skyward and down. Rockets skittered across the mesa.

"Booster," said Des Grieux. "Topo blow-up of six-six-one. Break. Driver—"

A large-scale plan of the mesa filled the left-hand display. Warrior was a blue dot, wandering across a ruin of wrecked equipment and demolished bunkers.

"—put us there—" Des Grieux stabbed a point on

the southwestern margin of the mesa. He had to reach across his body to do so, because his left hand was welded to the tribarrel's controls "—and hold. Break. Booster—"

Kuykendall swung the tank. *Warrior* now rode nose-down by a few degrees. The bow skirts were too crumpled to seal at the normal attitude.

"—give me maximum magnification on the main screen."

Debris from previous explosions still flapped above Hill 661 like bat-winged Death. A fuel store ignited. The pillar of flame expanded in slow motion by comparison with the previous ammunition fires.

Though the main screen was in high-magnification mode, the right-hand display—normally the commo screen, but De Grieux had shut off external commo— retained a 120° panorama of *Warrior*'s surroundings. Images shifted as the tank reversed through the ruin its guns had created. Air spilling beneath the skirts stirred the flames and made their ragged tips bow in obeisance.

A Rep with the green tabs of a Central Command officer on his epaulets knelt with his hands folded in prayer. He did not look up as *Warrior* slid toward him, though vented air made his short-sleeved khaki uniform shudder.

Des Grieux touched his left joystick. The Rep was already too close to *Warrior* for the tribarrel to bear; and anyway . . .

And anyway, one spaced-out man was scarcely worth a bolt.

*Warrior* howled past the Rep officer. A cross-wind rocked the tank minusculy from Kuykendall's intended line, so that the side skirt drifted within five meters of the man.

Sensors fired a section of the automatic defense
system. Pellets blew the Republican backward, as
loose-limbed as a rag doll.

Kuykendall ground the skirts to bring the tank to
a safe halt at the edge of the mesa. *Warrior* lay
across a zigzag trench, empty save for a sprawled
corpse. The drive fans could stabilize a tank in still
air, but shockwaves and currents rushing to feed
flames whipped the top of Hill 661.

Des Grieux depressed the muzzle of his main gun
slightly. On *Warrior's* gunnery screen, the hollow
pipper slid over a high-resolution view of Republican
positions on Hill 504.

The mesa on which *Warrior* rested was 150
meters higher than the irregular hillock on which the
Reps had placed their western firebase. The twelve
kilometers separating the two peaks meant nothing
to the tank's powerguns.

On Hill 504, a pair of bombardment rockets leapt
from their launching tubes toward the Federal
encampment. The holographic image was silent, but
Des Grieux had been the target of too many similar
rounds not to imagine the snarling roar of their passage. He centered his ring sight on the munitions
truck bringing another twenty-four rounds to the
launchers—

And toed the foot trip.

*Warrior* rocked with the trained lightning of its
main gun. The display blanked in a cataclysm: pure
blue plasma; metal burning white hot; and red as
tonnes of warheads and solid rocket fuel exploded
simultaneously. The truck and everything within a
hundred meters of it vanished.

Des Grieux shifted his sights to what he thought
was the Republican command post. He was smiling.

He fired. Sandbags blew outward as shards of glass. There were explosives of some sort within the bunker, because a moment after the rubble settled, a secondary explosion blew the site into a crater.

Concussion from the first blast had stunned or killed the crew of the single calliope on Hill 504. The weapon was probably unserviceable, but Des Grieux's third bolt vaporized it anyway.

"I told you bastards . . ." the tanker muttered in a voice that would have frightened anyone who heard him.

Dust and smoke billowed out in a huge doughnut from where the truckload of rockets had been. The air-suspended particles masked the remaining positions on Hill 504. Guns and bunker sites vanished into the haze like ships sinking at anchor. The main screen provided a detailed vision of whorls and color variations within the general blur.

"Booster," Des Grieux said. "Feed me targets."

*Warrior*'s turret was supported by superconducting magnetic bearings powered by the same fusion plant that drove the fans. The mechanism purred and adjusted two degrees to starboard, under control of the artificial intelligence recalling the terrain before it was concealed. The hollow pipper remained centered on the gunnery screen, but haze appeared to shift around it.

The circle pulsed. Des Grieux fired the twenty-CM gun. Even as the tank recoiled from the bolt's release, the AI rotated the weapon toward the next unseen victim.

"Booster!" Des Grieux snarled. His throat was raw with gunnery fumes and the human waste products of tension coursing through his system. "*Show* me the bloody—"

The pipper quivered again. Des Grieux fired by reflex. A flash and a mushroom of black smoke penetrated the gray curtain.

"—targets!"

The main gun depressed minutely. To Des Grieux's amazement, a howitzer on Hill 504 banged a further shell toward the Federal positions. *Warrior*'s AI obediently supplied the image of the weapon to Des Grieux's display as it steadied beneath the orange circle.

A bubble of gaseous metal sent the howitzer barrel thirty meters into the air.

With only one calliope to protect them, the Reps on 504 had dug in somewhat better than their fellows on Hill 661. Despite that, there was still a suicidal amount of ready ammunition stacked around the fast-firing guns. The tank's data banks fed each dump to the gunnery screen.

Des Grieux continued to fire. The haze over the target area darkened, stirred occasionally by sullen red flames. A red 0 replaced the green numeral 1 on the lower right corner of the screen. The interior of the fighting compartment stank like the depths of Hell.

"I told you bastards . . ." Des Grieux repeated, though his throat was so swollen that he had to force the words out. "And I told that bastard Lindgren."

"Sarge?" Kuykendall said.

Des Grieux threw the charging lever to refill the ready magazine. Just as well if he didn't use the main gun until the bore was relined; but the status report gave it ten percent of its original thickness, a safe enough margin for a few bolts, and you did what you had to do. . . .

"Yeah," he said aloud. "Get us somewhere outa the way. In the morning we'll rejoin. Somebody."

Kuykendall adjusted the fans so that they bit into the air instead of slicing through it with minimum disruption. She'd kept the power up while *Warrior* was grounded. In an emergency, they could hop off the mesa with no more than a quick change of blade angle.

The smoke-shrouded ruin of Hill 661 was unlikely to spawn emergencies, but in the four hours remaining till dawn some Rep officer might muster a tank-killer team. No point in making trouble for yourself. There were hundreds of kilometers of arid scrub which would hide *Warrior* until the situation sorted itself out.

And there were no longer any targets around *here* worthy of *Warrior's* guns. Of that, Des Grieux was quite certain.

Kuykendall elected to slide directly over the edge of the mesa instead of returning to the logistics route by which they had attacked. The immediate slope was severe, almost 1:3, but there were no dangerous obstacles and the terrain flattened within a hundred meters.

There were bound to be scores of Rep soldiers on the road, some of them seeking revenge. A large number might fly into a lethal panic if they saw *Warrior's* gray bow loom through the darkness. A smoother ride to concealment wasn't worth the risk.

"Sarge?" asked Kuykendall. "What's going on back at 541 North?"

"How the hell would I know?" Des Grieux snarled.

But he could know, if he wanted to. He reached to reconnect the commo buss . . . and withdrew his hand. He could adjust a screen, and he started to

do that—manually, because his throat hurt as if he'd
been swallowing battery acid.

Instead of carrying through with the motion, Des
Grieux lifted the crash bar to open the hatch and
raise his seat to cupola level. The breeze smelled so
clean that it made him dizzy.

Kuykendall eased the tank toward the low ground
west of Hill 661. With a swale to shelter them, they
could drive north a couple kays and avoid the stragglers from the Republican disaster.

For it had been a disaster. The Federal artillery
on Hill 541N was in action again, lobbing shells
toward the Rep staging areas. Fighting still went on
within the encampment, but an increasing volume
of fire raked the eastern slope up which the Reps
had carried their initial assault objectives.

The weapons which picked over the remnants of
the Republican attacks were machine guns firing
white tracers, standard Federal issue; and at least a
dozen tribarreled powerguns. A platoon of Slammers' combat cars had entered the Federal encampment and was helping the defenders mop up.

The relief force had finally arrived.

"In the morning . . ." Des Grieux muttered. He
was as tired as he'd ever been in his life.

And he knew that he and his tank had just won a
battle singlehandedly.

*Warrior* proceeded slowly up the eastern slope of
Hill 541 North. The brush had burned to blackened
spikes. Ash swirled over the ground, disintegrating
into a faint shimmer in the air.

Given the amount of damage to the landscape,
there were surprisingly few bodies; but there were

some. They sprawled, looking too small for their uniforms; and the flies had found them.

Half an hour before dawn, Des Grieux announced in clear, on both regimental and Federal frequencies, that *Warrior* was reentering the encampment. The AI continued to transmit that message at short intervals, and Kuykendall held the big vehicle to a walking pace to appear as unthreatening as possible.

There was still a risk that somebody would open fire in panic. The tank was buttoned up against that possibility.

It was easier when everybody around you was an enemy. Then it was just a matter of who was quicker on the trigger. Des Grieux never minded playing *that* game.

"Alpha One-six to Oyster Two commander," said a cold, bored voice in Des Grieux's helmet. "Dismount and report to the CP as soon as you're through the minefields. Over."

"Oyster Two to One-six," Des Grieux replied. Alpha One-six was the callsign of Major Joaquim Steuben, Colonel Hammer's bodyguard. Steuben had no business being here. . . . "Roger, as soon as we've parked the tank. Over."

"Alpha One-six to Oyster Two commander," the cold voice said. "I'll provide your driver with ground guides for parking, Sergeant. I suggest that this time, you obey orders. One-six out."

Des Grieux swallowed. He wasn't afraid of Steuben, exactly; any more than he was afraid of a spider. But he didn't like spiders either.

"Driver," he said aloud. "Pull up when you get through the minefield. Somebody'll tell you where they want *Warrior* parked."

"You bet," said Kuykendall in a distant voice.

Federal troops drew back at the tank's approach. They'd been examining what remained of the perimeter defenses and dragging bodies cautiously from the wire. There were thousands of unexploded mines scattered across the slope. Nobody wanted to be the last casualty of a successful battle.

Successful because of what Des Grieux had done.

Something about the Feds seemed odd. After a moment, Des Grieux realized that it was their uniforms. The fabric was green—not clean, exactly, but not completely stained by the sandy red soil of Hill 541 North either. These were troops from the relieving force.

A few men of the original garrison watched from the bunker line. It was funny to see that many troops in the open sunlight; not scuttling, not cowering from snipers and shellfire.

The bunkers were ruins. Sappers had grenaded them during the assault. When the Federals counterattacked, Reps sheltered in the captured positions until tribarrels and point-blank shellfire blew them out. The roofs had collapsed. Wisps of smoke still curled from among the ruptured sandbags.

A Slammers' combat car—unnamed, with fender number 116—squatted in an overwatch position on the bunker line. The three tribarrels were manned, covering the troops in the wire. Bullet scars dented the side of the fighting compartment. A bright swatch of SpraySeal covered the left wing gunner's shoulder.

A figure was painted on the car's bow slope, just in front of the driver's hatch: a realistically-drawn white mouse with pink eyes, nose, and tail.

The White Mice—the troops of Alpha Company, Hammer's Regiment—weren't ordinary line soldiers.

Nobody ever said they couldn't fight—but they, under their CO, Major Steuben, acted as Hammer's field police and in other internal security operations.

A dozen anti-personnel mines went off under *Warrior*'s skirts as the tank slid through the perimeter defenses. Kuykendall tried to follow a track Rep sappers blew the night before, but *Warrior* overhung the cleared area on both sides.

The surface-scattered mines were harmless, except to a man who stepped on one. Even so, after the third *bang!* one of the Feds watching from the bunker line put his hands over his face and began to cry uncontrollably.

Three troopers wearing Slammers' khaki and commo helmets waited at the defensive perimeter. One of them was a woman. They carried sub-machine guns in patrol slings that kept the muzzles forward and the grips close to their gunhands.

They'd been sitting on the hillside when Des Grieux first noticed them. They stood as *Warrior* approached.

"Driver," Des Grieux said, "you can pull up here."

"I figured to," Kuykendall replied without emotion. Dust puffed forward, then drifted downhill as she shifted nacelles to brake *Warrior*'s slow pace.

Des Grieux climbed from the turret and poised for a moment on the back deck. The artillery shell that bounced from *Warrior* on Hill 661 had dished in a patch of plating a meter wide. Number seven intake grating ought to be replaced as well. . . .

Des Grieux hopped to the ground. One of the White Mice sat on *Warrior*'s bow slope and gestured directions to the driver. The tank accelerated toward the encampment.

"Come on, Sunshine," said the female trooper. Her features were blank behind her reflective visor. "The Man wants to see you."

She jerked her thumb uphill.

Des Grieux fell in between the White Mice. His legs were unsteady. He hadn't wanted to eat anything with his throat feeling as though it had been reamed with a steel bore brush.

"Am I under arrest?" he demanded.

"Major Steuben didn't say anything about that," the male escort replied. He chuckled.

"Naw," added the woman. "He just said that if you give us any crap, we should shoot you. And save him the trouble."

"Then we all know where we stand," said Des Grieux. Soreness and aches dissolved in his body's resumed production of adrenaline.

The encampment on Hill 541 North had always been a wasteland, so Des Grieux didn't expect to notice a change now.

He was wrong. It was much worse, and the forty-odd bodies laid in rows in their zipped-up sleeping bags were only part of it.

The smell overlaid the scene. Explosives had peculiar odors. They blended uneasily with ozone and high-temperature fusion products formed when bolts from the powerguns hit.

The main component of the stench was death.

Bunkers had been blown closed, but the rubble of timber and sandbags didn't form a tight seal over the shredded flesh within. The morning sun was already hot. In a week or two, a lot of wives and parents were going to receive a coffin sealed over seventy kilos of sand.

That wasn't Des Grieux's problem, though; and without him, there would have been plenty more corpses swelling in Federal uniforms.

General Wycherly's command post had taken a direct hit from a heavy shell. A high-sided truck with multiple antennas parked beside the smoldering wreckage. Federal troops in clean uniforms stepped briskly in and out of the vehicle.

The real authorities on 541N wore Slammers khaki. Major Joachim Steuben was short, slim, and so fine-featured that he looked like a girl in a perfectly-tailored uniform among Sergeant Broglie and several Alpha Company officers. They looked up as Des Grieux approached.

Steuben's command group stood under a tarpaulin slung between a combat car and Lieutenant Lindgren's tank. The roof of Lindgren's bunker was broken-backed from the fighting, but his tank looked all right at first glance.

At a second look—

"Via!" Des Grieux said. "What happened to *Queen City*?"

There were tell-tale soot stains all around the tank's deck, and the turret rested slightly askew on its ring. *Queen City* was a corpse, as sure as any of the staring-eyed Reps out there in the wire.

The female escort sniffed. "Its luck ran out. Took a shell down the open hatch. All they gotta do now is jack up what's left and slide a new tank underneath."

"Dunno how anybody can ride those fat bastards," the other escort muttered. "They maneuver like blind whales."

"Glad you could rejoin us, Sergeant," Major Steuben said. He gave the data terminal in his left hand to a lieutenant beside him. His voice was lilting and as *pretty* as Steuben's appearance, but it cut through any thought Des Grieux had of snarling a response to the combat-car crewman beside him.

"Sir," Des Grieux muttered. The Slammers didn't salute. Salutes in a war zone targeted officers for possible snipers.

"Would you like to explain your actions during the battle last night, Sergeant?" the major asked.

Steuben stood arms akimbo. His pose accentuated the crisp tuck of his waist. The fall of the slim right hand almost concealed the pistol riding in a cut-out holster high on Steuben's right hip.

The pistol was engraved and inlaid with metal lozenges in a variety of colors. In all respects but its heavy one-CM bore, it looked as surely a girl's weapon as its owner looked like a girl.

Joachim Steuben's eyes focused on Des Grieux. There was not a trace of compassion in the eyes or the soul beneath them. Any weapon in Steuben's hands was Death.

"I was winning a battle," Des Grieux said as his eyes mirrored Steuben's blank, brown glare. "Sir. Since the relieving force was still sitting on its hands after three weeks."

Broglie slid his body between Des Grieux and the major. Broglie was fast, but Steuben's pistol was socketed in his ear before the tanker's motion was half complete.

"I think Sergeant Des Grieux and I can continue our discussion better without you in the way, Mister Broglie," Steuben said. He didn't move his eyes from Des Grieux.

The White Mice hadn't bothered to remove the pistol from the holster on Des Grieux's equipment

belt. Now Des Grieux knew why. *Nobody could be
that fast. . . .*

"Sir," Broglie rasped through a throat gone dry.
"*Warrior* did destroy both the Rep firebases. That's
what took the pressure off here at the end."

Broglie stepped back to where he'd been standing.
He looked straight ahead, not at either Des Grieux
or the major.

"You've named your tank *Warrior*, Sergeant?"
Steuben said. "Amusing. But right at the moment
I'm not so much interested in what you did so much
as I am in why you disobeyed orders to do it."

He reholstered his gorgeous handgun with a
motion as precise and delicate as that of a bird
preening its feathers.

"You got some people killed, you know," the
major added. His voice sounded cheerful, or at least
amused. "Your lieutenant and his driver, because
nobody was dealing with the shells from Hill 504."

He smiled coquettishly at Des Grieux. "I won't
blame you for the other one. Hawes, was it?"

"Hawes, sir," Broglie muttered.

"Since Hawes was stupid enough to leave his position also," Steuben went on. "And I don't care a
great deal about Federal casualties, except as they
affect the Regiment's contractual obligations. . . ."

The pause was deadly.

"Which, since we *have* won the battle for them,
shouldn't be a problem."

"Sir," Des Grieux said, "they were wide open. It
was the one chance we were going to have to pay the
Reps back for the three weeks we sat and took it."

Major Steuben turned his head slowly and sur-
veyed the battered Federal encampment. His tongue
went *tsk, tsk, tsk* against his teeth.

*Warrior* was parked alongside Broglie's *Honey Girl* in the center of the hill. *Warrior*'s bow skirts had cracked as well as bending inward when 170 tonnes slammed down on them. Kuykendall had earned her pay, keeping the tank moving steadily despite the damage.

Des Grieux's gaze followed the major's. *Honey Girl* had been hit by at least three buzzbombs on this side. None of the sun-hot jets seemed to have penetrated the armor. Broglie had been in the thick of it, with the only functional tank remaining when the Reps blew their way through the bunker line. . . .

The Federal gun emplacements were nearby. The Fed gunners had easily been the best of the local troops. They'd hauled three howitzers up from the gun pits to meet the Republican assault with canister and short-fused high explosive.

That hadn't been enough. Buzzbombs and grenades had disabled the howitzers, and a long line of bodies lay beside the damaged hardware.

"You know, Sergeant?" Steuben resumed unexpectedly. "Colonel Hammer found the relief force's progress a bit leisurely for his taste also. So he sent me to take command . . . and a platoon of Alpha Company, you know. To encourage the others."

He giggled. It was a terrible sound, like gas bubbling through the throat of a distended corpse.

"We were about to take Hill 541 South," Steuben continued. "In twenty-four hours we would have relieved the position here with minimal casualties. The Reps knew that, so they made a desperation assault . . . which couldn't possibly have succeeded against a bunker line backed up by four of our tanks."

Joachim's eyes looked blankly through Des Grieux.

"That's why," the delicate little man said softly, "I really think I ought to kill you now, before you cause other trouble."

"Sir," said Broglie. "Slick cleared our left flank. That had to be done."

Major Steuben's eyes focused again, this time on Broglie. "Did it?" the major said. "Not from outside the prepared defenses, I think. And certainly not against orders from a superior officer, who was—"

The cold stare again at Des Grieux. No more emotion in the eyes than there would be in the muzzle of the pistol which might appear with magical speed in Joachim's hand.

"Who was, as I say," the major continued, "passing on *my* orders."

"But . . ." Des Grieux whispered. "I *won*."

"No," Steuben said in a crisply businesslike voice. Moods seemed to drift over the dapper officer's mind like clouds across the sun. "You ran, Sergeant. *I* had to make an emergency night advance with the only troops I could fully trust—"

He smiled with cold affection at the nearest of his White Mice.

"—in order to prevent Hill 541 North from being overrun. And even then I would have failed, were it not for the actions of Mister Broglie."

"Broglie?" Des Grieux blurted in amazement.

"Oh, yes," Joachim said. "Oh, yes, Mister Broglie. He took charge here after the Federal CP was knocked out and Mister Lindgren was killed. He put *Susie Q*'s driver back into the turret of the damaged tank and used that to stabilize the left flank. Then he led the counterattack which held the Reps on the right flank until my platoon arrived to finish the business.

"I don't like night actions when local forces are involved, Sergeant," he added in a frigid voice. "It's dangerous because of the confusion. If my orders had been obeyed, there would have been no confusion."

Steuben glanced at Broglie. He smiled, much as he had done when he looked at his White Mice. "I'm particularly impressed by the way you controlled the commo net alone while fighting your vehicle, Mister Broglie," he said. "The locals might well have panicked when they lost normal communications along with their command post."

Broglie licked his lips. "It was okay," he said. "Booster did most of it. And it had to be done—*I* couldn't stop the bastards alone."

"Wait a minute," Des Grieux said. "Wait a bloody minute! *I* wasn't just sitting on my hands, you know. I was fighting!"

"Yes, Sergeant," Major Steuben said. "You were fighting like a fool, and it appears that you're still a fool. Which doesn't surprise me."

He smiled at Broglie. "The Colonel will have to approve your field promotion to lieutenant, Mister Broglie," he said, "but I don't foresee any problems. Of course, you'll have a badly understrength platoon until replacements arrive."

Des Grieux swung a fist at Broglie. The White Mice had read the signs correctly. The male escort was already holding Des Grieux's right arm. The woman on the other side bent the tanker's left wrist back and up with the skill of long practice.

Joachim set the muzzle of his pistol against Des Grieux's right eye. The motion was so swift that the cold iridium circle touched the eyeball before reflex could blink the lid closed.

Des Grieux jerked his head back, but the pistol

followed. Its touch was as light as that of a butterfly's wing.

"Via, sir," Broglie gasped. "*Don't*. Slick's the best tank commander in the regiment."

Steuben giggled again. "If you insist, Mister Broglie," he said. "After all, you won the battle for us here."

He holstered the pistol. A warrior's frustrated tears rushed out to fill Des Grieux's eyes. . . .

# PART II

Xingha was the staging area for the troops on the Western Wing: a battalion of the Slammers and more than ten thousand of the local Han troops the mercenaries were supporting.

The city's dockyard district had a way to go before it adapted to the influx of soldiers, but it was doing its manful—womanly, childish, and indeed bestial—best to accommodate the sudden need. Soon the entertainment facilities would reach the universal standard to which war sinks those who support the fighters; in all places, in every time.

Sergeant Samuel Des Grieux had seen the pattern occur often during his seven years in the Slammers. He could describe the progression as easily as an ecologist charts the process by which lakes become marshes, then forests.

Des Grieux didn't care one way or the other. He drank what passed for beer; listened to a pair of Oriental women keen, *"Oh where ha you been, Laird Randall, me son?"* (Hammer's Slammers came to the

Han contract from seven months of civil war among the Scottish colonists of New Aberdeen); and wondered when he'd have a chance to swing his tank into action. It'd been a long time since he had a tank to command. . . .

"Hey, is there anybody here from Golf Company?" asked a trooper, obviously a veteran but wearing new-issue khaki. His hair was in a triple ponytail, according to whim or the custom of some planet unfamiliar to Des Grieux. The fellow was moving from one table to the next in the crowded cantina. Just now, he was with a group of H Company tankers next to Des Grieux, bending low and shouting to be heard over the music and general racket.

"Hey, lookit that," said Pesco, Des Grieux's new driver. He pointed to the flat, rear-projection screen in the corner opposite the singers. "That's Captain Broglie, isn't he? What's he doing on local video?"

"Who bloody cares?" Des Grieux said. He finished his beer and refilled his glass from the pitcher.

If you tried, you could hear Broglie's voice—though not that of the Han interviewer—over the ambient noise. Despite himself, Des Grieux found himself listening.

"Hey, Johnnie," chirped a woman in a red dress as she draped her arm around Des Grieux's shoulders. She squeezed her obviously-padded bosom to his cheek. She was possibly fourteen, probably younger. "Buy me a drink?"

"Out," said Des Grieux, stiff-arming the girl into the back of a man at the next table. Des Grieux stared at the video screen, getting cues from Broglie's lips to aid as he fitted together the shards of speech.

"No, on the contrary, the Hindis make very respectable troops," Broglie said. "And as for Baffin's Legion, they're one of the best units for hire. I don't mean the Legion's in our class, of course. . . ."

A fault in the video screen—or the transmission medium—gave the picture a green cast. It made Broglie look like a three-week corpse. Des Grieux's lips drew back in a smile.

Pesco followed the tank commander's stare. "You served under him before, didn't you?" he asked Des Grieux. "Captain Broglie, I mean. What's he like?"

Des Grieux slashed his hand across the air in brusque dismissal. "I never served under him," he said. "When he took over the platoon I was in, I transferred to . . . infantry, Delta Company. And then combat cars, India and Golf."

". . . Baffin's tank destroyers are first-class," Broglie's leprous image continued. "Very dangerous equipment."

"Yeah, but look," Pesco objected. "With him, under him, it don't matter. What's he like, Broglie? Does he know his stuff, or is he gonna get somebody killed?"

Near where the singers warbled, *"Mother, make my bed soon . . ."* a dozen troopers had wedged two of the round tables together and were buying drinks for Sergeant Kuykendall. Des Grieux had heard his former driver'd gotten a twelve-month appointment to the Military Academy on Nieuw Friesland, with a lieutenancy in the Slammers waiting when she completed the course.

He supposed that was OK. Kuykendall had combat experience, so she'd be at least a cunt-hair better than green sods who'd never been on the wrong end of a gun muzzle.

Of course, she didn't have the experience Des Grieux himself did. . . .

*"For I'm sick at the heart, and I fain would lie down,"* the singers chirped through fixed smiles.

"Slick?" Pesco pressed. "Sarge? What about the new CO?"

Des Grieux shrugged. "Broglie?" he said. "He's a bloody good shot, I'll tell you that. Not real fast—not as fast as I am. But when he presses the tit, he nails what he's going after."

"Either of you guys from Golf?" asked the veteran in new fatigues. "I just got back from leave and I'm lookin' for my cousin, Tip Rasidi."

"We're Hotel Company, buddy," Pesco said. "Tanks. Why don't you try the Adjutant?"

"Because the bloody Adjutant lost half his bloody records in the transit," the stranger snapped, "and the orderly sergeant tells me to bugger off until he's got his bloody office sorted out. So I figure I'll check around till I find what's happened to Tip."

The stranger scraped his way over to the next table, rocking Pesco forward in his chair. The driver grimaced sourly.

"I don't know if the Hindis are brave or not," said Captain Broglie's image. "I suppose they're like everybody else, some braver than others. What I do know is that their troops are highly disciplined, and *that* causes me some concern."

"C'mon, what about him, then?" Pesco said. "Broglie."

"He'll do what he's told," Des Grieux said, staring at the video screen. His voice was clear, but it came from far away. "He's smart and he's got balls, I'll give him that. But he'd rather kiss the ass of whoever's giving orders than get out and fight. He coulda been really something, but instead . . ."

Sergeant Kuykendall got up from her table. She was wearing a red headband with lettering stitched in black. The others at the table shouted, "Speech! Speech!" as Kuykendall tried to say something.

"Yeah, but what's Broglie gonna be like as an officer?" Pesco demanded. "He just transferred to Hotel, you know. He'd been on the staff."

"Sure, courage is important," Broglie said on the screen. Though his words were mild enough, his tone harshly dismissed the interviewer's question. "But in modern warfare discipline is absolutely crucial. The Hindi regulars are quite well disciplined, and I fear that's going to make up for some deficiencies in their equipment. As for Baffin's Legion—"

Kuykendall broke away from her companions. She came toward Des Grieux, stepping between tables with the care of someone who knows how much she's drunk. The letters on her headband read "SIR!"

"—they're first rate in equipment *and* unit discipline. The war on the Western Wing isn't going to be a walk-over."

"Kid," said Des Grieux in a voice that grated up from deep within his soul, "I'll give you the first and last rule about officers. The more they keep outa your way and let you get on with the fighting, the better they are. And when things really drop in the pot, they're always too busy to get in your way. Don't worry about them."

". . . from Golf Company?" trailed the stranger's voice through a fissure in the ambient noise.

Sergeant Kuykendall bent over the table. "Hello, Slick," she said in measured tones. "I'm glad to see you're back in tanks. I always thought you belonged with the panzers."

Des Grieux shrugged. He was still looking at the screen, though the interview had been replaced by a stern-faced plea to buy War Stamps and support the national effort.

"Tanks," Des Grieux said, "combat cars. . . . I ran a gun jeep once. It don't really matter."

Pesco looked up at Kuykendall. "Hey, Sarge," he said to her. "Congrats on the appointment. Want a beer?"

"Just wanted to say hi to Slick," she said. "Me and him served with Captain Broglie way back to the dawn of time, y'know."

"Hey," Pesco said, his expression brightening. "You know Broglie, then? Looks to me he's got a lot of guts, telling 'em like it is on the video when they musta been figuring on a puff piece, is all. Likely to piss off Hammer, don't you think?"

Kuykendall glanced at the screen, though it now showed only a desk and a newsreader who mumbled unintelligibly. "Oh," she said, "I don't know. I guess the Colonel's smart enough to know that telling the truth now that the contract's signed isn't going to do any harm. May help things if we run into real trouble; and we might, Baffin's outfit's plenty bloody good."

She looked at Pesco, then Des Grieux, and back to Pesco. There were minute crow's feet around Kuykendall's eyes where the skin had been smooth when she drove for Des Grieux. "But Broglie's got guts, you bet."

Des Grieux shoved his chair backward. "If guts is what it takes to toady t' the brass, he's got 'em, you bet," he snarled as he rose.

He turned. "Hey, buddy!" he shouted. "You looking for Tip Rasidi?"

Voices stilled, though clattering glass, the video screen, and the singers' recorded background music continued at a high level.

The stranger straightened to face the summons.

Des Grieux said, "Rasidi drove for me on Aberdeen. We took a main-gun hit and burnt out. There wasn't enough of Tip to ship home in a matchbox."

The stranger continued to stand. His expression did not change, but his eyes glazed over.

The girl in the red dress sat at the table where Des Grieux had pushed her, wedged in between a pair of female troopers. Des Grieux gripped the girl by the shoulder and lifted her. "Come on," he snarled. "We're going upstairs."

One of the seated troopers might have objected, but she saw Des Grieux's face and remained silent.

The girl's face was resigned. She knew what was coming, but by now she was used to it.

*"The tow and the halter,"* sang the entertainers, *"for to hang on yon tree. . . ."*

The gravel highway steepened by a couple degrees before the switchback. The Han driving the four-axle troop transport just ahead of Des Grieux's tank opened his exhaust cut-outs to coax more power from the diesel.

As the unmuffled exhaust rattled, several of the troops on the truck bed stuck their weapons in the air and opened fire. A jolt threw one of the Han soldiers backward. His backpack laser slashed a brilliant line across the truck's canvas awning.

The lieutenant in command of the troops leaned from the cab and shouted angrily at his men, but they were laughing too hard to take much notice. Somebody tossed an empty bottle over the side in enough of a forward direction that the officer disappeared back within the cab.

The awning smoldered to either side of the long, blackened rent, but the treated fabric would not sustain a fire by itself.

The truck ground through the switchback, spewing gravel. Both forward axles were steerable. The vehicle was a solid piece of equipment, well-designed and manufactured. The local forces in this contract were a cursed sight better equipped than most of those you saw. Mostly the off-planet mercenaries stood out from the indig troops like diamonds on a bed of mud.

Both sets of locals, these Han and their Hindi rivals. . . .

"Booster," Des Grieux muttered as he sat in the cupola of his tank. "Hindi combat vehicles, schematics. Slow crawl. Out."

He manually set his commo helmet to echo the artificial intelligence's feed onto the left side of the visor. Des Grieux's cold right eye continued to scan the line of the convoy and the terraces that they had passed farther down the valley.

A soldier tossed another empty bottle from the truck ahead. Because the truck was higher and the road had reversed direction at the switchback, the brown-glazed ceramic shattered on the turret directly below Des Grieux. A line of heads turned from the truck's rail, shouting apologies and amused warnings to the soldier farther within the vehicle who'd thrown the bottle without looking first.

Des Grieux squeezed his tribarrel's grips, overriding its present Automatic Air-Defense setting. He slid the holographic sight picture across the startled Han faces which disappeared as the men flung themselves flat onto the truck bed.

Pesco shifted his four rear nacelles and pivoted the tank around its bow, following the switchback. They swung in behind the truck again. Des Grieux released the grips and let the tribarrel shift back to its normal search attitude: muzzles forward, at a forty-five degree elevation.

Des Grieux had only been joking. Had he been serious, he'd have put the first round into the fuel tank beneath the truck's cab. Only then would he rake his bolts along the men screaming as they tried to jump from the inferno of blazing kerosene.

He'd done that often enough before.

The artificial intelligence rotated three-dimensional images of Hindi armor onto the left side of the visor in obedience to Des Grieux's command. The schematic of a tank as flat as a floor tile lifted to display the balloon tires, four per axle, which supported its weight. In particularly marshy soils—and the rice paddies on both sides of the border area were muddy ponds for most of the year—the tires could be covered with one-piece tracks to lower the ground pressure still further.

The tank did not have a rotating turret. Its long, slim gun was mounted along the vehicle's centerline. The weapon used combustion-augmented plasma to drive armor-piercing shots at velocities of several thousand meters per second.

Comparable Han vehicles mounted lasers in small turrets. Neither technology was quite as effective as the powerguns of the Slammers—and Baffin's Legion; but they would serve lethally, even against armor as thick as that of Des Grieux's tank.

The AI began to display a Hindi armored personnel carrier, also running on large tires behind a thin
shield of armor. Des Grieux switched his helmet to
direct vision. The images continued to flicker un-
watched on the left-hand screen below in the fighting compartment. Adrenaline from the bottle
incident left the mercenary too restless to pretend
interest in mere holograms.

There were hundreds of vehicles behind Des
Grieux's tank. The convoy snaked down and across
the valley floor for as far as he could see without
increasing his visor's magnification. Most of the column was of Han manufacture: laser vehicles, troop
transports, maintenance vans. Huge articulated supply trucks with powerplants at both ends of the load;
*they'd* be bitches to get up these ridges separating
the fertile valleys.

Des Grieux didn't care about the logistics vehicles,
whether indigenous or the Slammers' own. His business was with things that shot, things that fought. If
he had a weapon, the form it took didn't matter. A
tank like the one he commanded now was best; but
if Des Grieux had been an infantryman with nothing
but a semi-automatic powergun, he'd have faced a
tank and not worried about the disparity in equipment. So long as he had a chance to fight. . . .

The convoy contained a Han mechanized brigade,
the Black Banner Guards: the main indig striking
force on the Western Wing. The tanks of Hammer's
H Company were spread at intervals along the order
of march to provide air and artillery defense.

Out of sight of the convoy, two companies of combat cars and another of infantry screened the force's
front and flanks. Hammer's air cushion vehicles were
much more nimble on the boggy lowlands than the

wheeled and track-laying equivalents with which the indigs made do.

No doubt the locals would rather have built their own ACVs, but the technology of miniaturized fusion powerplants was beyond the manufacturing capacity of any but the most sophisticated handful of human worlds. Without individual fusion bottles, air-cushion vehicles lacked the range and weight of weapons and armor necessary for front-line combat units.

So they hired specialists, the Han and Hindis both. If one side in a conflict mortgaged its future to hire off-planet talent, the other side either matched the ante-or forfeited that future.

The rice on the terraces had a bluish tinge that Des Grieux didn't remember having seen before, though he'd fought on half a dozen rice-growing worlds over the years. . . .

His eyes narrowed. An air-cushion jeep sped up the road from the back of the column. It passed trucks every time the graded surface widened and gunned directly up-slope at switchbacks to cut corners. Des Grieux thought he recognized the squat figure in the passenger seat.

He looked deliberately away.

Des Grieux's tank was nearing the last switchback before the crest. The vehicle ahead began to blat through open exhaust pipes again, though its engine note didn't change. Han trucks used hydraulic torque converters instead of geared transmissions, so their diesels always stayed within the powerband. Lousy troops, but good equipment. . . .

Des Grieux imagined the jeep passing his tank—spinning a little in the high-pressure air vented beneath the tank's skirts—sliding under the wheels of the Han truck and then, as *Captain* Broglie

screamed, being reduced to a millimeters' thick
streak as the tank overran the wreckage despite all
Pesco did to avoid the obstacle.

Des Grieux caught himself. He was shaking. He
didn't know what his face looked like, but he suddenly realized that the soldiers in the truck ahead
had ducked for cover again.

The truck turned hard left and dropped down the
other side of the ridge. Brakelights glowed. The dis-
advantage of a torque coverter was that it didn't permit compression braking. . . .

From the crest, Des Grieux could see three more
ridgelines furrowing the horizon to the west. The
last was in Hindi territory. Three centuries ago, this
planet had been named Friendship and colonized by
the Pan-Asian Cooperative Settlement Authority.
The organizers' plans had worked out about as well
as most notions that depended on the Brotherhood
of Man.

More business for Hammer's Slammers. More
chances for Slick Des Grieux to do what he did better than anybody else. . . .

Pesco pivoted the tank, changing its attitude to
follow the road before sliding off the crest. As the
huge vehicle paused, the jeep came up along the
port side. Des Grieux expected the jeep to pass
them. Instead, the passenger—Broglie, as Des Grieux
had known from the first glimpse—gripped the
mounting handholds welded to the tank's skirts and
pulled himself aboard.

The jeep dropped back. For a moment, Des
Grieux could see nothing of his new company commander except shoulders and the top of his head as
Broglie found the steps behind their spring-loaded
coverplates. If he slipped now—

Broglie lifted himself onto the tank's deck. Unless Pesco was using a panoramic display—which he shouldn't be, not when the road ahead was more than enough to occupy anybody driving a vehicle of the tank's bulk—he didn't know what was going on behind him. The driver would have kittens when he learned, since at least half the blame would land on him if something went wrong.

Des Grieux would have taken his share of the trouble willingly, just to see the red smear where *that* human being had been ground into the gravel.

Broglie braced one foot on a turret foothold and leaned toward the cupola. "Hello, Slick," he said. He shouted to be heard over the rush of air into the fan intakes. "Since we're going to be working together again, I figured I'd come and chat with you. Without going through the commo net and whoever might be listening in."

Des Grieux looked at his new company commander. The skin of Broglie's face was red. Des Grieux remembered that the other man never seemed to tan, just weathered. He looked older, too; but Via, they all did.

"I didn't know you were going to be here when I took the transfer to Hotel," Des Grieux blurted. He hadn't planned to say that; hadn't *planned* to say anything, but the words came out when he looked into Broglie's eyes and remembered how much he hated the man.

"Figured that," said Broglie, nodding. He looked toward the horizon, then added, "You belong in tanks, Slick. They're the greatest force multiplier there is. A man who can use weapons like you ought to have the best weapons."

It wasn't flattery; just cold truth, the way Des

Grieux had admitted that Broglie was a dead shot. It occurred to Des Grieux that his personal feelings about Broglie were mutual and always had been.

He said nothing aloud. If the company commander had come to talk, the company commander could talk.

"What's your tank's name, Slick?" Broglie asked.

Des Grieux shrugged. "I didn't name her," he said. "The guy I replaced did. I don't care cop about her name."

"That's not what I asked," Broglie said. "Sergeant."

"Right," said Des Grieux. His eyes were straight ahead, toward the horizon in which the far wall of the valley rose. "The name's *Gangbuster*. *Gangbuster II*, since you care so much. Sir."

"Glad to be back in tanks?" Broglie asked. His voice was neutral, but it left no doubt that he expected answers, whether or not Des Grieux saw any point in giving them.

"Any place is fine," Des Grieux said, turning abruptly toward Broglie again. "Just so long as they let me do my job."

The anger in Des Grieux's tone surprised even him. He added more mildly, "Yeah, sure, I like tanks. And if you mean it's been five years—don't worry about it. I haven't forgotten where the controls are."

"I don't worry about you knowing how to handle any bloody weapon there is, Slick," Broglie said. They stared into one another's eyes, guarded but under control. "I might worry about the way you took orders, though."

Des Grieux swallowed. A billow of dust rose around *Gangbuster*'s bow skirts and drifted back as Pesco slowed to avoid running over the truck ahead.

Des Grieux let the grit settle behind them before he said, "Nobody has to worry about *me* doing my job, Captain."

"A soldier's job is to obey orders, Slick," Broglie said flatly. "The time when heroes put on their armor and went off to single combat, that ended four thousand years ago. D'ye understand me?"

Des Grieux fumbled within the hatch and brought up his water bottle. The refrigerated liquid washed dust from his mouth but left the sour taste of bile. He stared at the horizon. It rotated sideways as Pesco negotiated a switchback.

"Do you understand me, Slick?" Captain Broglie repeated.

"I understand," Des Grieux said.

"I'm glad to hear it," Broglie said.

Des Grieux felt the company commander step away from the turret and signal to the driver of his jeep. All Des Grieux could see was the red throb of the veins behind his own eyes.

Ten kilometers to the west, the Han and Hindi outpost lines slashed at one another in a crackling barely audible through the darkness.

"These are the calculated enemy positions," said Captain Broglie. The portable projector spread a holographic panorama in red for Broglie and the three tank commanders of H Company, 2nd Platoon.

Ghosts of the coherent light glowed on the walls of the tent. The polarizing fabric gave the Slammers within privacy but allowed them to see and hear the world outside.

"And here's Baffin's Legion," Broglie continued.

A set of orange symbols appeared to the left, map West, of the red images. The Legion, a combined-arms force of battalion strength, made a relatively minor showing on the map, but none of the Slammers were deceived. Almost any mercenary unit was better than almost any local force; and Baffin's Legion was better than almost any other mercenaries.

Almost.

"Remember," Broglie warned, "Baffin can move just as fast as we can. In fifteen minutes, he could be driving straight through the friendly lines."

A battery of the Slammers' rocket howitzers was attached to the Strike Force. The hogs chose this moment to send a single round apiece into the night. The white glare of their simultaneous muzzle flashes vanished as suddenly as it occurred, but afterimages from the shells' sustainer motors flickered purple and yellow across the retinas of anyone without eye protection who had been looking in the direction of those brilliant streaks.

"Are they shelling Morobad?" asked Platoon Sergeant Peres. Peres had been in command of 2nd Platoon ever since the former platoon leader vanished in an explosion on New Aberdeen that left a fifty-foot crater where his tank had been. She gestured toward the built-up area just west of the major canal that the map displayed. Morobad was the only community in the region that was more than mud houses and a central street.

Hundreds of Han soldiers started shooting as though the artillery signalled a major attack. Small arms, crew-served weapons, and even the soul-searing throb of heavy lasers ripped out from the perimeter. Flashes and the dull glow of self-sustaining brushfires marked the innocent targets downrange.

"Stupid bastards," Des Grieux muttered, his tone

too flat to be sneering. "If they're shooting at anything, it's their own people."

"You got that right, Slick," Broglie agreed as he
stared for a moment through the pervious walls of
the tent. His face was bleak; not angry, but as determined as a storm cloud.

Han officers sped toward the sources of gunfire on
three-wheeled scooters, crying orders and blowing
oddly-tuned whistles. Some of the shooting came
from well within the camp.

A rifle bullet zinged through the air close enough
to the Slammers' tent that the fabric echoed the ballistic crack. Medrassi, the veteran commander of *Dar
es Salaam*—House of Peace—swore and hunched his
head lower on his narrow shoulders.

"What we oughta do," Des Grieux said coldly, "is
leave these dumb clucks here and handle the job
ourself. That way there's only half the people around
likely t' shoot us."

Cyan streaks quivered over the horizon to the
west. The light wasn't impressive until you remembered it came from ten kilometers away. Shells burst
in puffs of distant orange.

Broglie lifted his thumb toward the western horizon. "I think that's what they were after, Perry," he
said to Sergeant Peres. "Just checking on how far
forward Baffin's artillery defenses were."

"Calliopes?" Medrassi asked.

Firing from the Han positions slackened. In the
relative silence, Des Grieux heard the *pop-pop-pop*
of shells, half a minute after powergun bolts had detonated them.

"Baffin uses twin-barrel three-CM rigs," Broglie
explained. "They're really light anti-tank guns converted to artillery defense. He's got about eight of

them. They're slow firing, but they pack enough punch that a single bolt can do the job."

He smiled starkly. "And they still retain their anti-tank function, of course."

Des Grieux spit on the ground.

"The reason that we're not going to leave our brave allies parked here out of the way, Slick," Broglie continued, "is that we're going to need all the help we can get. Indigenous forces may include an entire armored brigade. The Hindis are tough opponents in their own right—don't judge them by the Han *we're* saddled with. And Baffin's Legion by itself would be a pretty respectable opponent—even for a Slammers' battalion combat team."

"Great," Peres said, kneading savagely at the scar on the back of her left hand. "Let's do it the other way, then. We keep the hell outa the way while our indig buddies mix it with Baffin and get all this wild shooting outa their system."

"What we're going to do," Broglie said, taking charge of the discussion again, "is turn a sow's ear into a . . . nice synthetic purse, lets say. Second Platoon is going to do that."

He looked at his subordinates. "And I am, because I'm going to be with you tomorrow."

The holographic display responded to Broglie's gestures. Blue arrows labeled as units of the Black Banner Guards wedged their way across the map toward the Hindi lines. Four gray dots, individual Slammers' tanks, advanced beyond the arrows like pearls on a velvet tray.

"The terrain is pretty much what we've seen in each of the valleys we crossed on the Han side of the boundary," Broglie said. "Dikes between one and two meters high. Some of them broad enough to carry a tank but *don't* count on it. Mostly the dikes are planted with hedges that give good cover, and Hindi troops are dug into the mud of the banks. At least Hindi troops—Baffin may be stiffening them."

"Morobad's not the same," Medrassi said through the hedge of his dark, gnarled fingers. "Fighting in a city's not the same as nothing. 'Cept maybe fighting in Hell."

"Don't worry," said Broglie dismissively. "Nobody's going anywhere near that far."

He looked at his tank commanders. "What the Strike Force is going to do, guys," he said. "You, me, and the Black Banner Guards . . . is move up—" blue arrows came in contact with the red symbols "—hit 'em—" the arrows flattened "—and retreat in good order, Lord willing and we all do our jobs."

"We'll do *our* jobs," Sergeant Peres grunted, "but where the hell's the rest of H Company?"

She raised her eyes from the horrid fascination of the holographic display, where blue symbols retreated eastward across terrain markers and red bars formed into arrows to pursue. "Where the *hell* is the rest of the battalion, Echo, Foxtrot, and Golf?"

The blue arrows on the display had attacked ahead of the gray tank symbols. As the Han forces began to pull back, the tanks provided the bearing surface on which the advancing Hindis ground in an increasingly desperate attempt to reach their planetary enemies.

"Fair question," Broglie said, but he didn't cue the holographic display. Symbolic events proceeded at their own pace.

Outside the Slammers' shelter, a multi-barreled

machine gun broke the near silence by firing skyward. Loops of mauve tracers rose until the marking
mixture burned out two thousand meters above the
camp. Han officers went off again in their furious
charade of authority.

Des Grieux sneered at the lethal fireworks on the
other side of the one-way fabric. The bullets would
be invisible when they fell; but they were going to
fall, in or bloody close to the Han lines. Broglie was
a fool if he thought *this* lot was going to do the
Slammers' fighting for them.

Red arrows forced their way forward over holographic rice paddies. The counterattack spread sideways as Han symbols accelerated their retreat. The
gray pearls of the four tanks shifted back more
quickly under threat of being overrun on both flanks.
Orange arrows joined the red when the computer
model estimated that Baffin would commit his far-
more-mobile forces to exploit the Hindi victory.

"The rest of our people are here," Broglie said as
lines and bars of gray light sprang into place to the
north, south, and east of the enemy salient. "Waiting
in low-observables mode until Baffin's got too much
on his plate to worry about fine-tuning his sensor
data. Waiting to slam the door."

On either flank of the red-and-orange thrust was
a four-tank platoon from H Company and a full company of combat cars. Gray arrows curving eastward
indicated combat cars racing across rice paddies in
columns of muddy froth, moving to rake the choke
point just east of Morobad where enemy vehicles
bunched as reinforcements collided with units at-
tempting a panicked retreat.

The dug-in infantry of the Slammers' Echo Company blocked the Hindi eastward advance. On the

holographic display, blue Han symbols halted their
retreat, then moved again to attack their trapped
opponents in concert with Hammer's infantry and
the tanks of 2nd Platoon.

The display still showed Second to have four vehicles. Everybody in the shelter knew that rear-guard
actions always meant casualties—and didn't always
mean survivors.

Medrassi grunted into his hands.

"The hogs'll provide maximum effort when the
time comes," Broglie said. "The locals have about
thirty self-propelled guns also, but their fire direction may leave something to be desired."

"It's not," Peres said, "going t' be a lot of fun.
Until the rest of our people come in."

"The battle depends on 2nd Platoon," Broglie said
flatly. "You're all highly experienced, and mostly
your drivers are as well. Slick, how do you feel about
your driver, Pesco? He's the new man."

Des Grieux shrugged. "He'll do," he said. Des
Grieux was looking at nothing in particular through
the side of the tent.

Broglie stared at Des Grieux for a moment without
expression. Then he resumed, "Colonel Hammer
put Major Chesney in command of this operation,
but it's not going to work unless Second does its job.
That's why I'm here with you. We've got to convince
the Hindis—and particularly Baffin—that the attack
is real and being heavily supported by the Slammers.
After the locals pull back—"

He looked grimly at the display, though its
image—enemy forces trapped in a pocket while artillery hammered them into surrender—was cheerful
enough for Pollyanna.

"After the Han pull back," the captain continued

softly, "it's up to us to keep the planned withdrawal from turning into a genuine rout. Echo can't hold by itself if Baffin's Legion slams into them full-tilt . . . and if that happens—"

Broglie smiled the hard, accepting smile of a professional describing events which would occur literally over his own dead body.

"—then Baffin can choose which of our separated flanking forces he swallows up first, can't he?"

A Han laser slashed the empty darkness from the perimeter.

"Bloody marvelous," Peres murmured. "But I suppose if they knew what they was doing, they wouldn't need us t'do it for them."

Medrassi laughed. "Dream on," he said.

"Do you all understand our mission, then?" Broglie asked. "Sergeant Peres?"

"Yessir," Peres said with a nod.

"Sergeant Medrassi?"

"Yeah, sure. I been in worse."

"Slick?"

Des Grieux stared at the wall of the shelter. His mind was bright with the rich, soul-devouring glare of a tank's main gun.

"Sergeant Des Grieux," Broglie said. His voice was no louder than it had been a moment before, but it cut like an edge of glass. "Do you understand the operation we will carry out tomorrow?"

Des Grieux looked at his commanding officer. "Chesney never came up with anything this cute," he said mildly. "This one was your baby? Sir."

"I had some input in the planning, that's right," Broglie said tonelessly. "Do you understand the operation, Slick?"

"I understand that it makes a real pretty picture,

Cap'n Broglie," Des Grieux replied. "Tomorrow we'll see how it looks on the ground, won't we?"

Outside the shelter, machine gun fire etched the sky in pointless response.

The Han armored personnel carrier was supposed to be amphibious, but it paused for almost thirty seconds on the first dike. The wheels of the front two axles spun in the air; those of the rear pair churned in a suspension of mud and water with the lubricating properties of motor oil.

A Hindi anti-tank gun ripped the APC with a fifty-MM osmium penetrator. Half of the carrier's rear-mounted engine blew through the roof of the tilted vehicle with a *crash* much louder than the Mach 4 ballistic crack of the shot.

The driver hopped out of the forward hatch and fell down on the dike. His legs continued to piston as though he were running instead of thrashing in mud. Sidehatches opened a fraction of a second later and a handful of unhurt infantrymen flopped clear as well.

Inertia kept the APC's front wheels rotating for some seconds. A rainbow slick of diesel fuel covered the rice paddy behind the vehicle. It did not ignite.

Des Grieux smiled like a shark from his overwatch position on the first terrace east of the floodplain. He traversed his main gun a half degree. The Hindi anti-tank gun was a towed piece with optical sights. It had no electronic signature to give it away, and *Gangbuster II*'s magnetic anomaly detector was far too coarse a tool to provide targeting information at a range of nearly a kilometer.

When the weapon fired, though—

Des Grieux stroked his foot trip and converted the anti-tank gun into a ball of saturated cyan light.

Han vehicles hosed the landscape with their weapons. Bullets from APC turrets and the secondary armament of laser-vehicles flashed as bright explosions among the foliage growing on dikes and made the mud bubble.

High-powered lasers raised clouds of steam wherever their pale beams struck, but they were not very effective. The lasers were line of sight weapons like the Slammers' powerguns. The gunners could hit nothing but the next hedge over while the firing vehicles sheltered behind dikes themselves.

The entire Han advance stopped when the Hindis fired their first gun.

Des Grieux had a standard two-CM Slammers' carbine clipped to the side of his seat. Over his head, *Gangbuster*'s tribarrel pumped short bursts into the heavens in automatic air-defense mode. The sky, still a pale violet color in the west, was decorated with an applique of shell tracks and the bolts of powerguns which detonated the incoming.

Both sides' artillery fired furiously. Neither party had any success in breaking through the webs of opposing defenses, but there was no question of taking *Gangbuster II* out of AAD. The infantry carbine and the tank's main gun were the only means of slaughter under Des Grieux's personal control.

"Blue Two," Captain Broglie's voice ordered. "On command, advance one dike. Remaining elements look sharp."

Blue Two, *Dar es Salaam*, was on the southern edge of the advance, half a kilometer from *Gangbuster II*. Broglie's command tank, *Honey Girl*, was a similar distance to starboard of Des Grieux; and Blue

One, Peres, backstopped the Han right flank a full kilometer north of *Gangbuster II*. The causeway carrying the main road to Morobad was the axis of the Strike Force advance.

The dikes turned the floodplain into a series of ribbons, each about a hundred meters wide. By advancing one at a time from their overwatch positions behind the Black Banner Guards, maybe the Slammers' tanks could get the Han force moving again. . . .

Though if instead the four tanks burst straight ahead in a hell-for-leather dash, they'd open up the Hindi lines like so many bullets through a can of beans.

"Blue Two, *go*."

Medrassi's tank lurched forward at maximum acceleration. The driver—Des Grieux didn't know his name; *her* name, maybe—had backed thirty meters in the terraced paddy to give himself a run before they hit the dike.

Water and bright green rice shoots, hand-planted only days before, spewed to either side as the fans compressed a cushion of air dense enough to float 170 tonnes. For a moment, *Dar es Salaam*'s track through the field was a barren expanse of wet clay; then muddy water slopped back to cover the sudden waste.

The tank didn't lift quite high enough to clear the dike, but the driver didn't intend to. The belly plates were the vehicle's thinnest armor. Hindi gunners, much less the Legion mercenaries, could penetrate even a Slammers' tank if it waved too much of its underside in the direction of the enemy.

*Dar es Salaam*'s bow skirts rammed the top layer of the bank ahead of the tank. Fleshy-branched native osiers flailed desperately as they fell with the dike in which they had grown.

*Honey Girl* fired its main gun. Des Grieux didn't see Broglie's target but there *was* a target, because the bolt detonated an anti-tank gun's 400-liter bottle of liquid propellant in a huge yellow flash. The barrel of the Hindi weapon flew toward the Han lines. The bodies of the gun crew shed parts all around the hemispherical blast.

Des Grieux didn't have a target. That bastard Broglie was good, Lord knew.

A pair of Han laser-vehicles resumed the planned advance; or tried to, they'd bogged in the muck when they stopped. Spinning wheels threw brown undulations to either side but contributed nothing to the forward effort. The Han vehicles were supposed to be all-terrain, but they lacked the supplementary treads the Hindi tanks used. The paddies might have been too much for the balloon tires even if the heavy vehicles had kept moving.

Four APCs grunted into motion—drawn by *Dar es Salaam* and encouraged by the deadly 20-CM powerguns on the mercenary tanks. The carriers found the going difficult also, but their lower ground pressure made them more mobile than the laser-vehicles were.

Thirty or more of the APCs joined the initial quartet. The advance, one or two vehicles revving into motion at a time, looked like individual drivers and officers making their own decisions irrespective of orders from above—but it had the effect of a planned leapfrog assault.

"Blue One," Broglie ordered. "On command, advance one dike. Remaining elements look sharp."

Only buzzbombs and a few light crew-served

weapons replied to the empty storm of Han fire. The Hindis kept their heads down and picked their targets.

Bullet impacts glittered on the glacis plate of an APC driving parallel to the causeway. The commander had been conning his vehicle with his head out of the cupola hatch. He ducked down immediately. The driver must have ducked also, even though he was using his periscopes. The APC ran halfway up the side of the causeway and overturned.

"Blue One, *go!*"

As Peres' driver kicked *Dixie Dyke* forward, Des Grieux's gunnery screen marked a target with a white carat. The barrel of a Hindi gun was rotating to bear when Peres' tank exposed its belly. Excellent camouflage concealed the motion from even the Slammers' high-resolution optics, but the magnetic anomaly detector noticed the shift against the previous electromagnetic background.

*Gangbuster II*'s turret traversed four degrees to starboard on its magnetic gimbals. The cupola tribarrel snarled up at incoming artillery fire, but the only sound within the fighting compartments was the whine of the turret drive motors and the whistling intake of Des Grieux's breath as he prepared to kill a—

The target vanished in the blue-white glare of *Honey Girl*'s bolt. Broglie had beaten Des Grieux to the shot again, and *fuck* that the target was in *Honey Girl*'s primary fire zone.

"Blue Three," Broglie ordered with his usual insouciant calm. "On command, advance two, I repeat two, dikes. Remaining elements, look sharp."

"Driver," Des Grieux ordered, "you heard the bastard."

Medrassi fired, but he didn't have a bloody target

for a main-gun bolt, there *wasn't* one. A section of dike flash-baked and blew outward as ceramic shards, but Via! what did a couple Hindi infantry matter?

Des Grieux ordered, "Booster, echo main screen, left side of visor, out," and pulled up hard on the seat-control lever. The seat rose. Des Grieux's head slid out of the hatch just as the cupola rotated around him and the tribarrel spat three rounds into the western sky with an acrid stench from the ejected empties.

"Blue Three, *go!*"

"Goose it, driver!" Des Grieux said as he un-clipped the shoulder weapon from his seat and felt *Gangbuster II* rise beneath him on the thrust of its eight drive fans to mount the dike.

The Han advance was proceeding in reasonable fashion, though at least a score of APCs hung back at the start point. Several laser-vehicles were moving also. The inaction of the rest was more likely the bog than cowardice, though cowardice was never an unreasonable guess when unblooded troops ran into their first firefight.

One laser-vehicle balanced on top of a dike. The fore and aft axles spun their tires in the air, while the grip of the central wheels was too poor to move them off the slick surface. Hindi skirmishers lobbed their buzzbombs at long range toward the teetering vehicle, but the anti-tank guns contemptuously ignored it to wait for a real threat.

To wait for the Slammers' tanks.

Des Grieux's eyes were four meters above the ground surface, higher than the tank's own sensors, when *Gangbuster II* humped itself over the dike. Through the clear half of his visor Des Grieux *saw* the movement, the glint of the plasma generator trunnion-mounted to an anti-tank gun, as it swung beneath its overhead protection.

The little joystick in the cupola was meant as a manual control for the defense array, but it was multi-function at need—and Des Grieux needed it. He rotated and depressed the main gun with his left hand as *Gangbuster II* started her fierce rush down the reverse side of the dike and the Hindi weapon traversed for the kill.

The pipper on the left side of Des Grieux's visor merged in a stereo image with the view of his right eye. He thumbed the firing tit with a fierce joy, knowing that *nobody* else was that good.

But Slick Des Grieux was. As the tank bellied down into the spray of her fans, a yellow fireball lifted across the distant fields. A direct hit, snap-shooting and on the move, but Des Grieux was the best!

Broglie fired also, from the other side of the empty road to Morobad. He must've got something also, because a secondary explosion followed the bolt, but the Hindis—strictly locals, no sign at all of the Legion—weren't done yet. A hypervelocity shot *spang*ed from *Gangbuster*'s turret. Kinetic energy became heat with a flash almost as bright as that of a plasma bolt, rocking Des Grieux backward.

He turned toward the shot, pointing his short-barreled shoulder weapon as though it were a heavy pistol. The tank bottomed on the paddy, then bounced upward nearly a meter as water rushed in to fill the cavity, sealing the plenum chamber to maximum efficiency.

The Hindi weapon was dug in low; it had fired through a carefully-cut aisle. Now the gunners waited to shoot again, hoping for more of a target

than Des Grieux's helmeted head bobbing over the
planted dikes between them. None of the three
Slammers' tanks providing the base of fire could bear
on the anti-tank gun even now that it had exposed
itself by firing.

*Gangbuster II*'s main gun was masked by the vegetation also, but Des Grieux's personal weapon spat
three times on successive bounces as the tank por-
poised forward. The gun's frontal camouflage flashed
and burned when a two-CM bolt flicked it.

Han officers, guided by the powergun, sent a
dozen ropes of tracer arcing toward the Hindi
weapon from the cupolas of their APCs. Hindi gunners splashed away from the beaten zone, hampered
by the mud and raked by the hail of explosive
bullets.

The *peepeepeep* in Des Grieux's earphones warned
him to attend to the miniature carat on his visor:
Threat Level I, a laser rangefinder painting *Gangbuster II* from the hedge boarding the causeway. No
way to tell what weapon the rangefinder served, but
somebody thought it could kill a Slammers'
tank. . . .

Des Grieux rotated the turret with the joystick,
thrusting hard as though his muscles rather than the
geartrain were turning the massive weight of iridium. "Driver, hard right!" he screamed, because the
traversing mechanism wasn't going to slew the main
gun fast enough by itself.

And maybe nothing was going to slew the main
gun fast enough.

Des Grieux shot twice with the carbine in his right
hand. His bolts splashed near the bottom of the
hedge. One round blew glassy fragments of mud in
the air; the other carbonized a gap the size of a pie

plate at the edge of the interwoven stems of native shrub.

The laser emitter itself was two meters high in the foliage, but that was only a bead connected to the observer's hiding place by a coaxial optical fiber. The observer was probably *close* to the emitter, though; and if the weapon itself was close to the observer, it would simply set-up and parallax corrections.

Soldiers liked things simple.

Pesco was trying to obey Des Grieux's order, but *Gangbuster II* had enormous forward momentum and there was the dike they were approaching to consider also. A sheet of spray lifted to the tank's port side as the driver dumped air beneath the left skirt. The edge of the right skirt dipped and cut yellow bottom clay to stain the roostertail sluicing back on that side.

*Gangbuster II* started to lift for the dike. That was almost certainly the Hindi aiming point, but Des Grieux had the sight picture he wanted, he *needed*—

Des Grieux tripped the main gun. Five meters of mud and vegetation exploded as the twenty-CM bolt slanted across the base of the hedge.

The jolt of sun-hot plasma certainly blinded the laser pick-up. It probably incinerated the observer as well: no mud burrow could withstand the impact of a tank's main gun.

The causeway was gouged as if a giant shark had taken a bite out of it. The soil steamed. Fragments of hedge blazed and volleyed orange sparks for twenty meters from where the bolt hit.

The weapon the observer controlled, a rack of four hypervelocity rockets dug into the edge of the causeway ten meters west of the rangefinder, was not damaged by the bolt. The observer's dying reflex must have closed the firing circuit.

A section of causeway collapsed from the rockets' backblast. *Gangbuster II*'s automatic defense system fired—too late to matter. The sleet of steel pellets disrupted the razor-sharp smoke trails, but the projectiles themselves were already past.

The exhaust tracks fanned out slightly from the launcher. One of the four rockets missed *Gangbuster*'s turret by little more than the patina on the iridium surface. The sound of their passage was a single brittle *c-c-crack*!

Because *Gangbuster II* was turning in the last instant before the missiles fired—and because the main gun had blasted the observer into stripped atoms and steam before he could correct for the course change—the tank was undamaged, and Des Grieux was still alive to do what he did best.

It was time to do that now, whatever Broglie's orders said.

"Driver, steer for the road!" Des Grieux ordered. "Highball! We're gonna gut 'em like fish, all the way t' the town!"

"Via, we can't do that!" Pesco blurted.

*Gangbuster II* dropped off the dike in a flurry of dirt, water, and vegetation diced by the fans. "Cap'n Broglie said—"

Des Grieux craned his body forward and aimed his carbine. He fired, dazzling the direct vision sensors built into the driver's hatch coaming. The bolt vaporized a tubful of water ahead of *Gangbuster II* and sent cyan quivers through a semicircle of the paddy.

"Drive, you son of a bitch!" Des Grieux shouted.

Pesco resumed steering to starboard, increasing

the slant *Gangbuster II* had taken to bring the twenty-CM gun to bear. The gap that bolt had blown in the causeway's border steadied across the tank's bow slope.

A dozen Hindi machine guns in the dikes and causeway rang bullets off *Gangbuster II*'s armor. One round snapped the air close enough to Des Grieux's face to fluff his moustache. It reminded him that he was still head and shoulders out of the cupola.

He shoved down the crash bar and dumped himself back into the fighting compartment. The hatch clanged above him, shutting out the sound of bullets and *Gangbuster II*'s own tribarrel plucking incoming artillery from the air.

Des Grieux slapped the AAD plate to put the tribarrel under his personal control again.

All three of the tanks in overwatch fired within split seconds of one another. A column of flame and smoke mounted far to the north, suggesting fuel tanks rather than munitions were burning.

Of course, the victim might have been one of the Han vehicles.

The topographic display on *Gangbuster II*'s left-hand screen showed friendly units against a pattern of fields and hedges. The entire Han line was in motion, spurred by the mercenaries' leapfrog advance and the Han's own amateur enthusiasm for war.

They'd learn. At least, the survivors would learn.

"General push," Des Grieux said, directing the tank's artificial intelligence to route the following message so that everyone in the Strike Force—locals as well as mercenaries—could receive it. "All units, follow me to Morobad!"

His hand reached into the breaker box and disconnected *Gangbuster II* from incoming communications.

The flooded rice paddies slowed the tank considerably. One hundred seventy tonnes were too much for even the eight powerful drive fans to lift directly. The vehicle floated on a cushion of air, but that high-pressure air required solid support also.

The water and thin mud of the paddies spewed from the plenum chamber. *Gangbuster II* rode on the clay undersurface—but the liquid still created drag on the outside of the skirts as the tank drove through it. To make the speed Des Grieux knew it needed to survive, *Gangbuster II* had to have a smooth, hard surface beneath her skirts.

The causeway was such an obvious deathtrap that none of the Han vehicles had even attempted it— but the locals didn't have vehicles with the speed and armor of a Slammers' tank.

And anyway, they didn't have Des Grieux's awareness of how important it was to keep the enemy off-balance by punching fast as well as often.

Des Grieux latched the two-CM carbine back against his seat. The barrel, glowing from the half magazine the veteran had fired through it, softened the patch of cushion it touched. The stench intertwined with that oozing from the main-gun empties on the floor of the turret basket.

*Gangbuster II* was now leading the Han advance instead of supporting it. Three Hindi soldiers got up and ran, left to right, across a dike two hundred meters west of the tank. All were bent over, their bodies tiger-striped by foliage. The trailing pair carried a long object between them, a machine gun or rocket launcher.

Maybe the Hindis thought they were getting into

a better position from which to fire at *Gangbuster II*. Des Grieux's tribarrel, *his* tribarrel again, sawed the men down in a tangle of flailing limbs and blue-white flashes.

Des Grieux didn't need to worry about indirect fire anymore, because the Hindi artillery wouldn't fire into friendly lines . . . and besides, *Gangbuster II* was moving too fast to be threatened by any but the most sophisticated terminally-guided munitions. The locals didn't have anything of that quality in their arsenals.

Baffin's Legion *did* have tank-killing rounds that were up to the job. Still, the cargo shells which held two or three self-forging fragments—shaped by the very blasts that hurled them against the most vulnerable spots in a tank's armor—were expensive, even for mercenary units commanding Baffin's payscale, or Hammer's. For the moment, the guns on both sides were flinging cheap rounds of HE Common at one another, knowing that counterfire would detonate the shells harmlessly in the air no matter what they were.

It'd take minutes—tens of seconds, at least—for Legion gunners to get terminally-guided munitions up the spout. That would be plenty of time for the charge Des Grieux led to blast out the core of enemy resistance.

"Hang on!" Pesco cried as though Des Grieux couldn't see for himself that *Gangbuster II* was about to surge up onto the causeway.

A Hindi soldier stood transfixed, halfway out of a spider hole in the hedge on the other side of the road. His rifle was pointed forward, but he was too terrified to sight down it toward the tank's huge, terrible bow. Des Grieux cranked the tribarrel with his right joystick.

*Gangbuster II* rose in a slurp of mud as dark and fluid as chocolate cake dough. The Hindi disappeared, not into his hole but by jumping toward the paddies north of the causeway. A Han gunner, lucky or exceptionally skillful, caught the Hindi in mid-leap. A splotch of blood hung in the air for some seconds after the corpse hit the water.

An anti-tank shot struck the rear of *Gangbuster II*'s turret. The bustle rack tore away in a scatter of the tankers' personal belongings, many of them afire. Impact of the dense penetrator on comparably dense armor heated both incandescent, enveloping the clothes and paraphernalia in a haze of gaseous osmium and iridium.

The projectile had only a minuscule direct effect on the inertia of *Gangbuster*'s 170 tonnes, but the shock made Pesco's hand twitch on the control column. The tank lurched sideways. The lights in the fighting compartment darkened and stayed out, but the screens only flickered as the AI routed power through pathways undamaged when the jolting impact severed a number of conduits.

The second shot blew through the northern hedge a half-second later. Pesco was fighting for control. The projectile hit, but only a glancing blow this time. The shot ricocheted from high on the rear hull, leaving a crease a half-meter long glowing in the back deck.

Des Grieux spun the tribarrel because the cupola responded more quickly than the massive turret forging, but he didn't have a clear target—and the anti-tank gunner didn't need one.

Powergun bolts would dump all their energy on

the first solid object they touched. It was pointless trying to shoot at a target well to the other side of dense vegetation. Heavy osmium shot, driven by a jolt of plasma generated in a chamber filled with liquid propellant, carried through the hedge with no significant degradation of its speed or stability.

*Gangbuster II* hesitated while Pesco swung the bow to port, following the causeway, and coarsened the fan pitch to regain the speed lost in climbing the embankment. The tank was almost stationary for the moment.

Hindi soldiers rose from spiderholes in the hedge and raised buzzbomb launchers. One of the rocketeers was a hundred meters ahead of *Gangbuster II*; the other was an equal distance behind, his position already enveloped by the Han advance.

Des Grieux's tribarrel was aimed directly to starboard, and even the main gun was twenty degrees wide of the man in front. The tanker's right hand strained against the joystick anyway. The Hindis fired simultaneously.

The third shot from the anti-tank gun punched in the starboard side of the tank's plenum chamber and exited to port in a white blaze of burning steel. Each hole was approximately the size of a human fist. Air roared out while *Gangbuster II* rang like a struck gong. The fan nacelles were undamaged, and the designers had overbuilt pressurization capacity enough to accept a certain amount of damage without losing speed or maneuverability.

The rocket from the man in the rear hit the hedge midway between launcher and the huge intended target. The buzzbomb's pop-out fins caught in the interlaced branches; the warhead did not go off.

The other buzzbomb was aimed well enough as to

line, but the Hindi soldier flinched upward as he squeezed the ignition trigger. The rocket sailed over *Gangbuster II* in a flat arc and exploded in the dirt at the feet of the other Hindi. The body turned legless somersaults before flopping onto the causeway again.

Des Grieux and Broglie fired their twenty-CM guns together. The Hindi rocketeer and thirty meters of hedge behind him blazed as *Gangbuster II*'s bolt raked along it. Through the sudden gap, Des Grieux saw the cyan-hearted fireball into which Broglie's perfect shot converted the Hindi gun that had targeted the tank on the causeway.

"Go, driver!" Des Grieux shouted hoarsely, but Pesco didn't need the order. Either he understood that their survival lay in speed, or blind panic so possessed him that he had no mind for anything but accelerating down the hedged three-kilometer aisle.

The Black Banner Guards were charging at brigade strength. It was a bloody shambles. The Hindis might have run when they saw the snouts of hundreds of armored personnel carriers bellowing toward them—

But they hadn't. More than a score of anti-tank guns unmasked and began firing, now that the contest was clearly a slugging match and not a game of cat-and-mouse. It took less than a second to purge the chamber of a Hindi gun, inject another projectile and ten liters of liquid propellant, and convert a tungsten wire into plasma in the center of the fluid.

Each shot was sufficiently powerful to lance through four APCs together if they chanced to be lined up the wrong way. Broglie, Peres, and Medrassi ripped away at the luxuriance of targets as fast as they could, but the paddies were already littered with torn and blazing Han vehicles.

The heavy anti-tank weapons were only part of the problem. Hindi teams of three to six men crouched in holes dug into the sides of the dikes, then rose to volley buzzbombs into the oncoming vehicles at point-blank range. Some of the rockets missed, but the hollow *whoomp!* of a single warhead was enough to disable any but the luckiest APC.

For those targets which the first volley missed, additional buzzbombs followed within seconds.

The jet of fire from a shaped charge would rupture fuel cells behind an APC's thin armor. Diesel fuel atomized an instant before it burst into flame. Hindi machine gunners then shot the Han crews to dog-meat as they tried to abandon their burning vehicles.

Des Grieux *knew* that green locals always broke if you charged them. His mind hadn't fully metabo-lized the fact that these Hindis might not be particu-larly accurate with their weapons, but they sure as *blood* weren't running anywhere.

As for the Han, who'd already lost at least a quarter of their strength in an unanswered turkey shoot . . . well, Des Grieux had problems of his own.

"Booster!" he said. "Clear vision!"

The images echoed onto the left side of his visor from *Gangbuster II*'s central screen vanished, leav-ing the screen itself sharp and at full size. Normally Des Grieux would have touched a finger to his hel-met's mechanical controls, but this wasn't normal and both his hands were on the gunnery joysticks.

*Gangbuster II* was so broad that the tank's side skirts brushed one, then the other, hedge bordering the causeway. Morobad was a distant haze at the end of an aisle as straight as peasants with stakes and string could draw it. Des Grieux's right hand stroked the main gun counterclockwise to center its hollow pipper on the community. He didn't need or dare to increase the display's magnification to give him actual images.

A Hindi soldier aimed a buzzbomb out of the left-hand hedge. The man's mottled green uniform was so new that the creases were still sharp. His dark face was as fixed and calm as a wooden idol's.

*Gangbuster II*'s sensors noted a human within five meters. They tripped the automatic defense system attached to a groove encircling the tank just above the skirts. A $50 \times 150$-MM strip of high explosive fired, blowing its covering of steel polygons into the Hindi like the blast of a huge shotgun.

The Hindi and his rocket launcher, both riddled by shrapnel, hurtled backward. Leaves and branches stripped from the hedge danced in the air, hiding the carnage.

A second rocketeer leaned out of the hedge three steps beyond the first. The ADS didn't fire because the cell that bore on the new target had just been expended on his comrade. The Hindi launched his buzzbomb from so close that the stand-off probe almost touched the tank's hull.

The distance was too short for the buzzbomb's fuze to arm. The missile struck *Gangbuster II*'s gun mantle and ricocheted upward instead of exploding. A bent fin made the buzzbomb twist in crazy corkscrews.

*Now* another explosive/shrapnel cell aligned. The automatic defense system went off, shredding the rocketeer's torso. Useless, except as revenge for the way the Hindi had made Des Grieux's heart skip a beat in terror—

But revenge had its uses.

Des Grieux put one, then another twenty-CM bolt

into Morobad without bothering to choose specific targets—if there were any. All he was trying to do for the moment was shake up the town. Some of the Legion's anti-artillery weapons were emplaced in Morobad. If the other side kept its collective head, *Gangbuster II* was going to get a hot reception.

Deafening, dazzling bolts from a tank's main gun pretty well guaranteed that nobody in the impact zone would be thinking coolly.

That was all right, and Des Grieux's tank was all right so far, seventy KPH and accelerating. *Gangbuster II* pressed a broad hollow down the causeway. The surface of dirt and rice-straw matting rippled up to either side under the tank's 170 tonnes, even though the weight was distributed as widely as possible by the air cushion.

The Han brigade that Des Grieux had led to attack was well and truly fucked.

Smoke bubbled from burning vehicles, veiling and clearing the paddies like successive sweeps of a bullfighter's cape. Some APCs had been abandoned undamaged. Their crews cowered behind dikes while Hindi buzzbomb teams launched missile after missile at the vehicles.

The rocketeers weren't particularly skillful: buzzbombs were reasonably accurate to a kilometer, but hits were a toss-up for most of the Hindis at anything over 100 meters. Determination and plenty of reloads made up for deficiencies in skill.

Han gunfire was totally ineffective. The officer manning the cupola machine gun also had his vehicle itself to command. As the extent of the disaster became clear, finding a way to safety overwhelmed any desire to place fire on the Hindis concealed by earth and foliage.

The infantry in the APC cargo compartments had individual gunports, but the Lord himself couldn't have hit a target while looking through a viewslit and shooting from the port beneath it. The APCs bucked and slipped on the slimy terrain. In the compartments, men jostled one another and breathed the hot, poisonous reek of powdersmoke and fear. Their bullets and laser beams either vanished into the landscape or glanced from the sideplates of friendly vehicles.

Des Grieux hadn't a prayer of a target either. He was trapped within the strait confines of the hedges for the two minutes it would take *Gangbuster II* to travel the length of the causeway.

His tribarrel raked the margins of the road, bursts to the right and left a hundred meters ahead of the tank's bluff bow. Stems popped like gunfire as they burned. That might keep a few heads down, but it wasn't a sufficient use for the most powerful unit on the battlefield.

Des Grieux could order his driver into the paddies again, but off the road the tank would wallow like a pig. This time there would be Hindi rocketeers launching buzzbombs from all four sides. Des Grieux no longer thought the local enemy would panic because it was a shark they had in the barrel to shoot at.

By contrast, the remaining Slammers' tanks were having a field day with the targets Des Grieux and the Han had flushed for them. Tribarrels stabbed across a kilometer of paddies to splash cyan death across Hindis focused on nearby APCs. Straw-wrapped packets of buzzbombs exploded, three and four at a time, to blow gaps in the dikes.

The left-hand situation display in *Gangbuster*'s

fighting compartment suddenly lighted with over a
hundred red carats. The tanks of a Hindi armored
brigade, lying hidden on the east side of the canal
which formed the eastern boundary of Morobad, had
been given the order to advance. When the drivers
lighted their gas turbine powerplants, *Gangbuster*'s
sensors noted the electronic activity and located the
targets crawling up onto prepared firing steps.

Morobad was less than a kilometer away. Hindi
tanks maneuvered on both sides of the causeway to
bring the guns fixed along the centerline of their
hulls in line with *Gangbuster II*. The Hindi vehicles
mounted combustion-augmented plasma weapons,
like the anti-tank guns but more powerful because a
tank chassis permitted a larger plasma generator than
that practical on a piece of towed artillery.

Des Grieux's situation display showed the condition clearly. The visuals on his gunnery screen were
the same as they'd been for the past minute and a
half: unbroken hedgerows which would stop bolts
from his powerguns as surely as thirty centimeters
of iridium could.

A Hindi shot *crack*ed left-to-right across the road
a tank's length behind *Gangbuster II*. Somebody'd
gotten a little previous with his gunswitch, but the
tank that had fired was still backing one track to slew
its weapon across the Slammers' vehicle.

Des Grieux traversed his main gun, panning the
target, and rocked the foot-trip twice. Instinct and
the situation display at the corner of his eye guided
him: the orange circle on the gunnery screen showed
only foliage.

The first bolt flash-fired the wall of hedge. The
second jet of cyan plasma crashed through the gap
and made a direct hit on the Hindi tank.

The roiling orange fireball rose a hundred meters. The column of smoke an instant later mounted ten times as high before flattening into an anvil shape which dribbled trash back onto the paddies. The compression wave of the explosion flattened an expanding circle of new-planted rice. Rarefaction following the initial shock jerked the seedlings upright again.

A tank on the north side of the causeway slammed a shot into *Gangbuster II*'s bow. A hundred kilos of iridium armor and #2 fan nacelle turned into white-hot vapor which seared leaves on which it cooled.

Pesco shouted and briefly lost control of his vehicle. The tank's enormous inertia resisted turning and kept the skirts on the road despite a nasty shimmy because of the drop in fan pressure forward.

Des Grieux tried to traverse his main gun to bear on the new danger, but the turret had seventy-five degrees to swing clockwise after its systems braked the momentum of the opposite rotation. He wasn't going to make it in the half-second before the next Hindi shot transfixed *Gangbuster II*'s relatively thin side armor—

But he didn't have to, because Captain Broglie's command tank nailed the Hindi vehicle. Plates of massive steel armor flew in all directions even though the bolt failed to detonate the target's munitions.

Score one for Broglie, *the bastard*; and if he'd brought the rest of the platoon along with Des Grieux, maybe *Gangbuster II* wouldn't be swinging in the breeze right now.

Hindi tanks were firing all along the line. They ignored *Gangbuster II* because the tanks destroyed to the immediate north and south of the causeway blocked the aim of their fellows.

The Hindi CAP guns were useless except against armored vehicles—their solid projectiles had no area effect whatever. Against armor, they were neither quite as effective shot for shot, nor quite as quick-firing as the Slammers' twenty-CM guns.

They were effective enough, though, and there was a bloody swarm of them.

Broglie and his two overwatching companions hit half a dozen of the Hindi vehicles, destroying them instantly even though most of the cyan bolts struck the thickest part of the targets' frontal armor. Then the surviving Hindis got the range and volleyed their replies.

A shot hit the cupola above Broglie. Ammo burned in the feed tube of *Honey Girl*'s tribarrel. A blue-white finger poked skyward, momentarily dimming the rising sun. Des Grieux's display cross-hatched *Dixie Dyke* as well, indicating the north-flank tank had been damaged as Peres raked Hindi lines with both main gun and tribarrel. All three units jerked backward to turret-down positions as quickly as their drivers could cant their fans.

"Driver!" Des Grieux said as *Gangbuster II*, its front skirts dragging sparks from the stone road surface, crossed the canal bridge. "Turn us and we'll hit the bastards from behind. Booster, gimme a fucking city map!"

The cheap buildings of Morobad's canal district were ablaze. Some of the walls were plastered wattle-and-daub; other builders had hung painted sheet-iron on scantlings of flimsy wood. Neither method could resist the two main-gun rounds Des Grieux snapped toward the town when *Gangbuster II* started its rush. The bolts had the effect of flares dropped into a tinder box.

The tank drove into a curtain of flame at ninety KPH. There was something in the way, a wrecked vehicle or the corner of a building. *Gangbuster*'s skirts shunted it aside with no more commotion than the clang the automatic defense system made when it went off.

The tank's AI obediently replaced the topographic display on the left screen with a map of Morobad from *Gangbuster II*'s data banks. The streets were narrow and twisting, even the thoroughfare leading west from the causeway.

Two hundred meters from the canal was a market square bordered by religious and governmental buildings. That would give Pesco room to turn. When *Gangbuster II* roared out of the city again and took the turretless Hindi tanks in the rear, it'd be all she wrote.

The air cleared at street level. *Gangbuster II* scraped the brick facade of a three-story tenement which started to collapse on them. At least a score of Hindi soldiers opened fire with automatic weapons. Bullets ricocheted from the sloped iridium armor, scything down the shooters and their fellows. Cells of the automatic defense system fired, louder and more lethal still.

Haze closed in momentarily, but a tell-tale in the fighting compartment informed Des Grieux that Pesco had already switched to sonic imaging instead of using the electro-optical spectrum to drive. *Gangbuster II* swept into the market square, pulling whorls of smoke into the clear, sunlit air.

A six-tube battery of 170-MM howitzers was set up in the square. Empty obturator disks and unneeded booster charges in white silk littered the cobble-stones behind the weapons. The crews were desperately cranking their muzzles down to fire point-blank at *Gangbuster II*. Hindi infantry cut loose with small arms from all windows facing the square and from the triple tile overhangs of the large temple behind the walled courtyard to the south.

As Des Grieux squeezed both firing tits, a hundred-kilogram shell hit the turret. The round was a thin-cased HE, what the crew happened to have up the spout when they got warning of the tank's approach. The red flash destroyed thirty percent of *Gangbuster II*'s forward sensors and rocked the tank severely, but the hatches were sealed and the massive turret armor was never even threatened.

"Driv—" Des Grieux started to say as his hazy screens showed him Hindi gunners doubling up, flying apart, burning in puffs of vaporized steel as the powergun sights slid across the battery.

A legless Hindi battery captain jerked the lanyard of his last howitzer. The shell was a capped armor-piercing round. Even so, the round would not have penetrated *Gangbuster II*'s frontal armor if it had struck squarely. Instead, it hit Pesco's closed hatch edge-on and spalled the backing plate down through the driver's helmet and skull.

Pesco convulsed at the controls of *Gangbuster II*. The tank skidded across the square, swapping ends several times. The courtyard wall braked but did not stop the careening vehicle. Des Grieux shouted curses, but words had no effect on the tank or its dead driver.

*Gangbuster II* slid bow-first into the stone-built temple. Blocks and tiles from the multiple roofs cascaded onto the tank and over the courtyard beyond.

All *Gangbuster II*'s systems crashed at the massive overload.

Des Grieux knew nothing about that. Despite his shock harness, his head slammed sideways into the map display so that he shut down an instant before his tank did.

Existence was a pulsing red blur until Des Grieux opened his eyes. The pulsing continued every time his heart beat, but now he could see real light: the tiny yellow beads of *Gangbuster II*'s stand-by illumination system.

The air in the fighting compartment was hot and foul. When the power went off, so did the air conditioning. The expended twenty-CM casings on the floor continued to radiate heat and complex gases.

Des Grieux reached for the reset switch to bring *Gangbuster II*'s systems alive again. Movement brought blinding pain. The tank's shock harness had retracted when movement stopped, but the straps left tracks in the form of bruises and cracked ribs where they had gripped Des Grieux to prevent worse.

His mouth tasted of blood, and there seemed to be a layer of ground glass between his eyes and their lids.

"Blood and martyrs," Des Grieux whispered. The taste in his mouth came from his tongue, which had swollen to twice its normal size because he had bitten it.

When the world ceased throbbing and his stomach settled again, Des Grieux finished his movement to the reset switch. Pain just meant you were alive. If you were alive, you could do for the bastard who'd done *you*.

The snarl of powerguns dimly penetrated to the tank's interior. Neither of the indig forces had powerguns of their own. Either the Slammers had entered Morobad, or Baffin had committed his Legion to exploit the ratfuck the Black Banner Guards had made when they tried to follow *Gangbuster II*'s lead.

Des Grieux knew which alternative *he'd* put his money on.

*Gangbuster II* came to life crisply and fast. That was better than the man in her fighting compartment had managed.

"Booster," Des Grieux said. His injured tongue slurred his words. "Order of Battle on Number One."

Screen #1, the left-hand unit, came up with the map of Morobad Des Grieux had ordered onto it before the crash and shut-down. The new overlay showed Des Grieux just what he'd bloody expected, the orange symbols of Legion vehicles streaming through the town and fanning out when they crossed the canal.

This was no feint or stiffening force. Baffin was committing his entire battalion-strength command to end the war here on the Western Wing.

"Like bloody hell . . ." Des Grieux muttered. "Driver! Report!"

Nothing. "Pesco?"

Nothing. Des Grieux would have to crawl forward and see what the hell was going on; but first he checked the condition of his tank.

*Gangbuster II* was fully operable. The tank was down one fan and had five fist-sized holes in her skirts. Des Grieux had no recollection of several of those hits. Both guns were all right, and sixty percent of the massively-redundant sensor suite checked out as well.

The only problem was that, according to the echo-ranging apparatus, the tank was covered by several meters of variegated rubble: bricks, tiles, wooden beams, and the bodies of Hindi soldiers who'd been shooting from the temple roofs up to the moment *Gangbuster II* brought the building's facade down on itself. All the visual displays were blank because the pickups were buried.

Of course, if the Slammers' vehicle hadn't been so completely concealed, Baffin's troops would have finished Des Grieux off by reflex. Veteran mercenaries were generally men who'd survived by never trusting a corpse until they'd put in a bayonet of their own.

A four-ship platoon of Baffin's tank destroyers slid eastward across the map of Morobad. They were air-cushion vehicles mounting fifteen-CM powerguns behind frontal armor almost as thick as that of the Slammers' tanks. The main guns were in centerline mountings like those of the Hindi tanks—turrets were relatively heavy, and an air-cushion vehicle could rotate easily in comparison to wheeled or track-laying armor.

Companies of infantry preceded and followed the tank destroyers in four air-cushion carriers apiece. Baffin carried his infantry in large, lightly-armored vehicles; Hammer mounted his men on one-man skimmers with their heavy weapons on air-cushion jeeps. Either method worked well with good troops; and both *these* units were very good indeed.

*Gangbuster II* showed brightly on Des Grieux's display as a cross-hatched blue symbol, but the Legion troops advancing through Morobad showed no sign of awareness. Their screens would be tuned to the Han/Slammers defenses kilometers to the east . . . if there were any Han troops left to thicken the line of cursing Slammers infantry and the survivors of 2nd Platoon.

Not all the Legion equipment in the square outside the collapsed temple was moving. Des Grieux's #1 display marked four of Baffin's three-CM twin guns, half the Legion's anti-artillery defenses, with neat orange symbols. The weapons were emplaced to either side of the thoroughfare. Support troops had hastily bulldozed the wreckage of the Hindi battery out of the way.

Ideally, artillery-defense guns should have a clear view to the horizon on all sides. In practice, crews preferred to set up in defilade where they were safe from hostile direct-fire weapons. Even so, the buildings surrounding the market square reduced the defended area to what seemed at first an unusually narrow cone.

Three command vehicles, armored air-cushion vans filled with communications gear, were parked back-to-back in a trefoil at the northwest corner of the square. *That* was what the three-CM guns were protecting: Baffin in his advanced command post.

Des Grieux's muscles began to tremble with reaction. He no longer felt the pain in his ribs; fresh adrenaline smoothed the knotted veins flowing to his brain. Baffin himself, a hundred and fifty meters from *Gangbuster II*'s main gun. . . .

"Pesco, you lazy bastard!" Des Grieux snarled, but he'd already given up on raising a response from his driver. He climbed out of his seat and slid between the hull and the frame of the turret basket.

Thick twenty-CM disks littered the deck, the

empty matrixes that had aligned the copper atoms which the powerguns released as plasma. One disk blocked the small hatch separating the fighting compartment from the driver's compartment. Des Grieux tossed the empty angrily behind him. The polyurethane was hot and still tacky; it clung to his fingertips.

As soon as he opened the hatch, the smell told Des Grieux that his driver was dead. Pesco had voided his bowels when the fragment sliced off the upper half of his skull. The liters of blood his heart pumped before the autonomic nervous system shut down had already begun to rot in the warm compartment.

Des Grieux swore. The hatch—the part of it that hadn't decapitated Pesco—was jammed beyond opening by anything short of rear-echelon maintenance. He didn't know what the *bloody* hell he was going to do with the driver's body.

He released the seat latch so that the back flopped down. The remaining contents of Pesco's cranial cavity slopped over Des Grieux's hands. He rotated the seat forty-five degrees to its stop, then tilted the corpse sideways out onto the forward deck of the compartment. There it blocked the foot pedals, but Des Grieux wouldn't be able to use those anyway.

Des Grieux leaned over the bloody seat, set the blade angles at zero incidence, and switched on the drive fans. All the necessary controls were on the column; the duplicate nacelle-attitude controls on the foot pedals permitted a driver to do four things simultaneously in an emergency—

But *Gangbuster II* didn't have a driver any more.

Seven green lights and a red one marked the fan status screen beneath the main driving display, but that was only half the story. Des Grieux knew the intake ducts were blocked as surely as *Gangbuster II*'s hatches. That didn't matter at the moment, but it would as soon as he rotated the pitch control and the fans started to suck wind.

No choice. Des Grieux could only hope that vibration as the nacelles drew against the rubble above them would help to clear the vehicle.

Because that was what he needed to do first.

Des Grieux breathed deeply. He didn't really notice the smell; other things could get in his way, but not that. He adjusted the nacelle angle to a balance between lift and thrust. He hoped he had the mixture right, but whatever he came up with would have to do.

Des Grieux had been a lousy driver; he was far too heavy handed, forcing the controls the way he forced himself.

For this particular job, a heavy hand was the only choice.

The fans hummed, running at full speed though the throttles were at their idle setting. With the pitch at zero, the leading edges of the blades knifed the air with minimal resistance. *Gangbuster II* began to resonate with a bell-note deeper than usual because the hull didn't hang free in the air.

Des Grieux sucked in another breath. His right hand drew the linked throttles full on, while his left thumb adjusted the pitch to sixty degrees. The tank wheezed and bucked like a choking lion. Des Grieux scrambled backward out of the hatch.

The empties jounced on the floor with the violence of *Gangbuster II*'s attempts to draw air through choked intakes. Des Grieux threw himself into his seat and grasped the gunnery joysticks. The orange pippers glowed against a background of uniform gray because the visual pick-ups were shrouded.

Des Grieux twisted the left joystick. Metal screeched as the turret began to swing clockwise against its weight of rubble. Hot insulation tinged the atmosphere of the fighting compartment as the turret drive motors overloaded.

Des Grieux twisted the control in the opposite direction. The turret reversed a few centimeters. There was a squawling crash as the mass of overburden shifted and slid away from *Gangbuster II*'s turret and deck. The tank bobbed like a diver surfacing through a sea of rubble.

The fan blades bit the air for which they had been starving. Uncontrolled, *Gangbuster II* lurched backward at an accelerating pace.

Des Grieux shouted with glee as he rotated his turret and cupola controls again. Now he had a sight picture and targets.

*Gangbuster II* had hit the temple facade nose on. Now it backed through the hole it had torn in the wall, bucking over and plowing through tiles and masonry from the building's upper stories.

The Hindis were using the temple's forecourt as a field hospital for casualties from Des Grieux's initial attack. Medics and the wounded who could move under their own power ran or crawled from *Gangbuster II*'s bellowing reappearance.

Des Grieux ignored them. The gap his tank had smashed in the courtyard wall showed at one edge of his gunnery screen, and a pair of Legion three-CM carriages were visible through it. The Legion guns were firing upward at a forty degree angle, snapping incoming shells from the air as soon as they notched the horizon.

The tribarrel's solid sight indicator covered the Legion weapons an instant before the main gun swung on target. Brilliant cyan bolts raked the Legion crews and the receivers of their guns. A pannier of ammunition exploded with a flash like that of a miniature nova. It destroyed everything within a five-meter sphere, pavement included.

*Gangbuster II* slewed across the courtyard in a scraping, sparking curve. The tank wasn't going to follow the track by which it had plunged in from the market square. The gap in the courtyard wall foreshortened into solidity as the damaged skirts slid the tank toward a point twenty meters west of its initial entry. The screams of wounded men in the vehicle's path were lost in the howl of steel on stone.

Des Grieux took his right hand from the joystick long enough to close the commo breaker. "Blue Three to Big Dog One-Niner!" he shouted hoarsely to battalion fire control. "Get some arty on top of us! Get us—"

*Gangbuster II* struck the courtyard wall for the second time. The shock threw Des Grieux forward into his harness. Redoubled pain shrank objects momentarily to pinhead size in his vision, but he did not black out.

The tank's iridium hull armor smashed through the brickwork, but the impact stripped off the already-damaged skirts. Momentum drove *Gangbuster II* partway into the market square. The vehicle halted there because half the plenum chamber was gone.

"—some firecracker rounds!" Des Grieux gasped to artillery control, demanding anti-personnel shells as his hands worked his joysticks.

Two of the three-CM pieces were undamaged. The

crew of the gun nearest the ammunition blast was dead or writhing shriveled on the pavement, but the gunners of the fourth piece were cranking down their twin muzzles to bear on the unexpected threat.

A bolt from *Gangbuster II*'s main gun struck the shield just below the stubby barrels of the artillery-defense weapon. The gun seemed to suck in, then flash outward as a ball of sunbright vapor.

A loader had turned to run when she saw death pointing down *Gangbuster II*'s twenty-CM bore. Gaseous metal enveloped all of the Legion soldier but her outflung hand. When the glowing ball condensed and vanished, the hand remained like a wax dummy on a framework of carbonized sticks.

Des Grieux's tribarrel raked the Legion command group. The plating of the vehicles' boxy sides was thick enough to turn about half the two-CM bolts—but at this short range, *only* half.

*Gangbuster II*'s main gun continued to rotate on-target. One of the three vans already sparkled with electrical shorts, while another puffed black smoke from the holes the powergun had blown across its flank.

"Blue Leader to Blue Three," Captain Broglie cried across the crackling, all-band static of powergun discharges. "Abandon your vehicle immediately! Anti-tank rounds are incoming on your location!"

"Screw you, Broglie!" Des Grieux screamed as his main gun slammed a bolt into the central command track, the one that was bow-on with its thicker frontal armor toward *Gangbuster II*'s tribarrel. The twenty-CM bolt blew out the vehicle's back and sides with a piston of vaporized metal which had been the glacis plate a micro-second earlier.

The Legion tank destroyer entering the square

from the west snapped a bolt from its fifteen-CM powergun into *Gangbuster II*'s turret. The tank rocked backward under the impact.

Des Grieux slammed into the seat. The screens and regular lighting went out, but the inner face of the turret armor glowed a sulphurous yellow.

Heat clawed at the skin of Des Grieux's face and hands. He started to draw in a breath. The air was fire, but he had to breathe anyway.

*Gangbuster II*'s nacelles stopped bucking in the stripped plenum chamber when the power shut off. Now the tank shuddered with heat stresses.

Des Grieux punched the reset switch. A conduit across the turret burst with a green flash. The holographic displays quivered to life, then went blank.

A salvo of shells landed near enough to rock the tank with their *crumpcrumpcrump*-CRUMP! They were HE Common, not anti-tank. The rounds had been in flight before the battery commander knew there was a hole blasted in the Legion's artillery defenses.

The seat controls were electrical; nothing happened when Des Grieux tugged the bar. He reached up—his ribs hurt almost as much as his lungs did—and slid the cupola hatch open manually.

Buildings around the market square were burning. Smoke mingled with ozone from the powerguns, organic residues from propellants and explosive, and the varied stench of bodies ripped open as they died.

It was like a bath in cool water compared to the interior of the tank.

The iridium barrel of *Gangbuster II*'s main gun was shorter by eighty centimeters. That was what saved Des Grieux's life. At this range, the tank destroyer's bolt would have penetrated if it had struck the turret face directly.

The stick of shells that just landed had closed the boulevard entering the square from the west. The tank destroyer that hit *Gangbuster II* wriggled free of collapsed masonry fifty meters away. The vehicle was essentially undamaged, though shrapnel had pecked highlights from its light-absorbent camouflage paint, and the cupola machinegun hung askew.

Bodies, and the wreckage of equipment too twisted for its original shape to be discerned, littered the pavement of the square.

Des Grieux set the tribarrel's control to thermal—self-powered—operation. It wouldn't function well, but it was better than nothing.

The manual traverse wheel refused to turn; the fifteen-CM bolt had welded the cupola ring to the turret. The elevating wheel spun, though, lowering the triple muzzles as the tank destroyer's own forward motion slid it into Des Grieux's sight picture.

Cargo shells popped open high in the heavens. Des Grieux ignored the warning. He squeezed the butterfly triggers to rip the tank destroyer's skirts. Bolts which might not have penetrated the vehicle's heavy iridium hull armor tore fist-sized holes in the steel.

Des Grieux got off a dozen rounds before his tribarrel jammed. They were enough for the job. The tank destroyer vented its air cushion through the gaps in the plenum chamber and grounded with a squealing crash.

Des Grieux bailed out of *Gangbuster II*, carrying his carbine. He slid down the turret and hit the pavement on his feet, but his legs were too weak to support him. He sprawled on his face.

The anti-tank submunition, one of three drifting down from the cargo shell by parachute, went off a hundred meters in the air. The *whack!* of the blast knocked Des Grieux flat as he started to get up. The supersonic penetrator which the explosion forged from a billet of depleted uranium had already punched through the thin upper hull of *Gangbuster II*.

Ammunition and everything else flammable within the tank *whuffed* out in a glare that seemed to shine through the armor. The fusion bottle did not fail. The turret settled again with a clang, askew on its ring.

Secondary explosions to the east and further west within Morobad marked other effects of the salvo, but none of the submunitions had targeted the disabled tank destroyer. Des Grieux sat up and crossed his legs to provide a stable firing position. He wasn't ready to stand, not quite yet. Heat from his tank's glowing hull washed across his back.

What sounded like screaming was probably steam escaping from a ruptured boiler. Humans couldn't scream that loud. Des Grieux knew.

He pointed his carbine.

The tank destroyer's forward hatch opened. The driver started to get out. Des Grieux shot him in the face. The body fell backward. Its feet were still within the hatch, but the arms flailed for a time.

The hull side hatch—the tank destroyer had no turret—opened a crack. Des Grieux covered the movement. Cloth—it wasn't white, just a gray uniform jacket, but the meaning was clear—fluttered from the opening.

"We've surrendered!" a woman called from inside. "Don't shoot!"

"Come on out, then," Des Grieux ordered.

His voice was a croak. He wasn't sure the vehicle crew could hear him, but a woman wearing lieutenant's insignia extended her head and shoulders from the hatch.

Her face was expressionless. When she saw that Des Grieux did not fire, she climbed clear of the tank destroyer. A male commo tech followed her. If they had sidearms, they'd left them within the vehicle.

"We've all surrendered," she repeated.

"Baffin's surrendered?" Des Grieux asked. He had trouble hearing. He wanted to order his prisoners closer, but he couldn't stand up and he didn't want them looking down at him.

"Via, Colonel Baffin was *there*," the lieutenant said, gesturing toward the three command vehicles. The center unit that Des Grieux hit with his main gun was little more than bulged sidewalls above the running gear.

She shook her head to clear it of memories. "The Legion's surrendered, that's what I mean," she said. "We must've lost ten percent of our equipment from that one salvo of artillery. No point in just getting wasted by shells. There'll be other battles. . . ."

The lieutenant's voice trailed off as she considered the implications of her own words. The commo tech stared at her in cow-eyed incomprehension.

Des Grieux leaned against a slope of shattered brick. The corners were sharp.

That was good. Perhaps their jagged touch would prevent him from passing out before friendly troops arrived to collect his prisoners.

Regimental HQ was three command cars backed against a previously-undamaged two-story school building. Flat cables snaked out of the vehicles, through windows and along corridors.

The combination wasn't perfect. Still, it provided Hammer's staff with their own data banks and secure commo, while permitting them some elbow room in the inevitable chaos at the end of a war—and a contract.

"Yeah, what is it?" demanded the orderly sergeant.

The lobby was marked off by a low bamboo barrier. Three Han clerks sat at desks in the bullpen area, while the orderly sergeant relaxed at the rear in the splendor of his computer console. Behind the staff was a closed door marked HEADMASTER in Hindi script and ADJUTANT/HAMMER'S REGIMENT in stenciled red.

Des Grieux withdrew the hand which he'd stretched toward the throat of the Han clerk. "I'm looking for my bloody unit," he said, "and this bloody wog—"

"C'mon, c'mon back," the orderly sergeant demanded with a wave of his hand. "Been partying pretty hard?"

Des Grieux brushed a bamboo post and knocked it down as he stepped into the bullpen. The local clerks jabbered and righted the barrier.

"Wasn't a party," Des Grieux muttered. "I been in a POW camp the past week."

The orderly sergeant blinked. "A *Han* POW camp," Des Grieux amplified. "Our good wog buddies here—" he kicked out at the chair of the nearest clerk; the boot missed, and Des Grieux almost overbalanced "—picked me up when they swept Morobad. Baffin's troops got paroled out within twenty-four hours, but *I* got stuck with the Hindi prisoners 'cause nobody knew I was there."

The orderly sergeant's name tag read Hechinger.

His nose wrinkled as Des Grieux approached. The Han diet of the POW camp differed enough from what the Hindi prisoners were used to that it gave most of them the runs. Latrine facilities within the camp were wherever you wanted to squat.

"Well, why didn't you tell them you were a friendly?" Hechinger asked in puzzlement.

Des Grieux's hands trembled with anger. "Have you ever tried to tell a wog *anything*?" he whispered. "Without a gun stuck down their throat when you say it?"

He got a grip on himself and added, more calmly, "And don't ask me for my ID bracelet. One of the guards lifted that first thing. Thought the computer key was an emerald, I guess."

Hechinger sighed. "Mary, key data," he ordered the artificial intelligence in his console. "Name?"

"Des Grieux, Samuel, Sergeant-Commander," the tanker said. "H Company, 2nd Platoon, Platoon Sergeant Peres commanding. She *was* commanding, anyhow. She may've bought it last week."

The console hummed and projected data. Des Grieux, standing at the back of the unit, could see the holograms only as refractions in the air.

"One of our trucks was going by and I shouted to the driver," Des Grieux muttered, glaring at the clerks. The three of them hunched over their desks, pretending to be busy. "He didn't know me, but he knew I wasn't a wog. I could've been there forever."

"Well," said the orderly sergeant, "three days longer and you'd sure've been finding your own transport back to the Regiment. We're pulling out. Got a contract on Plessy. Seems the off-planet workers there're getting uppity and think they oughta have a share in the shipyard profits."

"Anyplace," Des Grieux said. "Just so long as I've got a gun and a target."

"Well, we got a bit of a problem here, trooper," Hechinger said as he frowned at his display. "Des Grieux, Sergeant-Commander, is listed as dead."

"I'm not bloody *dead*," Des Grieux snarled. "Blood 'n Martyrs, ask Sergeant Peres."

"Lieutenant Peres, as she'll be when she comes off medical leave," the orderly sergeant said, "isn't a lotta help right now either. And if you're going to ask about—" he squinted at the characters on his display "—Sergeant-Commander Medrassi, he bought the farm."

Hechinger smirked. "Like you did, y'see? Look, don't worry, we'll—"

"Look, I just want to get back to my unit," Des Grieux said, hearing his voice rise and letting it. "Is Broglie around? *He* bloody knows me. I just saved his ass—again!"

The orderly sergeant glanced over his shoulder. "Captain Broglie we might be able to round up for you, trooper," he said carefully. He nodded back toward the Adjutant's office.

"Anyhow," Hechinger continued, "he was captain when he went in there. Don't be real surprised if he comes out with major's pips on his collar, though."

"That *bastard* . . ." Des Grieux whispered.

"Captain Broglie's very much the fair-haired boy just now, you know, buddy," Hechinger continued in his careful voice. "He stopped near a brigade of Hindi armor with one tank platoon. It was kitty-bar-the-door, all the way back to Xingha, if it hadn't been for him."

The office door opened. Sergeant Hechinger straightened at his console, face forward.

Des Grieux looked up expecting to see either the Adjutant or Broglie—

And met the eyes of Major Joachim Steuben, as cold and hard as beads of chert. Hammer's bodyguard looked as stiffly furious as Des Grieux had ever seen a man who was still under control.

Des Grieux didn't think that Steuben would recognize him. It had been years since the last time they were face to face. There was crinkled skin around the corners of the major's eyes, though his was still a pretty-boy's face if you didn't look closely; and Des Grieux just now looked like a scarecrow. . . .

Joachim was more than just a sociopathic killer, though the Lord knew he was *that*. He looked at the tanker and said, "Well, well, Des Grieux. Seeking our own level, are we?"

The way Joachim shot his hip could have been an affectation . . . but it also shifted the butt of his pistol a further centimeter clear of the tailored blouse of his uniform. Des Grieux met his eyes. Anyway, there was no place to run.

"Well, I understand your decision, Luke," said Colonel Hammer as he came out of the Adjutant's office with his hand on the arm of the much larger Broglie. The moon-faced Adjutant followed them, nodding to everything Hammer said. "But believe me, I regret it. Remember you've always got a bunk here if you change your mind."

Broglie wore no rank insignia at all.

Hechinger had to say *something* to avoid becoming part of the interchange between Steuben and Des Grieux. Nobody in his right mind—except maybe the Colonel—wanted to be part of Joachim's interchanges, even as a spectator.

"Okay, Des Grieux," he said in a voice just above

a whisper. "I'll cut you some temporary orders so's you can get chow and some kit."

Broglie heard the name. He glanced at Des Grieux. His face blanked and he said, in precisely neutral tones, "Hello, Slick. I didn't think you'd make it back from that one."

"Oh, you ought to show more warmth than *that*, Mister Broglie," Joachim drawled. He didn't look at Broglie and Hammer behind him. "After all, without Sergeant Des Grieux here to create that monumental screw-up, you wouldn't have been such a hero for straightening things out. Would you, now?"

"What d'ye mean screw-up?" Des Grieux said, *knowing* that Steuben was looking for an excuse to kill something. "*I'm* the one who blew the guts outa Baffin's Legion!"

"That's the man?" Hammer said, speaking to Broglie.

The Colonel's eyes were gray. They had none of the undifferentiated hatred for the world that glared from Major Steuben's, but they were just as hard as the bodyguard's when they flicked over Des Grieux.

"Yessir," Broglie murmured. "Joachim—Major Steuben? I'm not taking the job the Legion offered me out of any disrespect for the colonel. If you like, I'll promise that the Legion won't take any contracts against the Slammers so long as I'm in charge."

Joachim turned as delicately as a marionette whose feet dangle above the ground. "Oh, my . . ." he said, letting his left hand dangle on a theatrically limp wrist. "And a traitor's promise is *so* valuable!"

"I'm not—" said Broglie.

"Joachim!" said the Colonel, stepping in front of Steuben—and between Steuben and Broglie, though that might have been an accident, if you believed

Colonel Alois Hammer did things by accident. "Go to the club and have a drink. I'll join you there in half an hour."

Steuben grimaced as though he'd been kicked in the stomach. "Sir," he said. "I'm . . ."

"Go on," Hammer said gently, putting his hand on the shoulder of the dapper killer. "I'll meet you soonest. No problem, all right?"

"Sir," Steuben said, nodding agreement. He straightened and strode out of the headquarters building. He looked like a perfect band-box soldier, except for his eyes. . . .

"And as for you, Luke," Hammer said as he faced around to Broglie again, "I won't have you talking nonsense. Your first duty is to your own troops. You'll take any bloody contract that meets your unit's terms and conditions . . . and I assure you, I'll do the same."

"Look, sir," Broglie said. He wouldn't meet Colonel Hammer's eyes. "I wouldn't feel right—"

"I said," Hammer snapped, "put a sock in it! Or stay with me—the Lord knows I'm going to have to replace Chesney anyway, after the lash-up he made when the wheels came off at Morobad."

Des Grieux was dizzy. The world had disconnected itself from him. He was surrounded by glassy surfaces which only seemed to speak and move in the semblance of people he had once known.

"Major Chesney—" Broglie began.

"Major Chesney had to be told twice," Hammer said, "first by you and then by *me*, a thousand kays away with 3d Operational Battalion, to set his flanking tank platoons to cover artillery defense for the center. You shouldn't have had to hold Chesney's hand while you were organizing Han troops into a real defense."

Broglie smiled. "Their laser-vehicles were mostly bogged," he said, "so they couldn't run. I just made sure they knew I'd shoot 'em faster than the Hindis could if they *tried* to run."

"Whatever works," said Hammer with an expression as cold as the hatred in Joachim's eyes a moment before.

The expression softened. "Listen to me, Luke," Hammer went on. "People are going to hire mercenaries so long as they're convinced mercenaries are a good investment. Having the Legion in first-rate hands like yours is good for all of us in this business. I'll miss you, but I gain from this, too."

Broglie stiffened. "Thank you, sir," he said.

"Listen!" Des Grieux shouted. "I'm the one who broke them for you! *I* killed Baffin."

"Oh, you killed a lot of people, Des Grieux," Colonel Hammer said in a deceptively mild voice. "And way too many of them were mine."

"Sir," said Broglie. "The disorganization in the Legion's rear really was Slick's doing. We pieced it together in post-battle analysis, and—"

"Saved about ten minutes, didn't it, Broglie?" the Colonel said. "Before the flanking units closed on Morobad?"

Broglie smiled again, thinly. "That was ten minutes I was real glad to have, sir," he said.

Hammer stared up and down at Des Grieux. The Colonel's expression did not change. "So, you think he's a good soldier, do you?" he asked softly.

"I think," said Broglie, "that . . . if he'd learn to obey orders, he'd be the best soldier I've ever seen."

"Fine, Mister Broglie," Hammer said. "I'll tell you what. . . ."

He continued to look at Des Grieux as if daring the tanker to move or speak again. Major Steuben was gone, but the White Mice at the outer doorway watched the discussion with their hands on the grips of their sub-machine guns.

"I'll let you have him, then," Hammer continued. "For Broglie's Legion."

Broglie grimaced and turned away. "No," he muttered. "Sorry, that wouldn't work out."

Hammer nodded crisply. "Hareway," he said to the Adjutant, "have Des Grieux here put in the lock-up until we lift. Then demote him to Trooper and put him to driving trucks for a while. *If* he cares to stay in the Slammers, as I rather hope he will not."

The lobby had a terrazzo floor. Hammer's boot-heels clacked on it as he strode off, arm and arm with Broglie. Their figures shrank in Des Grieux's eyesight, and he barely heard the orderly sergeant shout, "Watch it! He's fainting!"

# PART III

The Slammers' lockup was a sixty-meter shipping container. The paired outer leaves were open, and the single inner door had been replaced by a grate. The facility was baking hot when the white sun of Meridienne cast its harsh shadows across the landscape. At night, when the clear air chilled enough to condense out the dew on which most of the local vegetation depended, the lockup became a shivering misery.

If the conditions in the lockup hadn't been naturally so wretched, Colonel Hammer would have used technology to make them worse. A comfortable detention facility would be counterproductive.

"Rise 'n shine, trooper," called the jailor, a veteran of twenty-five named Daniels. "They want you there yesterday, like always."

Daniels' two prosthetic feet worked perfectly well—so long as they were daily retuned to match his neural outputs. He had the choice of moving to a high-technology world where the necessary electronics

127

were available, or staying with the Slammers in a
menial capacity. Since Daniels' only saleable skill—
firing a tribarrel from a moving jeep—had no civilian
application, he became one of the Regiment's jailers.

"Nobody's waiting for me," said Slick Des Grieux,
lying on his back with his knees raised. He didn't
open his eyes. "Nobody cares if I'm alive or dead.
Not even me."

"C'mon," Daniels insisted as he inserted his
microchip key in the lock. "Get moving or they'll be
on *my* back."

He clashed the grate as best he could. It was
formed of beryllium alloy, while the container itself
had been extruded from high-density polymers. The
combination made a tinny/dull rattle, not particularly
arousing.

Des Grieux got to his feet with a smooth grace
which belied his previous inertia. There was a three-
CM pressure cut above his right temple, covered
now with SpraySeal. His pale hair was cut so short
that there had been no need to shave the injured
portion before repairing it.

"What's going on, then?" Des Grieux asked. His
tongue quivered against his lips as the first wisps of
adrenaline began to dry his mouth. *There was going
to be action. . . .*

"Sounds like it really dropped in the pot," said
Daniels as he swung the grate outward. "Dunno
how. *I* thought it was gonna be a walkover this
time."

He nodded Des Grieux toward the climate-con-
trolled container that he used for an office. "I wonder," Daniels added wistfully, "if it's bad enough
they're gonna put support staff in the line. . . ?"

Des Grieux couldn't figure why he was getting

out of the lockup five days early. The Hashemite Brotherhood controlled the northern half of Meridienne's single continent and claimed the whole of it. They'd been raiding into territory of the Sincanmo Federation to the south—pin-pricks, but destructive ones. Unchecked vandalism had destabilized governments and economic systems more firmly based than anything the Sincanmos could claim.

In order to prevent the Sincanmos from carrying the fighting north, the Hashemites had hired off-planet mercenaries, the Thunderbolt Division, to guard their territory and deter the Sincanmos from escalating to all-out war with local forces. The situation had gone on for one and a half standard years, with the Hashemites chuckling over their cleverness.

The Thunderbolt Division was a good choice for the Hashemite purposes. It was a large organization which could be distributed in battalion-sized packets to stiffen local forces of enthusiastic irregulars; and the Thunderbolt Division was cheap, an absolute necessity. Meridienne was not a wealthy planet, and the Hashemites expected their "confrontation" to continue for five or more years before the Sincanmo Federation collapsed.

The Thunderbolt Division was cheap because it wasn't much good. Its equipment was low-tech, little better than what Meridienne's indigenous forces had bought for themselves. The mercenaries' main benefit to their employers was their experience. They *were* full-time, professional soldiers, not amateurs getting on-the-job training in their first war.

Then the Sincanmos met the threat head on: they

hired Hammer's Slammers and prepared to smash every sign of organization in the northern half of the continent in a matter of weeks.

Des Grieux didn't see any reason the Sincanmo plan wouldn't work. Neither did Captain Garnaud, the commanding officer of Delta Company.

Normally line troops expected to serve disciplinary sentences after the fighting was over. In this case, Garnaud had decreed immediate active time for Des Grieux. D Company didn't need the veteran against the present threat, and Garnaud correctly believed that missing the possibility of seven days' action was a more effective punishment for Slick Des Grieux than a year's down-time restriction.

But now he was getting out early. . . .

Des Grieux followed Daniels into the close quarters of the jailor's office. The communications display was live with the angry holographic image of a senior lieutenant in battledress.

The face was a surprise. The officer was Katrina Grimsrud, the executive officer of H Company, rather than one of D Company's personnel. "Where the bloody hell have you been?" she snarled as soon as the jailor moved into pickup range of the display's cameras.

Daniels sat down at the desk crammed into the half of the container which didn't hold his bed and living quarters. His artificial feet splayed awkwardly at the sudden movement; they needed tuning or perhaps replacement.

"Sorry, sir," he muttered as he manipulated switches. His equipment was old and ill-mated, castoffs from several different departments. Junk gravitated to this use on its way to the scrap pile. "Had to get the prisoner."

He adjusted the retinal camera. "Okay, Des Grieux," he said. "Look into this."

Des Grieux leaned his forehead against the padded frame. "What's going on?" he demanded.

Light flashed as the unit recorded his retinal pattern and matched it with the file in Central Records. Daniels' printer whined, rolling out hard copy. Des Grieux straightened, blinking as much from confusion as from the brief glare.

"Listen, Des Grieux," Lieutenant Grimsrud said. "We don't want any of your cop in this company. If you get cute, you're out. D'ye understand? Not busted, not in lockup: out!"

"I'm not *in* Hotel Company," Des Grieux snapped. He was confused. Besides, the adrenaline sparked by a chance of action had made him ready—as usual—to fight anybody or anything, including a circle saw.

"You are now, Sarge," Daniels said as he handed Des Grieux the hard copy.

"Get over to the depot soonest," Grimsrud ordered as Des Grieux stared at his orders. "Jailor, you've got transport, don't you? Carry him. We've got a replacement tank there with a newbie crew. Des Grieux's to take over as commander—the assigned commander'll drive."

Des Grieux frowned. He was transferred from Delta to Hotel, all right. It didn't matter a curse one way or the other; they were both tank companies.

Only . . . transfers didn't occur at finger-snap speed—but they did this time, with the facsimile signature of Colonel Hammer himself releasing Sergeant-Commander Samuel Des Grieux (retinal prints attached) from detention and transferring him to H Company.

"Look, sir," Daniels said, "it's not my job to dr—"

"It's bloody well your job if you *don't* get him to the depot ASAP, buddy!" Lieutenant Grimsrud said. "I can't spare the time or the man to send a driver back. D'ye understand?"

Des Grieux folded the orders into the right cargo pocket of his uniform. "*I* don't understand," he said to the holographic image. "Why such a flap over the Thunderbolt Division? We could put truck drivers in line and walk all over them."

"Too right," Grimsrud said forcefully. "Seems the towelheads figured that out for themselves in time to hire Broglie's Legion. Colonel Hammer wants all the veterans he's got in line—and with you, that gives my 3d Platoon one, I say again *one*, trooper with more than two years in the Regiment. Get your ass over to our deployment area *soonest*."

Lieutenant Grimsrud cut the connection. Des Grieux stared in the direction of blank air no longer excited by coherent light. His whole body was trembling.

"Don't sound like she's lookin' for excuses," Daniels grumbled as he got to his feet. "C'mon, Sarge, it's ten keys to the depot from here."

Des Grieux whistled tunelessly as he followed the jailor to an air-cushion jeep as battered as the equipment in Daniels' office. His kit was still in D Company. He didn't care. He didn't care about anything at all, except for the chance fate offered him.

Daniels started the jeep. At least one drive fan badly needed balancing. "Hey, Sarge?" he said. "I never asked you—what was the fight about? The one that landed you here?"

"Some bastard called me a name," Des Grieux said. He braced himself against the tubular seat frame worn through the upholstery. The jeep lurched into motion.

Des Grieux's eyes were closed. His face looked like the blade of a hatchet. "He called me 'Pops,' " Des Grieux said. Memory of the incident pitched his voice an octave higher than normal. "So I hit him."

Daniels looked at the tanker, then frowned and looked away.

"Thirty-two standard years don't make me an old man," Slick Des Grieux added in an icy whisper.

A starship tested its maneuvering jets on the landing pad beside the depot's perimeter defenses. The high screech was so loud that the air seemed to ripple. Though the lips of Warrant Leader Farrell, the depot superintendent, continued to move for several seconds, Des Grieux hadn't the faintest notion of what the man was saying.

Des Grieux didn't much care, either. There was only one tank among the depot's lesser vehicles and stacked shipping containers. He stepped past Farrell and tested the spring-loaded cover of a step with his fingertip. It gave stiffly.

"Right," said Farrell. He held Des Grieux's transfer orders and, on a separate flimsy, the instructions which Central had down-loaded directly to the depot. "Ah, here's the, ah, the previous crew."

Two troopers stood beside the depot superintendent. Both were young, but the taller, dark-haired one had a wary look in his eyes. The other man was blond, pale, and soft-seeming despite the obvious muscle bulging his khaki uniform.

Des Grieux gave them a cursory glance, then

returned his attention to the important item: the vehicle he was about to command.

The tank was straight out of the factory in Hamburg on Terra. Farrell's crew would have—should have—done the initial checks, but the bearings would be stiff and the electronics weren't burned in yet.

The tank didn't have a name, just a skirt number in red paint: H271.

"Trooper Wartburg will move to driver," Farrell said. The dark-haired man acknowledged the statement by raising his chin a centimeter. "Trooper Flowers here was going to drive, but he'll go back to Logistics till we get another vehicle in."

Des Grieux climbed deliberately onto the deck of H271. The bustle rack behind the turret held personal gear in a pair of reused ammunition containers.

"You got any experience, Wartburg?" Des Grieux asked without looking back toward the men on the ground.

"Year and a half," the dark-haired man said. "Wing gunner on a combat car, then I drove for a while. This was going to be my first command."

Wartburg's tone was carefully precise. If he was disappointed to be kicked back to driver at the last instant, he kept the fact out of his voice.

Des Grieux slid the cupola hatch closed and open, ignoring the others again.

"One question, Sarge," Wartburg called. The irritation he had hidden before was now obvious. "Grimsrud told us a veteran'd be taking over the tank, but she didn't say who. You got a name?"

"Des Grieux," the veteran said. The tribarrel rotated on its ring, even with the power off. That was good, and a little surprising in a tank that hadn't yet been broken in. "Slick Des Grieux. You just do what I tell you and we'll get along fine."

Wartburg laughed brittlely. "The bloody hell I will," he said as he hopped up to the tank's deck himself.

Des Grieux turned in surprise. His eyes were flat and wide open. All he was sure of was that he'd need to pay more attention than he wanted to his new driver.

Wartburg said nothing further. He reached into the bustle rack and pulled out one of the cases, then tossed it to the ground.

The container crashed down and bounced before it fell flat. Flowers jumped to avoid it. The dense plastic was designed to protect 3,000 disks of two-CM ammunition against anything short of a direct from another powergun. It withstood the abuse, and its hinged lid remained latched.

"What d'ye think you're doing?" Des Grieux demanded.

Wartburg threw down the other container. "I think I'm not doin' *any*bloodything with you, Des Grieux," he said. He jumped to the ground.

"Wait a minute, trooper!" said the outraged depot superintendent. "You've got your orders!"

He waggled the flimsies in his hand at Wartburg, though in fact neither of the documents directly mentioned that trooper.

Trooper Flowers looked from Wartburg to Des Grieux to Farrell—and back. His mouth was slightly open.

"Look, Warrant Leader," Wartburg said to Farrell. "I *heard* about this bastard. No way I'm riding with him. *No* way. You want me to resign from the

Regiment, you got it. You wanna throw me in the lockup, that's your business."

He turned and glared at the man still on the deck of H271. "But I don't ride with Slick Des Grieux. If I ever get that hot to die, I'll eat my gun!"

"Screw you, buddy," Des Grieux said softly. He looked at the depot superintendent. "Okay, Mister Farrell, you get me a driver. That's your job. If you can't do that, then I'll drive and fight this mother both, if that's what it takes."

The three men on the ground began speaking to one another simultaneously in rasping, nervous voices. Des Grieux lowered himself through the cupola hatch.

H271's fighting compartment had the faintly medicinal odor of solvents still seeping from recently-extruded plastics. Des Grieux touched control buttons, checking them for feel and placement. There were always production-line variations, even when two vehicles were ostensibly of the same model.

He heard the clunk of boot toes on the steps formed into H271's armor. Somebody was boarding the vehicle.

Des Grieux threw the main power switch. Gauges and displays hummed to life. There was a line of distortion across Screen #3, but it faded after ten seconds or so. A tinge of ozone suggested arcing somewhere, probably in a microswitch. It would either clear itself or fail completely in the next hundred hours.

A hundred hours was a lifetime for a tank on the same planet as Colonel Luke Broglie. . . .

A head shadowed the light of the open hatch. Des Grieux looked up, into the face of Trooper Flowers.

"Sarge?" Flowers said. "Ah, I'm gonna drive for you. If that's all right?"

"Yeah, that's fine," said Des Grieux without expression. He turned to his displays again.

"Only, I've just drove trucks before, y'see," Flowers added.

"I don't care if you rolled hoops," Des Grieux said. "Get in and let's get moving."

"Ah—I'll get my gear," said Flowers. "I off-loaded when they said I was back in Logistics."

"Booster," said Des Grieux, keying H271's artificial intelligence. "Course data on Screen One."

He watched the left-hand screen. He wasn't sure that the depot had gotten around to loading the course information into the tank's memory, but the route and topography came up properly. Des Grieux thought there was a momentary hesitation in the AI's response, but that might have been his own impatience.

The deck clanked as Flowers jumped directly to the ground in his haste. The way things were going, the kid probably slipped 'n broke his neck. . . .

The course to Base Camp Two and H Company was a blue line curving across three hundred kilometers of arid terrain. No roads, but no problems either. Gullies cut by the rare cloudbursts could be skirted or crossed.

Des Grieux spread his hands, closed his eyes, and rested his forehead against the cool surface of the main screen. Everything about H271 was smooth and cold. The tank functioned, but it didn't have a soul.

He shivered. He could remember when he had enough hair that it wasn't bare scalp that touched the hologram display when he leaned forward like this.

Tank H271 was the right vehicle for Slick Des Grieux.

In the gully beside H271, twenty or so Sincanmo troops sang around a campfire to the music of strings and a double flute. There'd been drums, too. Lieutenant Kuykendall threatened to send a tank through the group if the drummer didn't toss his instrument into the fire *immediately*.

That was one order from the commander of Task Force Kuykendall that Des Grieux would have cheerfully obeyed. Not that he had anything against this particular group of indigs.

There were thirty or forty other campfires scattered among the gullies like opals on a multistrand necklace. With luck, the force's camouflage film concealed the firelight from the hostile outpost two kilometers away on the Notch. Silencing the drums, whose low-frequency beat carried forever in the cool desert air, was as much of a compromise as Kuykendall thought she could enforce.

The Sincanmos were a militia organized by extended families. Each family owned four to six vehicles which they armed with whatever the individuals fancied and could afford. Medium-powered lasers; post-mounted missile systems, both guided and hypervelocity; automatic weapons; even a few mortars, each of a different caliber. . . .

Logistics would have been a nightmare—if the Sincanmo Federation had *had* a formal logistics system. On the credit side, each band was highly motivated, extremely mobile, and packed a tremendous amount of firepower for its size.

The families made decisions by conclave. They took orders from their own Federation rather more often than they ignored those orders; but as for an off-planet mercenary—and a *female*—Kuykendall's authority depended on her own platoon of combat cars and the four H Company tanks attached to her for this operation.

Des Grieux chewed a ration bar in the cupola of his tank. The Sincanmos made their fire by soaking a bucket of sand in motor fuel and lighting it. The flames were low and red and quivered with frustrated anger, much like Des Grieux's thoughts.

There was going to be a battle very soon. In days, maybe hours.

But not here. If Colonel Hammer had expected significant enemy forces to cross the Knifeblade Escarpment through the Notch, he wouldn't have sent Hotel Company's 3d Platoon with the blocking force. The platoon had been virtually reconstituted after a tough time on Mainstream during the previous contract. In a few years, some of these bloody newbies would be halfway decent soldiers. The ones who survived that long.

"Booster," Des Grieux muttered. "Ninety degree pan, half visor."

H271's artificial intelligence obediently threw a high-angle view of the terrain which Task Force Kuykendall guarded onto the left side of Des Grieux's visor. The nameless sandstone butte behind the blocking force was useless as a defensive position in itself, because the only way for military equipment to get up or down its sheer faces was by crane. The mass of rock would confuse the enemy's passive sensors—at least the sensors of the Thunderbolt Division; Broglie's hardware certainly had the discrimination to pick out tanks, combat cars, and the Sincanmo $4 \times 4$s, even though the vehicles were defiladed and backed by a 500-meter curtain of stone.

The butte also provided a useful pole on which to hang the Slammers' remote sensors, transmitting their multispectral information down jam-free, undetectable fiber optics cables. Des Grieux at ground level had as good a vantage point as that of the Hashemite outpost in the Notch; and because the image fed to the tanker's helmet was light-enhanced and computer sharpened, Des Grieux *saw* infinitely more.

Not that there was any bloody thing to see.

Gullies cut by the infrequent downpours meandered across the plain. They were shallow as well as directionless, because the land didn't really drain. Rain sluiced from the buttes and the Escarpment, flooded the whole landscape—and evaporated.

Winds had scoured away the topsoils to redeposit them thousands of kilometers away as loess. The clay substrates which remained were virtually impervious to water.

Seen from Des Grieux's high angle, the gullies were dark smears of gray-green vegetation against the lighter yellow-gray soil. Low shrugs with hard, waxy leaves grew every few meters along the gully floors, where they were protected from wind and sustained by the memory of moisture. The plants were scarcely noticeable at ground level, but they were the plain's only feature.

The butte was a dark mass at Des Grieux's back. In front of him, two kilometers to the south, was the Knifeblade Escarpment: a sheer wall of sandstone for a hundred kays east and west, except for the Notch carved by meltwater from a retreating glacier thirty millions of years in the past. A one in five slope led from the Notch to the plain below. It was barely negotiable by vehicles; but it *was* negotiable.

South of the escarpment, the Hashemites and their mercenaries faced the Sincanmo main force—and Hammer's Slammers. Task Force Kuykendall was emplaced to prevent the enemy from skirting the Knifeblade to the north and falling on the Slammers' flank and rear.

The Hashemites themselves would never think of that maneuver; the Thunderbolt Division could not possibly carry out such a plan in the time available. But Broglie was smart enough, and his troops were good enough . . . if he were willing to split his already outgunned force.

Alois Hammer wasn't willing to bet that Broglie wouldn't do what Hammer himself would do if the situation were desperate enough.

But neither did Hammer *expect* a real fight north of the escarpment. All odds were that Task Force Kuykendall, two platoons of armor and 600–800 Sincanmo irregulars, would wait in bored silence while their fellows chewed on Hashemites until the Brotherhood surrendered unconditionally.

Thunder rumbled far beyond the distant horizon. In this climate, a storm was less likely than the Lord coming down to appoint Slick Des Grieux as master of the universe.

No, it was artillery promising imminent action. For other people.

The most recent bite of ration bar was a leaden mass in Des Grieux's mouth. He spat it into the darkness, then tossed the remainder of the bar away also.

"Booster," he said. "Close-up of the Notch."

A view of flamelit rock replaced the panorama before the last syllable was out of the tanker's mouth. The Hashemites were as feckless and unconcerned as their planetary enemies; and unlike the Sincanmos, the Hashemites didn't have the Slammers' logistics personnel to dispense an acre of camouflage film which would conceal equipment, personnel, and campfires—from hostile eyes.

Of course, the Hashemites didn't think there *were* any hostile eyes. They had stationed an outpost here to prevent the Sincanmos from using the Notch as a back door for attack, but the force was a nominal one of a few hundred indig troops with no leavening of mercenaries. The real defenses were the centrally-controlled mines placed in an arc as much as a kilometer north of the Notch.

The outpost hadn't seen Task Force Kuykendall move into position in the dark hours this morning. In a few hours or days, when the main battle ground to a conclusion, they would *still* be ignorant of the enemy watching them from the north.

The troops of the outpost probably thanked their Lord that they were safely out of the action . . . and they were.

Des Grieux swore softly.

The outpost had a pair of heavy weapons, truck-mounted railguns capable of pecking a hole in tank armor in twenty seconds or so. Des Grieux wouldn't *give* them twenty seconds, of course, but while he dealt with the railguns, the remainder of the Hashemites would loose a barrage of missiles at H271. And then there were the mines to cross. . . .

If the platoon's other three tanks were good for anything—if one of the crews was good for anything—

it'd be possible to pick through the minefields with clearance charges, sonics, and ground-penetrating radar. Trusting *this* lot of newbies to provide covering fire would be like trusting another trooper with your girl and your bottle for the evening.

Kuykendall's platoon was of veterans, but she had orders to keep a low profile unless the enemy sallied out. Kuykendall took orders real good. She'd do fine with Colonel Bloody Broglie. . . .

Hashemites drank and played a game with dice and markers around fuel-oil campfires on the Notch. The sensor pack high on the mesa gave Des Grieux a beautiful view of the enemy, but they were beyond the line-of-sight range of his guns.

A salvo of artillery ricocheting from the sandstone walls would grind the towelheads to hamburger, but the shells would first have to get through the artillery defenses south of the Escarpment. Des Grieux remembered being told the first thing Broglie had done after taking command was to fit every armored vehicle in the Legion with a tribarrel capable of automatic artillery defense.

Guns muttered far to the south. When Des Grieux listened very carefully, he could distinguish the hiss-*crack* reports of big-bore powerguns. Tanks and tank destroyers were beginning to mix it—twenty kilometers away.

Des Grieux shivered and cursed; and after a time, he began to pray to a personal God of Battles. . . .

"Sir?" said Trooper Flowers from the narrow duct joining his station to H271's fighting compartment. The driver's shoulders were a tight fit in the passage. "I'm ready to take my watch, sir. Do you want me in the cupola, or . . . ?"

Des Grieux adjusted a vernier control on Screen #1, dimming the topographic display fractionally. "I'm not 'sir,'" he said. He didn't bother to look toward Flowers through the cut-out sides of the turret basket. "And *I'll* worry about keeping watch till I tell you different."

He returned his attention to Screen #3 on the right side of the fighting compartment. It was live but blank in pearly lustrousness; Des Grieux was missing a necessary link in the feed he wanted to arrange.

"Ah, S-sergeant?" the driver said. The only light in the fighting compartment was scatter from the holographic screens. Flowers' face appeared to be slightly flushed. "Sergeant Des Grieux? What do you want me to do?"

On the right—eastern—edge of the topo screen, a company of Slammers' infantry supported by combat cars moved up the range of broken hills held by the Thunderbolt Division. The advance seemed slow, particularly because the map scale was shrunk to encompass a ten-kilometer battle area; but it was as certain and regular as a gear train.

If navigational data passed to the map display, then there *had* to be a route for—

"Sir?" said Flowers.

"Go play with yourself!" Des Grieux snarled. He glared angrily at his driver.

As Des Grieux's mind refocused to deal with the interruption, the answer to the main problem flashed before him. *The information he wanted wasn't passing on the command channels he'd been tapping out of the Regiment's rear echelon back in Sanga: it was in the machine-to-machine data links, untouched by human consciousness. . . .*

"Right," Des Grieux said mildly. "Look, just stick close to the tank, okay, kid? Do anything you please."

Flowers ducked away, surprised at the tank commander's sudden change of temper. His boots scuffled hollowly as he backed through the internal hatch to the driver's compartment.

"Booster," Des Grieux ordered the tank's artificial intelligence, "switch to Utility Feed One and synthesize on Screen Three."

The opalescent ready status on the right-hand screen dissolved into multicolored garbage. Whatever data was coming through UF1 didn't lend itself to visual presentation.

"Via!" Des Grieux snarled. "Utility Feed Two."

He heard boots on H271's hull, but he ignored them because Screen #3 was abruptly live with what appeared to be a live-action view through the gunnery screen of another tank. The orange circle of the main-gun pipper steadied on a slab of rock kilometers away. There was no visible target—

Until the point of aim disintegrated in a gout of white-hot glass under the impact of the twenty-CM powergun of another tank. The ledge cracked from heat shock. Half of it slid away to the left in a single piece, while the remainder crumbled into gravel.

Iridium armor gleamed beneath the pipper. Des Grieux's boot trod reflexively on his foot trip, but the safety interlock still disengaged his guns.

The real gunner, kilometers away, was only a fraction of a second slower. The image blurred with the recoil of the sending tank's main gun, and the target—a Legion tank destroyer—erupted at the heart of the cyan bolt.

"Sergeant Des Grieux?" said a voice from the open

cupola hatch. "I'm just checking how all my people are—good Lord!"

Des Grieux looked up. Lieutenant Carbury, 3d Platoon's commanding officer and almost as new to the business of war as Des Grieux's driver was, stared at the images of Screen #3.

"What on earth is that?" Carbury begged/demanded as he turned to scramble backward into the fighting compartment of H271. "Is it happening now?"

"More or less," the veteran replied, deliberately vague. He pretended to ignore the lieutenant's intrusion by concentrating on the screen. His AI had switched the image feed to that from a gun camera on a combat car. Mortar rounds flashed in a series of white pulses from behind the hillcrest a hundred meters away.

The images were not full-spectrum transmissions. Each vehicle's artificial intelligence broadcast its positional and sensory data to the command vehicle of the unit to which it was attached. Part of the command vehicle's communications suite was responsible for routing necessary information—including sensory data stripped to digital shorthand—to the central data banks at the Slammers' rear-area logistical headquarters.

The route was likely to be long and poor, because communications satellites were the first casualties of war. Here on Meridienne, the Regiment depended on a chain of laser transponders strung butte to butte along the line of march. When sandstorms disrupted the chain of coherent light, commo techs made do with signals bounced from whichever of Meridienne's moons were in a suitable location.

The signals did get through to the rear, though.

Des Grieux had set his tank's artificial intelligence to enter Central through Task Force Kuykendall's own long data link. The AI sorted out gunnery feeds, then synthesized the minimal squibs of information into three-dimensional holograms.

On Screen #3, fuel blazed from a vehicle struck by the probing mortar shells. A moment later a light truck accelerated up the forward slope of the next hill beyond. A dozen Hashemite irregulars clung to the truck. Their long robes flapped with the speed of their flight.

Des Grieux expected the camera through which he watched to record a stream of cyan bolts ripping the vehicle. Nothing happened. The Hashemite truck ducked over the crest to more distant cover again.

Three half-tracked APCs of the Thunderbolt Division grunted up the forward slope, following the Hashemite vehicle. Their steel-cleated treads sparked wildly on the stony surface.

The tribarrel through which Des Grieux watched and those of the combat car's two wing gunners poured a converging fire into the center APC. It exploded, flinging out the fiery bodies of Thunderbolt infantrymen. The rest of the combat car platoon concentrated on the other two carriers. Their thin armor collapsed with similar results.

Slammers infantry on one-man skimmers slid forward to consolidate the new position just as Des Grieux's AI cut to a new viewpoint.

"How do you *do* that?" asked Lieutenant Carbury as he stared at the vivid scenes.

The platoon leader was as slim as Des Grieux and considerably shorter, but the fighting compartment of a line tank had not been designed for two-person occupancy. Des Grieux could have provided a little more room by folding his seat against the bulkhead, but he pointedly failed to do so.

"Prob'ly the same way they showed you at the Academy," Des Grieux said. *They didn't teach cadets how to use a tank's artificial intelligence to break into Central, but Via! they were fully compatible systems.* "Sir."

The sound of real gunfire whispered through the night.

"Wow," said Carbury. He was sucking in his belly so that he could lean toward Screen #3 without pressing the veteran's shoulder. "Exactly what is it that's happening, Sergeant? They, ah, they aren't updating me very regularly."

Des Grieux rotated his chair counterclockwise. The back squeezed Carbury against the turret basket until the lieutenant managed to slip aside.

"It's all right there," Des Grieux said, pointing toward the map display on Screen #1. "He's got Broglie held on the left—" orange symbols toward the western edge of the display "—but that's just sniping, no *way* they're gonna push Broglie out of ground that rugged."

He gathered spit in his mouth, then swallowed it. "The bastard's good," the veteran muttered to himself. "I give him that."

"Right," said Carbury firmly in a conscious attempt to assert himself. Strategy *was* a major part of the syllabus of the Frisian Military Academy. "So instead he's putting pressure on the right flank where the terrain's easier—"

Not a lot easier, but at least the hills didn't channel tanks and combat cars into a handful of choke points.

"—and there's only the Thunderbolt Division to worry about." Carbury frowned. "Besides the Hashemites themselves, of course."

"*You* worry about the towelheads," Des Grieux said acidly. He glared at the long arc of yellow symbols marking elements of the Thunderbolt Division.

Though the enemy's eastern flank was anchored on hills rising to join the Knifeblade Escarpment well beyond the limits of the display, the center of the long line stretched across terrain similar to that in which Task Force Kuykendall waited. Gullies; scattered shrubs; hard, wind-swept ground that rolled more gently than a calm sea.

Perfect country for a headlong armored assault.

"*That's* what he ought to do," Des Grieux said, more to himself than to the intruding officer. He formed three fingers of his left hand into a pitchfork and stabbed them upward past the line of yellow symbols.

On Screen #3 at the corner of his eye, an image flashed into a cyan dazzle as another main-gun bolt struck home.

"Umm," said Carbury judiciously. "It's not really that simple, Sergeant." His manicured index finger bobbed toward the left, then the right edge of the display. "They'd be enfiladed by fire from the Legion, and even the Thunderbolts have antitank weapons. You wouldn't want to do that."

Des Grieux turned and stared up at the lieutenant. "Try me," he said. The tone was unemotional, but Carbury's head jerked back from the impact of the veteran's eyes.

Screen #3 showed a distant landscape through the sights of a combat-car tribarrel. The image expanded suddenly as the gunner dialed up times forty magnification. The target was a—

Des Grieux's attention clicked instantly to the display. Freed from the veteran's glare, Carbury blinked and focused on the distant scene also.

The target was a Thunderbolt calliope, shooting upward from a pit that protected the eight-barreled weapon while it knocked incoming artillery shells from the air. The high ground which the combat car had gained gave its tribarrels a slanting view down at the calliope four kilometers away.

The line-straight bolts from a powergun cared nothing for distance, so long as no solid object intervened. A five-round burst from the viewpoint tribarrel raked the gun pit, reducing half the joined barrels and the crew to ions.

That would have been enough, but the calliope was in action when the bolts struck it. One of the weapon's own high-intensity three CM rounds discharged in a barrel which the Slammers' fire had already welded shut.

A blue-white explosion blew open the multiple breeches. That was only the momentary prelude to the simultaneous detonation of the contents of an ammunition drum. Plasma scooped out the sides of the gun pit and reflected pitilessly from rockfaces several kilometers away.

As if an echo, three more of the Thunderbolt Division's protective calliopes exploded with equal fury.

The Slammers' toehold on the eastern hills wasn't the overture to further slogging advances on the same flank: it was a vantage point from which to destroy at long range the artillery defenses of the entire hostile center.

"Good *Lord*," Lieutenant Carbury gasped. He

leaned forward in amazement for a closer view. Des Grieux shoved Carbury back with as little conscious volition.

H271's artificial intelligence switched its viewpoint to that of a jeep-mounted infantry tribarrel. Six red streaks fanned through the sky above the narrow wedge of vision, a full salvo from a battery of the Slammers' rocket artillery.

Powerguns fired from the hills to the west. Some of Broglie's defensive weapons had retargeted abruptly to help close the sudden gap in the center of the line. That was dangerous, though, since Hammer's other two batteries continued to pound the flanks of the enemy position.

Broglie's powerguns detonated two of the incoming shells into bright flashes and smears of ugly smoke. The help was too little, too late: the other four firecracker rounds popped open at preset altitudes and strewed their deadly cargo widely over the Thunderbolt lines.

For the moments that the anti-personnel bomblets took to fall, nothing seemed to happen. Then white light like burning magnesium erupted over four square kilometers. Hair-fine lengths of glass shrapnel sawed in all directions. The coverage was thin, but the blasts carved apart anyone within a meter of an individual bomblet.

Lieutenant Carbury jumped for the hatch, aiming his right boot at the back of the tank commander's seat but using Des Grieux's shoulder as a step instead. "Remote that feed to my tank *now*, Sergeant!" the lieutenant shouted as he pulled himself out of H271's cupola.

Des Grieux ignored Carbury and keyed his intercom. *Flowers had better be wearing his commo hel-*

*met.* "Driver!" the veteran snarled. "Get your ass aboard!"

On Screen #3, another salvo of anti-personnel shells howled down onto the Thunderbolt Division's reeling battalions.

Powerguns snapped and blasted at a succession of targets on H271's right-hand screen. For the past several minutes, the real excitement, even for Des Grieux, was on the map display on the other side of the fighting compartment.

The Hashemites and their mercenary allies were getting their clocks cleaned.

The AI's interpretation of data from the battle area cross-hatched all the units of the Thunderbolt Division which were still on the plain. A few minutes of hammering with firecracker rounds had reduced the units by twenty percent of their strength from casualties—

And to something closer to zero combat efficiency because of their total collapse of morale. The battle wasn't over yet, but it was over for *those* men and women. They retreated northward in disorder, some of them on foot without even their personal weapons. Their only thought was to escape the killing zone of artillery and long-range sniping from the Slammers' powerguns.

Half of the Thunderbolt Division remained as an effective fighting force on the high ground to the east—the original left-flank battalions and the troops which had retreated to their protection under fire. Even those units were demoralized, but they would hold against anything except an all-out attack from the Slammers.

If the mercenary commander surrendered now,

while his position was tenable and his employers were still fighting, the Thunderbolt Division would forfeit the performance bond it had posted with the Bonding Authority on Terra. That would end the division as an employable force—and shoot the career of its commander in the nape of the neck.

H271 quivered as its fans spun at idle. The tank was ready to go at a touch on the throttle and pitch controls. "Sarge?" Flowers asked over the intercom channel. "Are we gonna move out soon?"

"Kid," Des Grieux said as he watched holographic dots crawling across holographic terrain, "when I want to hear your voice, I'll tell you."

If he hadn't been so concentrated on the display, he would have snarled the words.

The Thunderbolt Division's employers weren't exactly fighting, but neither had they surrendered. The Hashemite Brotherhood was no more of a monolith than were their Sincanmo enemies; and Hashemite troops were concentrated on the plains, where their mobility seemed an advantage. Des Grieux suspected that the Hashemites *would* have surrendered by now if they'd had enough organization left to manage it.

Broglie's armored elements on what had been the Hashemite right flank, now cut off from friendly forces by the collapse of the center, formed a defensive hedgehog among the sandstone boulders. The terrain gave them an advantage that would translate into prohibitive casualties for anybody trying to drive them out—even the panzers of Colonel Hammer's tank companies. Broglie's Legion wasn't going anywhere.

But Broglie himself had.

Within thirty seconds of the time artillery defense

had collapsed in the center of the Hashemite line, four tank destroyers sped from the Legion's strongpoint to reinforce the Thunderbolt infantry. There was no time to redeploy vehicles already in the line, and Broglie had no proper reserve. These tank destroyers were the Legion's Headquarters/Headquarters Platoon.

The move was as desperate as the situation itself. Des Grieux wasn't surprised to learn Broglie had figured the only possible way out of Colonel Hammer's trap, but it was amazing to see that Broglie had the balls to put himself on the line that way. Des Grieux figured that Broglie obeyed orders because he was too chicken not to. . . .

By using gullies and the rolling terrain, three of the low-slung vehicles managed to get into position. The single loss was a tank destroyer that paused to spike a combat car five kilometers away on the Slammers' right flank. A moment later, the Legion vehicle vanished under the impact of five nearly-simultaneous twenty CM bolts from Slammers' tanks.

Tribarrels on the roofs of the three surviving tank destroyers ripped effectively at incoming artillery, detonating the cargo shells before they strewed their bomblets over the landscape. The tank destroyers' fifteen-CM main guns were a threat nothing, not even a bow-on tank, could afford to ignore. The leap-frog advance of Slammers' units toward the gap in the enemy center slowed to a lethal game of hide-and-seek.

But it was still too little, too late. The Hashemite and Thunderbolt Division troops were broken and streaming northward. All the tank destroyers could do was act as a rear guard, like Horatius and his two companions.

There was no bridge on their line of retreat, but the only practical route down from the Knifeblade Escarpment was through the Notch. Task Force Kuykendall and tank H271 had that passage sealed, as clever-ass *Colonel* Luke Broglie would learn within the next half hour.

Des Grieux began to chuckle hoarsely as he watched beads ooze across a background of coherent light. The sound that came from his throat blended well with the increasingly loud mutter of gunfire from south of the escarpment.

"Shellfish Six to all Oyster and Clam elements," Des Grieux's helmet said.

Des Grieux had ignored the chatter which broke out among the Slammers' vehicles—the combat cars were code-named Oyster; the tanks were Clam—as soon as Carbury gave the alarm. He couldn't ignore this summons, because it was the commander of Shellfish—Task Force Kuykendall—speaking over a unit priority channel.

"All blower captains to me at Golf Six-five ASAP. Acknowledge. Over."

*This was no bloody time to have all the senior people standing around in a gully, listening to some bitch with lieutenant's pips on her collar!*

There were blips of static on Des Grieux's headset. Several commanders used the automatic response set on their consoles instead of replying—protesting—in person.

"Clam Six to Shellfish Six . . ." said Lieutenant Carbury nervously. The tank-platoon commander was not only beneath Kuykendall in the chain of command, he was well aware that she was a ten-year veteran of the Slammers while he had yet to see action. "Suggest we link our vehicles for a virtual council, sir. Over."

"Negative," Kuykendall snapped. "I need to make a point to our employers and allies, here, Clam Six, and they're not in the holographic environment."

She paused, then added in a coldly neutral voice. "Break. This means you, too, Slick. Don't push your luck. Shellfish Six out."

Des Grieux cursed under his breath. After a moment, he slid his seat upward and climbed out of the tank. He'd grabbed a grenade launcher and a bandolier of ammunition at the depot; he carried them in his left hand.

He didn't acknowledge the summons.

Occasional flashes to the south threw the Knife-blade Escarpment into hazy relief, like a cloudbank lighted by a distant storm. Sometimes the wind sounded like human cries.

The gullies at the base of the butte twisted Task Force Kuykendall's position like the guts of a worm. Two combat cars and a tank were placed between H271 and Kuykendall's vehicle, *Firewalker*, in the rough center of the line. The gaps between the Slammers' units were filled by indigs in family battlegroups.

The restive Sincanmos had let their campfires burn down. The way through the gullies was marked by metal buckets glowing from residual heat. Men in bright, loose garments fingered their personal weapons and watched Des Grieux as he trudged past.

There was a group of fifty or more armed troops—all men except for Kuykendall and one of the tank commanders, and overwhelmingly indigs—gathered at *Firewalker* when Des Grieux arrived. Kuykendall had switched on the car's running lights with deep yellow filters in place to preserve the night vision of those illuminated.

"Glad you could make it, Slick," Kuykendall said. She perched on cargo slung to the side of her combat car. It was hard to make out Kuykendall's words over the burble of Sincanmo conversation because she spoke without electronic amplification. "I want all of you to hear what I just informed Chief Diabate."

The name of the senior Sincanmo leader in the task force brought a partial hush. Men turned to look at Diabate, white-bearded and more hawk-faced than most of his fellows. He wore a robe printed in an intricate pattern of black/russet/white, over which were slung a two-CM powergun and three silver-mounted knives in a sash.

"Colonel Hammer has ordered us back ten kays," Kuykendall continued. Two crewmen stood at *Firewalker*'s wing tribarrels, but the weapons were aimed toward the Notch. The air of the gathering was amazement, not violence. "So we're moving out in half an hour."

"Don't be bloody crazy!" Des Grieux shouted over the indig babble. "*You* saw what's happening south of the wall."

He pointed the barrel of his grenade launcher toward the Escarpment. The bandolier swung heavily in the same hand. "Inside an hour, there'll be ten thousand people trying t' get through the Notch, and *we're* here t' shut the door in their face!"

Sincanmo elders shook their guns in the air and cried approval.

Kuykendall's sharp features pinched tighter. She muttered an order to *Firewalker*'s AI, then—regard-

less of the Hashemites in the Notch—blared through
the combat car's external speakers, "*Listen* to me,
gentlemen!"

Her voice echoed like angry thunder from the face
of the butte. Shouting men blinked and looked at
her.

"The Colonel *wants* them to run away instead of
fighting like cornered rats," Kuykendall went on,
speaking normally but continuing to use amplification. "He wants a surrender, not a bloodbath."

"But—" Chief Diabate protested.

"What the Colonel orders," Kuykendall said firmly,
"I carry out. And I'm in charge of this task force, by
order of your own council."

"We know the Hashemites!" Diabate said. This
time, Kuykendall let him speak. "If they throw away
their guns and flee now, they will find more guns
later. Only if we kill them all can we be sure of
peace. This is the time to kill them!"

"I've got my orders," Kuykendall said curtly, "and
you've got yours. Slammers elements, saddle up. We
move out in twenty . . . seven minutes."

Khaki-uniformed mercenaries turned away, shrugging at the slings and holsters of their personal weapons. Des Grieux did not move for a moment.

"I wanted you to see," Kuykendall continued to
the shocked Sincanmo elders. "This isn't a tribal
council, this is war and *I'm* in charge. If you refuse
to obey my orders, *you're* in breach of the contract,
not me and Colonel Hammer."

Sincanmos shouted in anger and surprise. Des
Grieux strode away from the crowd, muttering com-
mands through his commo helmet to the artificial
intelligence in H271. The AI obediently projected a

view of the terrain still closer to the base of the mesa onto the left side of Des Grieux's visor.

Flowers waited with his torso out of the driver's hatch. "What's the word, Sarge?" he called as Des Grieux stepped around the back of a Sincanmo truck mounted with a cage launcher and a quartet of forty-kilo bombardment rockets.

"We're moving," Des Grieux said. He lifted himself to the deck of his tank. "There's a low spot twenty meters from the base of the butte. I'll give directions on your screen. Park us there."

He clambered up the turret side and thrust his legs through the hatch.

"Ah, Sarge?" Flowers called worriedly. The curved armor hid him from Des Grieux. "Should I take down the cammie film?"

Des Grieux switched to intercom. Screen #1 now showed the terrain in the immediate vicinity of H271. The site Des Grieux had picked was within two hundred meters of the tank's present location.

"It'll bloody come down when you bloody drive through it, won't it?" Des Grieux snarled. He slashed his finger across the topo map, marking the intended route with a glowing line that echoed on the driver's display. "Do it!"

The microns-thick camouflage film was strung, then jolted with high-frequency electricity which caused it to take an optical set in the pattern and colors of the ground underneath it. The film was polarized to pass light impinging on the upper surfaces but to block it from below. The covering was permeable to air as well, though it did impede ventilation somewhat.

H271's fans snorted at increased power, sucking

the thin membrane against its stretchers. Sincanmo troops moved closer to their own vehicles, eyeing the 170-tonne tank with concern.

Flowers rotated H271 carefully in its own length, then drove slowly up the back slope of the gully. The nearest twenty-meter length of camouflage film bowed, then flew apart when the stresses exceeded its limits. Gritty soil puffed from beneath the tank's skirts.

"Clam Four, this is Clam Six," said Lieutenant Carbury over the 3rd Platoon push. "What's going on there? Over."

Des Grieux closed the cupola hatch above him. This was going to be very tricky. Not placing the shot—he could do that at ten kays—but determining where the shot had to *be* placed.

H271 lurched as Flowers drove it down into a washout directly at the base of the mesa. Des Grieux let the tank settle as he searched the sandstone face through his gunnery screen.

"This where you want us, Sarge?" Flowers asked.

"Clam Four, this is Shellfish Six. Report! Over."

"Right," said Des Grieux over the intercom. "Shut her down. Is your hatch closed?"

The intake howl dimmed into the sighing note of fans winding down. Iridium clanged forward as Flowers slammed his hatch.

"Yessir," he said.

Des Grieux fired his main gun. Cyan light filled the world.

The rockface cracked with a sound like the planetary mantle splitting. The shattered cliff slumped forward in chunks ranging in size from several tons to microscopic beads of glass. H271 rang and shuddered as the wave of rubble swept across it, sliding up against the turret.

"Clam Four to Clam Six," Des Grieux said. He didn't try to keep his voice free of the satisfaction he felt at the perfect execution of his plan. "I've had an accidental discharge of my main gun. No injuries, but I'm afraid my tank can't be moved without mebbe a day's work by heavy equipment. Over."

"Slick," said Lieutenant Kuykendall, "you stupid son of a bitch."

She must have expected something like this, because she didn't bother raising her voice.

Kuykendall's right wing gunner worked over the Notch with his tribarrel as *Firewalker* idled at the base of the butte.

When H271 lighted the night with its main gun, the Hashemites guarding the Notch came to panicked alertness. During the ten minutes since, combat cars fired short bursts to keep enemy heads down while the Slammers pulled out.

This thirty-second slashing was different. The gunner's needless expenditure of ammunition was a way to let out his frustration—at what Des Grieux had done, or at the fact that the rest of the Slammers were running while Des Grieux and the indigs stayed to fight.

The troopers of Task Force Kuykendall were professional soldiers. If they'd been afraid of a fight, they would have found some other line of work.

Kuykendall squeezed the gunner's biceps, just beneath the shoulder flare of his body armor. The trooper's thumbs came off the butterfly trigger. The weapon's barrel-set continued to rotate for several seconds to aid in cooling. The white-hot iridium muzzles glowed a circle around their common axis.

Trooper Flowers lifted himself into *Firewalker*'s

fighting compartment. His personal gear—in a duf-
flebag; Flowers was too junior to have snagged large-
capacity ammo cans to hold his belongings—was
slung to the vehicle's side. Combat cars made room
for extra personnel more easily than Carbury's remaining tanks could.

Des Grieux braced his feet against the cupola
coaming and used his leg muscles to shove at a block
of sandstone the size of his torso. Thrust overcame
friction. The slab slid across a layer of gravel, then
toppled onto H271's back deck.

The upper surfaces were clear enough now that
Des Grieux could rotate the turret.

Lieutenant Carbury's *Paper Doll* was an old tank,
frequently repaired. An earlier commander had
painted kill rings on the stubby barrel of the main
gun. Holographic screens within the fighting compartment illuminated Carbury from below. His fresh,
youthful face was out of place peering from the veteran vehicle.

"Sergeant Des Grieux," the lieutenant said. His
voice was pitched too high for the tone of command
he wished to project. "You're acting like a fool by
staying here, and you're disobeying my direct orders."

Carbury spoke directly across the twenty meters
between himself and tank H271 instead of using his
commo helmet. The *hoosh* of lift fans idling almost
washed his voice away. In another few seconds,
minutes at most, Des Grieux would be alone with
fate.

The veteran brushed his palms against the front
of his jumpsuit. He had to be careful not to rub his
hands raw while moving rocks. He'd need delicate
control soon, with the opening range at two kays.

"Sorry, sir," he called. "I figure the accident's my

fault. It's my duty to stay with the tank since I'm the one who disabled it."

A combat car spat at the Notch. The Sincanmos, still under their camouflage film, were keeping as quiet as cats in ambush while the two platoons of armored vehicles maneuvered out of the gullies.

The Sincanmos didn't take orders real well, but they were willing to do whatever was required for a chance to kill. Des Grieux felt a momentary sympathy for the indigs, knowing what was about to happen.

But Via! if they hadn't been a bunch of stupid wogs, they'd have known, too. They weren't his problem.

"Clam Six," said Lieutenant Kuykendall remotely, "this is Shellfish Six." She used radio, a frequency limited to the Slammers within the task force. "Are all your elements ready to move? Over."

Carbury stiffened and touched the frequency key on the side of his commo helmet. "Clam Six to Six," he said. "Yessir, all ready. Over."

Instead of giving the order, Kuykendall turned to look at Des Grieux. She raised the polarized shield of her visor. "Goodbye, Slick," she called across the curtain of disturbed air. "I don't guess I'll be seeing you again."

Des Grieux stared at the woman who had been his driver a decade before. They were twenty meters apart, but she still flinched minutely at his expression.

Des Grieux smiled. "Don't count on that, Lieutenant-sir," he said.

Kuykendall slapped her visor down and spoke a curt order. Fan notes changed, the more lightly-loaded rotors of the combat cars rising in pitch faster than those of the tanks.

Moving in unison with a tank in the lead, the Slammers of Task Force Kuykendall howled off into the night. Their powerguns, main guns as well as tribarrels, lashed the Notch in an unmistakable farewell gesture. The sharp *crack* of the bolts and the dazzling actinics reflected back and forth between the Escarpment and the sheer face of the mesa.

For Des Grieux, the huge vehicles had a beauty like that of nothing else in existence. They skated lightly over the soil, gathering speed in imperceptible increments. Occasionally a skirt touched down and sparked, steel against shards of quartz. Then they were gone around the mesa, leaving the sharpness of ozone and the ghost-track of ionized air dissipating where a main gun had fired at the Hashemites.

Des Grieux felt a sudden emptiness; but it was too late now to change, and anyway, it didn't matter. He slid down into H271 and tried his gunnery controls again. Added weight resisted the turret motors briefly, but this time it was only gravel and smaller particles which could rearrange themselves easily.

The sight picture on H271's main screen rotated: off the blank wall of the butte and across open desert, to the Notch that marred the otherwise smooth profile of the Knifeblade Escarpment. Des Grieux raised the magnification. Plus twenty; plus forty, and he could see movement as Hashemites crawled forward, over rocks split and glazed by blue-white bolts, to see why the punishing fire had ceased; plus eighty—

A Hashemite wearing a turban and a dark blue

jellaba swept the night with the image-intensifying sight of his back-pack missile.

He found nothing. Des Grieux stared at the Hashemite's bearded face until the man put down his sight and called his fellows forward. His optics were crude compared to those of H271, and the Hashemite didn't know where to look.

Des Grieux smiled grimly and shut down all his tank's systems. From now until he slammed home the main switch again, Des Grieux would wait in a silent iridium coffin.

It wasn't his turn. Yet. He raised his head through the cupola hatch and watched.

Because of the patient silence the Sincanmos had maintained, Des Grieux expected the next stage to occur in about half an hour. In fact, it was less than five minutes after the Slammers' armored vehicles had noisily departed the scene before one of the outposts switched the minefield controls to Self Destruct. Nearly a thousand charges went off simultaneously, any one of them able to destroy a 4x4 or cripple a tank.

An all-wheel drive truck laden with towelheads lurched over the lip of the Notch and started for the plains below.

The locals on both sides were irregulars, but the Sincanmos in ambush had something concrete to await. All the Hashemite guards knew was that a disaster had occurred south of the Escarpment, and that they had themselves been released from a danger unguessed until the Slammers drove off through the night. *They* saw no reason to hold position, whatever their orders might be.

Three more trucks followed the first—a family bat-

tlegroup, organized like those of the Sincanmos. One
of the vehicles towed a railgun on a four-wheeled
carriage. The slope was a steep twenty percent. The
railgun threatened to swing ahead every time the
towing vehicle braked, but the last truck in the
group held the weapon's barrel with a drag line to
prevent upset.

The Sincanmos did not react.

A dozen more trucks grunted into sight. H271's
sensors could have placed and identified the vehicles
while they were still hidden behind the lip of rock,
but it didn't matter one way or the other to Des
Grieux. Better to keep still, concealed even from
sensors far more sophisticated than those available
to the indigs.

More trucks. They poured out of the Notch, three
and four abreast, as many as the narrow opening
would accept. Forty, sixty—still more. The entire
outpost was fleeing at its best speed.

The Hashemites must have argued violently. Should
they go or stay? Was the blocking force really gone,
or did it lurk on the other side of the butte, waiting
to swing back into sight spewing blue fire?

But somebody was bound to run; and when that
group seemed on the verge of successful escape, the
others would follow as surely as day follows night.

There would be no day for most of this group of
Hashemites. When their leading vehicles reached
the bottom of the slope, the Sincanmos opened up
with a devastating volley.

The two-kilometer range was too great for sidearms to be generally effective, though Des Grieux
saw a bolt from a semi-automatic powergun—perhaps Chief Diabate's personal weapon—light up a
truck cab. The vehicle went out of control and rolled

sideways. Upholstery and the driver's garments were afire even before ammunition and fuel caught.

Mostly the ambush was work for the crew-served weapons. For the Sincanmo gunners, it was practice with live pop-up targets. Dozens of automatic cannon punched tracers into and through soft-skinned vehicles, leaving flames and torn flesh behind them. Mortars fired, mixing high explosive and incendiary bombs. Truck-mounted lasers cycled with low-frequency growls, igniting paint, tires, and cloth before sliding across the rock to new targets.

A pair of perfectly-aimed bombardment rockets landed within the Notch itself, causing fires and secondary explosions among the tail end of the line of would-be escapees. The smooth, inclined surface of the Escarpment provided no concealment, no hope. Hashemites stood or ran, but they died in either case.

Des Grieux smiled like a sickle blade and pulled the hatch closed above him. He continued to watch through the vision blocks of the cupola.

Truckloads of Sincanmo troops drove up out of their concealment, heading for the loot and the writhing wounded scattered helplessly on the slope.

*Have fun while you can, wogs*, Des Grieux thought. *Because* you *won't see the morning either*.

Thirty-seven minutes after Chief Diabate sprang his ambush, Sincanmo troops in the Notch began firing southward. The shooters were the bands who'd penetrated farthest in their quest for loot and throats to cut.

Other bright-robed irregulars were picking over the bodies and vehicles scattered along the slope.

When the guns sounded, they looked up and began to jabber among themselves in search of a consensus.

Des Grieux watched through his vision blocks and waited. H271's fighting compartment was warm and muggy with the environmental system shut down, but a cold sweat of anticipation beaded the tanker's upper lip.

Half—apparently the junior half—of each Sincanmo battlegroup waited under camouflage film in the gullies to provide a base of fire for the looters. The Sincanmos were not so much undisciplined as self-willed, and they had a great deal of experience in hit-and-run guerrilla warfare.

The appearance of a well-prepared defense was deceptive, though. The heavy weapons that were effective at a two-kilometer range had expended much of their ammunition in the first engagement; and besides, the irregulars were about to find themselves out of their depth.

They were facing the first of the retreating Thunderbolt Division troops. The Thunderbolts weren't much; but they were professionals, and this lot had Luke Broglie with them. . . .

At first the Sincanmos in the Notch fired small arms at their unseen targets; automatic rifles pecked the night with short bursts. Then somebody got an abandoned Hashemite railgun working. The Notch lighted in quick pulses, the corona discharge from the weapon's generator. The *crackcrackcrack* of hypervelocity slugs echoed viciously.

A blue-white dazzle outlined the rock surfaces of the Notch. A Legion tank destroyer kilometers away had put a fifteen-CM bolt into the center of the captured outpost. Two seconds later the sound reached

Des Grieux's ears, the glass-breaking *crash* as rock shattered under unendurable heat stresses.

Three Sincanmo survivors scampered down the Escarpment. One man's robe smoldered and left a fine trail of smoke behind him. The men were on foot, because their trucks fed the orange-red flames lighting the Notch behind them.

The Sincanmo irregulars had gotten their first lesson. A siren on Chief Diabate's 8x8 armored car, halfway up the slope, wound slowly from a groan to a wail. Exhaust blatted through open pipes as the indigs leaped aboard their vehicles and started the engines.

The first salvo howled from the Thunderbolt Division's makeshift redoubt to the southeast. The shells burst with bright orange flashes in the empty plains, causing no casualties. The Sincanmos were either in the gullies well north of the impact area or still on the slope, where the height of the Knifeblade Escarpment provided a wall against shells on simple ballistic trajectories.

Indig vehicles grunted downslope as members of their crews threw themselves aboard. Another four-tube salvo of high explosive struck near where the previous rounds had landed. One shell simply dug itself into the hard soil without going off. Casing fragments rang against the side of a truck, but none of the vehicles slowed or swerved.

The camouflage film fluttered as indigs in the gullies packed their belongings. The trucks were both cargo haulers and weapons platforms for the battlegroups. When the Sincanmos expected action, they cached non-essentials—food, water, tents and bedding—beside the vehicles, then tossed them aboard again when it was time to leave.

Another round streaked across the Escarpment from the south*west*. The Sincanmos ignored the shell because it didn't come within a kilometer of the ground at any point in its trajectory.

Broglie's Legion had a single six-gun battery, very well equipped as to weapons (self-propelled 210-MM rocket howitzers) and the selection of shells those hogs launched. The battery's first response to the new threat was a reconnaissance round which provided real-time images through a laser link to Battery Fire Control.

Had Des Grieux powered up H271, his tribarrel in Automatic Artillery Defense mode could have slapped the spy shell down as soon as it sailed over the Escarpment. It was no part of the veteran's plan to give the tank's presence away so soon, however.

At least thirty guns from the Thunderbolt Division opened fire according to target data passed them by the Legion's fire control. Spurts of black smoke with orange hearts leaped like poplars among the Sincanmo positions, shredding camouflage film that had not deceived the Legion's recce package.

A truck blew up. Men were screaming. Vehicles racing back from the slope to load cached necessities skidded uncertainly as their crews wondered whether or not to drive into the shellbursts ahead of them.

The Legion's howitzers ripped out a perfect Battery Three, three shells per gun launched within a total of ten seconds. They were firecracker rounds. The casings popped high in the air, loosing approximately 7,500 bomblets to drift down on the Sincanmo forces.

For the most part, the Sincanmo looters under Chief Diabate didn't know what hit them. A blanket of white fire fell over the vehicles which milled across the plain for fear of Thunderbolt shells. Thousands of bomblets exploded with a ripping sound that seemed to go on forever.

For those in the broad impact zone, it *was* forever. Smoke and dust lifted over the soil when the explosive light ceased. A dozen Sincanmo vehicles were ablaze; more crashed and ignited in the following seconds. Only a handful of trucks were under conscious control, though run-while-flat tires let many of the vehicles careen across the landscape with their crews flayed to the bone by glass-filament shrapnel.

Fuel and munitions exploded as the Thunderbolt Division continued to pound the gully positions. A pair of heavy caliber shells landed near H271, but they were overs—no cause for concern. The indigs dying all across the plain provided a perfect stalking horse for the tank in ambush.

Chief Diabate's armored car—the only vehicle in the Sincanmo force with real armor—had come through the barrage unscathed. It wallowed toward the eastern flank of the butte with its siren summoning survivors from the gullies to follow it to safety. Sincanmo 4x4s lurched through the remnants of the camouflage film, abandoning their cached supplies to the needs of the moment.

Sparks and rock fragments sprang up before and beside the armored car. Diabate's driver swerved, but not far enough: a second three-round burst punched through the car's thin armor. A yellow flash lifted the turret, but the vehicle continued to roll on inertia until a larger explosion blew the remainder of the car and crew into pieces no larger than a man's hand.

Leading elements of the Thunderbolt Division had

reached the Notch. One of them was a fire support vehicle, a burst-capable ninety-MM gun on a half-tracked chassis. The gun continued to fire, switching from solid shot to high explosive as it picked its targets among the fleeing Sincanmo trucks. Other mercenary vehicles, primarily armored personnel carriers with additional troops riding on their roofs, crawled through the Notch and descended the slope littered by the bodies of indigs locked in the embrace of death.

It was getting to be time. Des Grieux closed his main power switch.

H271's screens came alive and bathed the fighting compartment with their light. Des Grieux lifted his commo helmet, ran his fingers through his close-cropped hair, and lowered the helmet again. He took the twin joysticks of the gunnery controls in his hands.

"Booster," Des Grieux said to the tank's artificial intelligence. "On Screen One, gimme vehicles on a four-kay by one strip aligned with the main gun."

The topographic map of the main battle area flicked out and returned as a narrow holographic slice centered on the Notch. The APCs and other vehicles already north of the Knifeblade Escarpment were sharp symbols that crawled down the holographic slope toward—unbeknownst to themselves—H271 waiting at the bottom of the display.

The symbols of vehicles on the other side of the sandstone wall were hollow, indicating the AI had to extrapolate from untrustworthy data. The electronics, pumps, and even ignition systems of Thunderbolt and Hashemite trucks had individual radio-frequency spectrum signatures which H271's sensor suite could read. Precise location and assignment was impossible at a four-kilometer range beyond an intervening mass of sandstone, however.

One vehicle was marked with orange precision: the Legion tank destroyer which had huffed itself to within five hundred meters of the Notch. The tank destroyer's tribarrel licked skyward frequently to keep shells from decimating the retreating forces. The lines of cyan fire, transposed onto the terrain map in the tank's data base, provided H271 with a precise location for the oncoming vehicle. The other two tank destroyers were at the very top of the display, where they acted as rear guard against the Slammers.

They would come in good time. As for the closest of the three—it would have been nice to take out the tank destroyer with the first bolt, the round that unmasked H271, but that wasn't necessary. Waiting for the Legion vehicle to rise into range would mean sparing some of the half-tracks that drove off the slope and disappeared into swales concealed from the tank.

Des Grieux didn't intend to spare anything that moved this night.

The gunnery screen shrank in scale as it incorporated both orange pippers, the solid dot that marked the tribarrel's target—the leading APC, covered by the flowing robes of a score of Hashemites riding on top of it—and the main gun's hollow circle, centered at the turret/hill junction on the fire support vehicle which still, from its vantage point in the Notch, covered the retreat.

Des Grieux fired both weapons together.

It took a dozen rounds from the tribarrel before the carrier blew up. By then, the screaming Hashemite riders were torches flopping over the rocks.

The main gun's twenty-CM bolt vaporized several square meters of the fire support vehicle's armor. Ammunition the Thunderbolts hadn't expended on Sincanmo targets were sufficient to blow a passing APC against the far wall of the Notch; the crumpled wreckage then slid forward, down the slope, shedding parts and flames.

Nothing remained of the fire support vehicle except its axles and wheels, stripped of their tires.

Des Grieux left his main gun pointed as it was. He worked the tribarrel up the line of easy targets against the slanted rock, giving each half-track the number of cyan bolts required to detonate its fuel, its on-board ammunition, or both. Secondary explosions leaped onto the slope like the footprints of a fire giant.

Nothing more came through the Notch after the twenty-CM bolt ripped it, but Screen #1 showed the Legion tank destroyer accelerating at its best speed to reach a firing position.

Des Grieux's face was terrible in its joy.

So long as H271 was shut down and covered by broken rock, it was virtually indetectable. When Des Grieux opened fire, anybody but a blind man could call artillery in on the tank's position. A number of Thunderbolt Division personnel survived long enough to do just that.

Four HE shells landed between ten and fifty meters of H271 as Des Grieux walked two-CM bolts across an open-topped supply truck with armored sides. His sight picture vanished for a moment in the spouting explosions. A fifth round struck in a scatter of gravel well up the side of the mesa. It brought down a minor rockslide, but no significant chunks landed near the tank.

Des Grieux ignored the artillery because he didn't have any choice. He'd ignited all eight of the supply truck's low-side tires with the initial burst. When the debris of the shellbursts cleared, the vehicle was toppling sideways. Its cargo compartment was full of wounded troops who screamed as they went over.

Twenty or thirty shells landed within a dozen seconds. A few of the Thunderbolt gun crews had switched to armor piercing, but none of those rounds scored a direct hit on the tank. A heavy shell burst on H271's rock-covered back deck. The shock made all the displays quiver. The air of the fighting compartment filled with dust shaken from every minute crevice.

Screen #1 showed the Legion tank destroyer's orange symbol entering the Notch from the south side. The heavy vehicle had collided with several Thunderbolt Division APCs in its haste to reach a position from which it could fire at the Slammers' tank.

Des Grieux slapped the plate that set his tribarrel on Automatic Artillery Defense. He said in a sharp, clear voice, "Booster, sort incoming from the southeast first," as his foot poised on the firing pedal for the main gun.

The twenty-CM weapon was already aligned. The eighty-times magnified tube of the tank destroyer's gun slid into the hollow circle on Screen #2. More shells burst near H271, but not very near, and the tribarrel was already snarling skyward at the anti-tank rounds which the Legion battery hurled.

The tank destroyer's glacis plate filled Des Grieux's display. He rocked forward on the foot trip. The saturated blue streak punched through the mantle of the fifteen-CM weapon before the Legion gunner could find his target.

The tank destroyer's ready magazine painted the Notch cyan. Then the reserve ammunition storage went off and lifted the vehicle's armored carapace a meter in the air before dropping it back to the ground.

The iridium shell glowed white. Nothing else remained of the tank destroyer or its crew.

Des Grieux laughed with mad glee. "Have to do better 'n that, Broglie!" he shouted as he slid his aiming point down the slope. He fired every time the hollow pipper covered an undamaged vehicle.

There were seventeen twenty-CM rounds remaining in H271's ready magazine. Each bolt turned a lightly-armored truck or APC into a fireball that bulged steel plates like the skin of a balloon. The last two half-tracks Des Grieux hit had already been abandoned by their crews.

Artillery fire slackened, though Des Grieux's tri-barrel snarled uninterruptedly skyward. A delay-fused armor-piercing shell struck short of H271 and punched five meters through the hard soil before going off. The explosion lifted the tank a hand's breadth despite the mass of rock overburden, but the vehicle sustained no damage.

Screen #1 showed a killing zone south of the Escarpment, where fleeing troops bunched and the Slammers maneuvered to cut them apart. Because the powerguns were deadly at any range so long as they had a sight line, every knob of ground Hammer's troops took cut a further swath through far-distant enemy positions.

When the Legion and Thunderbolt artillery directed its fire toward Des Grieux, the cupola guns of the tanks were freed to kill. The process of collapse accelerated as tanks and combat cars took the howitzer batteries themselves under direct fire.

Des Grieux waited. H271's fighting compartment was a stinking furnace. Empties from the rapidly-fired main gun loosed a gray haze into the atmosphere faster than the air conditioning could absorb it. The tank chuckled mechanically as it replenished the ready magazine from storage compartments deep in its armored core.

Fuel fires lighted the slope all the way to the Notch. Hashemite, Sincanmo, and Thunderbolt vehicles—all wrecked and burning. Flames wove a dance of victory over a landscape in which nothing else moved.

Hundreds of terrified soldiers were still alive in the wasteland. The survivors remained motionless. Incoming artillery fire had ceased, giving Des Grieux back the use of his tribarrel. He used it and H271's night vision equipment to probe at whim wherever a head raised.

Des Grieux waited as he watched Broglie's two tank destroyers.

They were no longer the rear guard for the Central Sector refugees. The tank destroyers moved up to the Notch at a deliberate pace which never exposed them to the guns of the panzers south of the Knifeblade Escarpment. Always a cunning bastard, Broglie. . . .

Ammunition in a supply truck near the bottom of the slope cooked off. The blast raised a mushroom-shaped cloud as high as the top of the Escarpment.

Two kilometers away, H271 shook.

The battle was going to be over very soon. The

Thunderbolt Division's horrendous butcher's bill gave its commander a legitimate excuse for surrendering whether his Hashemite employers did so or not. The bodies heaped on both sides of the Notch would ransom the lives of their fellows.

It occurred to Des Grieux that he could probably drive H271 away, now. Incoming shells had done a day's work for excavating equipment in freeing the tank from his deliberate rockfall.

There wasn't anyplace else in the universe that Des Grieux wanted to be.

Screen #1 showed the tank destroyers pausing just south of the Notch. A fifteen-CM bolt stabbed across the intervening kilometers and vaporized a portion of the mesa's rim. Sonic echoes of the plasma discharge rumbled across the plain below.

Des Grieux blinked, then understood. When the Slammers in Task Force Kuykendall moved out, they'd abandoned the sensor pack they'd placed on the butte. H271 wasn't connected to the pack, but Broglie didn't know that.

And trust that clever bastard not to miss a point before he made his move!

Des Grieux chuckled through a throat burned dry by ozone and the other poisons he breathed. His hands rested lightly on the two joysticks. The pippers were already locked together, solid in circle, where they needed to be.

The left-hand tank destroyer backed, then began to accelerate toward the Notch at high speed. The other Legion vehicle moved forward also, but at a relative crawl.

The right-hand tank destroyer had made the one-shot kill on the tiny sensor pack two kilometers away.

It happened the way Des Grieux knew it would happen. The tank destroyer rushing through the left side of the Notch braked so abruptly that its skirts rubbed off a shower of sparks against the smooth rock. The other tank destroyer, Broglie's own vehicle, continued to accelerate. It burst into clear sight while H271's gunner was supposed to be concentrating on the target ten meters to the side.

But it was Des Grieux below, and Des Grieux's pippers filled with the mass of iridium that slid into the sight picture. His tribarrel and main gun fired in unison at the massive target.

The interior of H271 turned cyan, then white, and finally red with heat like a hammer. The shockwave was not a sound but a blow that slammed Des Grieux down in his seat.

The cupola was gone. Warning lights glowed across Des Grieux's console. Screen #3 switched automatically to a damage-assessment schematic. The tribarrel had vaporized, but the main gun was undamaged and the turret rotated normally the few mills required to bring the hollow pipper onto its remaining target.

Luke Broglie was very good. He'd fired a fraction of a second early, but he must have known that he wouldn't get the additional instant he needed to center his sight squarely on the tank turret.

He must have known that he was meeting Slick Des Grieux for the last time.

Broglie's vehicle was a white glow at the edge of the Notch. The other crew should have bailed out of their tank destroyer and waited for the Hashemite surrender, but they tried to finish the job at which their Colonel had failed.

Three fifteen-CM bolts cut the night, two shots

before the tank destroyer *had* a sight picture and the last round thirty meters wide of H271. Des Grieux penetrated the tank destroyer's thick glacis plate with his first bolt, then sent a second round through the hole to vaporize the wreckage in a pyre of its own munitions.

They should have known it was impossible to do what Luke Broglie couldn't manage. Nobody was as good as Broglie . . . except Slick Des Grieux.

Des Grieux could see both north and south of the Knifeblade Escarpment from where he sat on top of the burned-out tank destroyer. Smudgy fires still burned over the sloping plain where the Slammers' artillery and sharpshooting powerguns had slashed the Hashemite center into retreat, then chaos.

Clots of surrendered enemies waited to be interned. Thunderbolt Division personnel rested under tarpaulins attached to their vehicles and a stake or two driven into the soil. The defeated mercenaries were not exactly lounging: there were many wounded among them, and every survivor from the punished battalions knew at least one friend who hadn't been so lucky.

But they would be exchanged back to their own command within hours or days. A mercenary's war ended when the fighting stopped.

The Hashemite survivors were another matter. They huddled in separate groups. Many of their trucks had been disabled by the rain of anti-personnel bomblets which the armor of the mercenary halftracks had shrugged off. The Hashemites' personal weapons were piled ostentatiously at a slight distance from each gathering.

That wasn't necessarily going to help. Sincanmo irregulars were doing the heavy work of interning prisoners: searching, sorting, and gathering them into coffles of two hundred or so to be transferred to holding camps. The Slammers overseeing the process wouldn't permit the Sincanmos to shoot their indig prisoners—here in public.

What happened when converted cargo vans filled with Hashemites were driven ten kays or so into the desert was anybody's guess.

A gun jeep whined its way up the south face of the Escarpment. Victorious troops and prisoners watched the vehicle's progress. The jeep's driver regarded them only as obstacles, and the passenger seated on the other side of the pintle-mounted tribarrel paid them no attention at all.

Des Grieux rolled bits of ivory between the ball of this thumb and his left hand. He turned his face toward the north, where H271 sat in the far distance with a combat car and a heavy-lift vehicle from the Slammers' maintenance battalion in attendance.

Des Grieux wasn't interested in the attempts to dig out H271, but he was unwilling to watch the jeep. Funny about it being a jeep. He'd expected at least a combat car; and Joachim Steuben present, not some faceless driver who wasn't even one of the White Mice.

The slope looked much steeper going down than it had when Des Grieux was on the plain two kilometers away. By contrast, the tilted strata on the south side of the Escarpment rose very gently, though they were as sure a barrier as the north edge that provided the name Knifeblade. There wasn't any way down from the Escarpment, except through the Notch.

And no way down at all, when Slick Des Grieux waited below with a tank and the unshakeable determination to kill everyone who faced him.

They'd rigged a bucket on the maintenance vehicle's shearlegs. A dozen Hashemite prisoners shoveled rock from H271's back deck into the bucket.

Des Grieux snorted. *He* could have broken the tank free in minutes. If he'd had to, if there were someplace he needed to be with a tank. While there was fighting going on, nothing mattered except a weapon; and the Regiment's panzers were the greatest weapons that had ever existed.

When the fighting was over, nothing mattered at all.

The sun had risen high enough to punish, and the tank destroyer's armor was a massive heat sink, retaining some of the fury which had devoured the vehicle. Nothing remained within the iridium shell except the fusion bottle, which hadn't ruptured when the tank destroyer's ammunition gang-fired.

The jeep was getting close. The angry sound of its fans changed every time the light vehicle had to jump or circle a large piece of debris. H271's main gun had seen to it that vehicle parts covered much of the surface of the Notch.

The heavy-lift vehicle arrived at dawn with several hundred Sincanmos and a platoon of F Company combat cars—not Kuykendall; Des Grieux didn't know where Kuykendall had gone. Des Grieux turned H271 over to the maintenance crew and, for want of anything better to do, wandered into the gully where the blocking force had waited.

A 4x4 with two bombardment rockets in their launching cage was still parked beside H271's initial location. The Sincanmo crew sprawled nearby, riddled by shrapnel too fine to be visible under normal lighting. One of them lay across a lute with a hemispherical sound chamber.

Des Grieux lifted the driver out of his seat and laid him on the ground with the blood-speckled side of his face down. The truck was operable. Des Grieux drove it up the steep slope to the Notch, shifting to compound low every time he had to skirt another burned-out vehicle or windrow of bodies.

Troopers in the combat cars watched the tanker, but they didn't interfere.

The gun jeep stopped. Its fans whirred at a deepening note as they lost power. Des Grieux heard boots hit the soil. He turned, but Colonel Hammer had already gripped a handrail to haul himself up onto the tank destroyer.

"Feeling proud of yourself, Des Grieux?" the Colonel asked grimly.

Hammer wore a cap instead of a commo helmet. There was a line of SpraySeal across his forehead, just above the pepper-and-salt eyebrows, where a helmet would have cut him if it were struck hard. His eyes were bloodshot and very cold.

"Not particularly," Des Grieux said. He wasn't feeling anything at all.

The driver was just a driver, a Charlie Company infantryman. He'd unclipped his carbine from the dash and pointed it vaguely in Des Grieux's direction, but he wasn't one of Joachim Steuben's field police.

Des Grieux had left his grenade launcher behind in H271. He was unarmed.

"They're trying to find Colonel Broglie," Hammer said. "The Legion command council is, and I am."

"Then you're in luck," Des Grieux said.

He opened his left hand. Bones had burned to lime in the glare of the tank destroyer's ammunition, but teeth were more refractory. Des Grieux had found three of them when he sifted the ashes within the tank destroyer's hull through his fingers.

Hammer pursed his lips and stared at the tanker. "You're sure?" he said. Then, "Yeah, you would be."

"Nobody else was that good, Colonel," Des Grieux said softly. His eyes were focused somewhere out beyond the moons' orbits.

Hammer refused to look down into Des Grieux's palm after the first brief glance. "You're out of here, you know," he snapped. "Out of the Slammers for good, and off-planet *fast* if you know what's good for you. I told Joachim I'd handle this my own way, but that's not the kind of instruction you can count on him obeying."

"Right," Des Grieux said without emotion. He closed his hand again and resumed rubbing the teeth against his palm. "I'll do that."

"I ought to let Joachim finish you, you know?" Hammer said. There was an edge in his voice, but also wonder at the tanker's flat affect. "You're too dangerous to leave alive, but I guess I owe something to a twelve-year veteran."

"I won't be joining another outfit, Colonel," Des Grieux said; a statement, not a plea for the mercy Hammer had already granted. "Not much point in it now."

Alois Hammer touched his tongue to his lips in

order to have time to process what he had just heard. "You know, Des Grieux?" he said mildly. "I really don't know why I don't have you shot."

Des Grieux looked directly at his commanding officer again. "Because we're the same, Colonel," he said. "You and me. Because there's nothing but war for either of us."

Hammer's face went white, then flushed except for the pink splotch of SpraySeal on his forehead. "You're a bloody fool, Des Grieux," he rasped, "and a bloody *liar*. I wanted to end this—" he gestured at the blackened wreckage of vehicles staggering all the way to the bottom of the slope "—by a quiet capitulation, not a bloodbath. Not like this!"

"You've got your way, Colonel," Des Grieux said. "I've got mine. Had mine. But it's all the same in the end."

He smiled, but there was only the memory of emotion behind his straight, yellowed teeth. "You haven't learned that yet. Have fun. Because when it's over, there isn't anything left."

Colonel Hammer pressed the SpraySeal with the back of his left hand, not quite rubbing it. He slid from the iridium carapace of the tank destroyer. "Come on, Des Grieux," he said. "I'll see that you get aboard a ship alive. You'll have your pension and discharge bonus."

Des Grieux followed the shorter man. The tanker walked stiffly, as though he were an infant still learning gross motor skills.

At the jeep, Hammer turned and said savagely, "And Via! Will you please throw those curst teeth away?"

Des Grieux slipped the calcined fragments into his

breast pocket. "I need them," he said. "To remind me that I was the best.

"Some day," he added, "you'll know just what I mean, Colonel."

His smile was terrible to behold.

## END

# LIBERTY PORT

Commandant Horace Jolober had just lowered the saddle of his mobile chair, putting himself at the height of the Facilities Inspection Committee seated across the table, when the alarm hooted and Vicki cried from the window in the next room, *"Tanks! In the street!"*

The three Placidan bureaucrats flashed Jolober looks of anger and fear, but he had no time for them now even though they were his superiors. The stump of his left leg keyed the throttle of his chair. As the fans spun up, Jolober leaned and guided his miniature air-cushion vehicle out of the room faster than another man could have walked.

Faster than a man with legs could walk.

Vicki opened the door from the bedroom as Jolober swept past her toward the inside stairs. Her face was as calm as that of the statue which it resembled in its perfection, but Jolober knew that only the strongest emotion would have made her disobey his orders to stay in his private apartments while the

189

inspection team was here. She was afraid that he was about to be killed.

A burst of gunfire in the street suggested she just might be correct.

"Chief!" called Jolober's mastoid implant in what he thought was the voice of Karnes, his executive officer. "I'm at the gate and the new arrivals, they're Hammer's, just came right through the wire! There's half a dozen tanks and they're shooting in the air!"

Could've been worse. Might yet be.

He slid onto the staircase, his stump boosting fan speed with reflexive skill. The stair treads were too narrow for Jolober's mobile chair to form an air cushion between the surface and the lip of its plenum chamber. Instead he balanced on thrust alone while the fans beneath him squealed, ramming the air hard enough to let him slope down above the staircase with the grace of a swooping hawk.

The hardware was built to handle the stress, but only flawless control kept the port commandant from up-ending and crashing down the treads in a fashion as dangerous as it would be humiliating.

Jolober was a powerful man who'd been tall besides until a tribarrel blew off both his legs above the knee. In his uniform of white cloth and lavish gold, he was dazzlingly obvious in any light. As he gunned his vehicle out into the street, the most intense light source was the rope of cyan bolts ripping skyward from the cupola of the leading tank.

The buildings on either side of the street enticed customers with displays to rival the sun, but the operators—each of them a gambler, brothel keeper, and saloon owner all in one—had their own warning systems. The lights were going out, leaving the plastic façades cold.

Lightless, the buildings faded to the appearance of the high concrete fortresses they were in fact. Repeated arches made the entrance of the China Doll, directly across the street from the commandant's offices, look spacious. The door itself was so narrow that only two men could pass it at a time, and no one could slip unnoticed past the array of sensors and guards that made sure none of those entering were armed.

Normally the facilities here at Paradise Port were open all day. Now an armored panel clanged down across the narrow door of the China Doll, its echoes merging with similar tocsins from the other buildings.

Much good that would do if the tanks opened up with their twenty-CM main guns. Even a tribarrel could blast holes in thumb-thick steel as easily as one had vaporized Jolober's knees and calves. . . .

He slid into the street, directly into the path of the lead tank. He would have liked to glance up toward the bedroom window for what he knew might be his last glimpse of Vicki, but he was afraid that he couldn't do that and still have the guts to do his duty.

For a long time after he lost his legs, the only thing which had kept Horace Jolober from suicide was the certainty that he had *always* done his duty. Not even Vicki could be allowed to take that from him.

The tanks were advancing at no more than a slow walk, though their huge size gave them the appearance of speed. They were buttoned up—hatches down, crews hidden behind the curved surfaces of iridium armor that might just possibly turn a bolt from a gun as big as the one each tank carried in its turret.

Lesser weapons had left scars on the iridium. Where light powerguns had licked the armor—and even a tribarrelled automatic was light in comparison to a tank—the metal cooled again in a slope around the point where a little had been vaporized. High-velocity bullets made smaller, deeper craters plated with material from the projectile itself.

The turret of the leading tank bore a long gouge that began in a pattern of deep, radial scars. A shoulder-fired rocket had hit at a slight angle. The jet of white-hot gas spurting from the shaped-charge warhead had burned deep enough into even the refractory iridium that it would have penetrated the turret had it struck squarely.

If either the driver or the blower captain were riding with their heads out of the hatch when the missile detonated, shrapnel from the casing had decapitated them.

Jolober wondered if the present driver even saw him, a lone man in a street that should have been cleared by the threat of one hundred and seventy tonnes of armor howling down the middle of it.

An air-cushion jeep carrying a pintle-mounted needle stunner and two men in Port Patrol uniforms was driving alongside the lead tank, bucking and pitching in the current roaring from beneath the steel skirts of the tank's plenum chamber. While the driver fought to hold the light vehicle steady, the other patrolman bellowed through the jeep's loudspeakers. He might have been on the other side of the planet for all his chance of being heard over the sound of air sucked through intakes atop the tank's hull and then pumped beneath the skirts forcefully enough to balance the huge weight of steel and iridium.

Jolober grounded his mobile chair. He crooked his left ring finger so that the surgically redirected nerve impulse keyed the microphone implanted at the base of his jaw. "Gentlemen," he said, knowing that the base unit in the Port Office was relaying his words on the Slammers' general frequency. "You are violating the regulations which govern Paradise Port. Stop before somebody gets hurt."

The bow of the lead tank was ten meters away—and one meter less every second.

To the very end he thought they were going to hit him—by inadvertence, now, because the tank's steel skirt lifted in a desperate attempt to stop but the vehicle's mass overwhelmed the braking effect of its fans. Jolober knew that if he raised his chair from the pavement, the blast of air from the tank would knock him over and roll him along the concrete like a trashcan in a windstorm—bruised but safe.

He would rather die than lose his dignity that way in front of Vicki.

The tank's bow slewed to the left, toward the China Doll. The skirt on that side touched the pavement with the sound of steel screaming and a fountain of sparks that sprayed across and over the building's high plastic façade.

The tank did not hit the China Doll, and it stopped short of Horace Jolober by less than the radius of its bow's curve.

The driver grounded his huge vehicle properly and cut the power to his fans. Dust scraped from the pavement, choking and chalky, swirled around Jolober and threw him into a paroxysm of coughing. He hadn't realized that he'd been holding his breath—until the danger passed and instinct filled his lungs.

The jeep pulled up beside Jolober, its fans kicking up still more dust, and the two patrolmen shouted words of concern and congratulation to their commandant. More men were appearing, patrolmen and others who had ducked into the narrow alleys between buildings when the tanks filled the street.

"Stecher," said Jolober to the sergeant in the patrol vehicle, "go back there—" he gestured toward the remainder of the column, hidden behind the armored bulk of the lead tank "—and help 'em get turned around. Get 'em back to the Refit Area where they belong."

"Sir, should I get the names?" Stecher asked.

The port commandant shook his head with certainty. "None of this happened," he told his subordinates. "I'll take care of it."

The jeep spun nimbly while Stecher spoke into his commo helmet, relaying Jolober's orders to the rest of the squad on street duty.

Metal rang again as the tank's two hatch covers slid open. Jolober was too close to the hull to see the crewmen, so he kicked his fans to life and backed a few meters.

The mobile chair had been built to his design. Its only control was the throttle with a linkage which at high-thrust settings automatically transformed the plenum chamber to a nozzle. Steering and balance were matters of how the rider shifted his body weight. Jolober prided himself that he was just as nimble as he had been before.

—Before he backed into the trench on Primavera, half wrapped in the white flag he'd waved to the oncoming tanks. The only conscious memory he retained of *that* moment was the sight of his right leg still balanced on the trench lip above him, silhouetted against the criss-crossing cyan bolts from the powerguns.

But Horace Jolober was just as much a man as he'd ever been. The way he got around proved it. And Vicki.

The driver staring out the bow hatch at him was a woman with thin features and just enough hair to show beneath her helmet. She looked scared, aware of what had just happened and aware also of just how bad it could've been.

Jolober could appreciate how she felt.

The man who lifted himself from the turret hatch was under thirty, angry, and—though Jolober couldn't remember the Slammers' collar pips precisely—a junior officer of some sort rather than a sergeant.

The dust had mostly settled by now, but vortices still spun above the muzzles of the tribarrel which the fellow had been firing skyward. "What're you doing, you bloody fool?" he shouted. "D'ye *want* to die?"

Not any more, thought Horace Jolober as he stared upward at the tanker. One of the port patrolmen had responded to the anger in the Slammer's voice by raising his needle stunner, but there was no need for that.

Jolober keyed his mike so that he didn't have to shout with the inevitable emotional loading. In a flat, certain voice, he said, "If you'll step down here, Lieutenant, we can discuss the situation like officers—which I am, and you will continue to be unless you insist on pushing things."

The tanker grimaced, then nodded his head and lifted himself the rest of the way out of the turret. "Right," he said. "Right. I . . ." His voice trailed off, but he wasn't going to say anything the port commandant hadn't heard before.

When you screw up real bad, you can either be afraid or you can flare out in anger and blame somebody else. Not because you don't know better, but because it's the only way to control your fear. It isn't pretty, but there's no pretty way to screw up bad.

The tanker dropped to the ground in front of Jolober and gave a sloppy salute. That was lack of practice, not deliberate insult, and his voice and eyes were firm as he said, "Sir. Acting Captain Tad Hoffritz reporting."

"Horace Jolober," the port commandant said. He raised his saddle to put his head at what used to be normal standing height, a few centimeters taller than Hoffritz. The Slammer's rank made it pretty clear why the disturbance had occurred. "Your boys?" Jolober asked, thumbing toward the tanks sheepishly reversing down the street under the guidance of white-uniformed patrolmen.

"Past three days they have been," Hoffritz agreed. His mouth scrunched again in an angry grimace and he said, "Look, I'm real sorry. I know how dumb that was. I just . . ."

Again, there wasn't anything new to say.

The tank's driver vaulted from her hatch with a suddenness which drew both men's attention. "Corp'ral Days," she said with a salute even more perfunctory than Hoffritz's had been. "Look, sir, *I* was drivin', and if there's a problem, it's my problem."

"Daisy—" began Captain Hoffritz.

"There's no problem, Corporal," Jolober said firmly. "Go back to your vehicle. We'll need to move it in a minute or two."

Another helmeted man had popped his head from the turret—surprisingly, because this was a line tank, not a command vehicle with room for several soldiers in the fighting compartment. The driver looked at her captain, then met the worried eyes of the trooper still in the turret. She backed a pace but stayed within earshot.

"Six tanks out of seventeen," Jolober said calmly. Things *were* calm enough now that he was able to follow the cross-talk of his patrolmen, their voices stuttering at low level through the miniature speaker on his epaulet. "You've been seeing some action, then."

"Too bloody right," muttered Corporal Days.

Hoffritz rubbed the back of his neck, lowering his eyes, and said, "Well, running . . . There's four back at Refit deadlined we brought in on transporters, but—"

He looked squarely at Jolober. "But sure we had a tough time. That's why I'm CO and Chester's up there—" he nodded toward the man in the turret "—trying to work company commo without a proper command tank. And I guess I figured—"

Hoffritz might have stopped there, but the port commandant nodded him on.

"—I figured maybe it wouldn't hurt to wake up a few rear-echelon types when we came back here for refit. Sorry, sir."

"There's three other units, including a regiment of the Division Legere, on stand-down here at Paradise Port already, Captain," Jolober said. He nodded toward the soldiers in mottled fatigues who were beginning to reappear on the street. "Not rear-echelon troops, from what I've heard. And they need some relaxation just as badly as your men do."

"Yes, sir," Hoffritz agreed, blank-faced. "It was real dumb. I'll sign the report as soon as you make it out."

Jolober shrugged. "There won't be a report, Captain. Repairs to the gate'll go on your regiment's damage account and be deducted from Placida's payment next month." He smiled. "Along with any chairs or glasses you break in the casinos. Now, get your vehicle into the Refit Area where it belongs. And come back and have a good time in Paradise Port. That's what we're here for."

"*Thank* you, sir," said Hoffritz, and relief dropped his age by at least five years. He clasped Jolober's hand and, still holding it, asked, "You've seen service, too, haven't you, sir?"

"Fourteen years with Hampton's Legion," Jolober agreed, pleased that Hoffritz had managed not to stare at the stumps before asking the question.

"Hey, good outfit," the younger man said with enthusiasm. "We were with Hampton on Primavera, back, oh, three years ago?"

"Yes, I know," Jolober said. His face was still smiling, and the subject wasn't an emotional one any more. He felt no emotion at all . . . "One of your tanks shot—" his left hand gestured delicately at where his thighs ended "—these off on Primavera."

"Lord," Sergeant Days said distinctly.

Captain Hoffritz looked as if he had been hit with a brick. Then his face regained its animation. "*No,* sir," he said. "You're mistaken. On Primavera, we were both working for the Federalists. Hampton was our infantry support."

Not the way General Hampton would have described the chain of command, thought Jolober. His smile became real again. He still felt pride in his old unit—and he could laugh at those outdated feelings in himself.

"Yes, that's right," he said aloud. "There'd been an error in transmitting map coordinates. When a company of these—" he nodded toward the great iridium monster, feeling sweat break out on his forehead and arms as he did so "—attacked my battalion, I jumped up to stop the shooting."

Jolober's smile paled to a frosty shadow of itself. "I was successful," he went on softly, "but not quite as soon as I would've liked."

"Oh, Lord and Martyrs," whispered Hoffritz. His face looked like that of a battle casualty.

"Tad, that was—" Sergeant Days began.

"Shut it *off*, Daisy!" shouted the Slammers' commo man from the turret. Days' face blanked and she nodded.

"Sir, I—" Hoffritz said.

Jolober shook his head to silence the younger man. "In a war," he said, "a lot of people get in the way of rounds. I'm luckier than some. I'm still around to tell about it."

He spoke in the calm, pleasant voice he always used in explaining the—matter—to others. For the length of time he was speaking, he could generally convince even himself.

Clapping Hoffritz on the shoulder—the physical contact brought Jolober back to present reality, reminding him that the tanker was a young man and not a demon hidden behind armor and a tribarrel—the commandant said, "Go on, move your hardware and then see what Paradise Port can show you in the way of a good time."

"Oh, *that* I know already," said Hoffritz with a

wicked, man-to-man smile of his own. "When we stood down here three months back, I met a girl named Beth. I'll bet she still remembers me, and the *Lord* knows I remember her."

"Girl?" Jolober repeated. The whole situation had so disoriented him that he let his surprise show.

"Well, you know," said the tanker. "A Doll, I guess. But believe me, Beth's woman enough for *me.*"

"Or for anyone," the commandant agreed. "I know just what you mean."

Stecher had returned with the jeep. The street was emptied of all armor except Hoffritz's tank, and that was an object of curiosity rather than concern for the men spilling out the doors of the reopened brothels. Jolober waved toward the patrol vehicle and said, "My men'll guide you out of here, Captain Hoffritz. Enjoy your stay."

The tank driver was already scrambling back into her hatch. She had lowered her helmet shield, so the glimpse Jolober got of her face was an unexpected, light-reflecting bubble.

Maybe Corporal Days had a problem with where the conversation had gone when the two officers started talking like two men. That was a pity, for her and probably for Captain Hoffritz as well. A tank was too small a container to hold emotional trouble among its crew.

But Horace Jolober had his own problems to occupy him as he slid toward his office at a walking pace. He had his meeting with the Facilities Inspection Committee, which wasn't going to go more smoothly because of the interruption.

A plump figure sauntering in the other direction tipped his beret to Jolober as they passed. "Ike,"

acknowledged the port commandant in a voice as
neutral as a gun barrel that doesn't care in the least
at whom it's pointed.

Red Ike could pass for human, until the rosy cast
of his skin drew attention to the fact that his hands
had only three fingers and a thumb. Jolober was surprised to see that Ike was walking across the street
toward his own brothel, the China Doll, instead of
being inside the building already. That could have
meant anything, but the probability was that Red
Ike had a tunnel to one of the buildings across the
street to serve as a bolthole.

And since all the *real* problems at Paradise Port
were a result of the alien who called himself Red
Ike, Jolober could easily imagine why the fellow
would want to have a bolthole.


Jolober had gone down the steps in a smooth
undulation. He mounted them in a series of hops,
covering two treads between pauses like a weary
cricket climbing out of a well.

The chair's powerpack had more than enough
charge left to swoop him up to the conference room.
It was the man himself who lacked the mental
energy now to balance himself on the column of
driven air. He felt drained—the tribarrel, the tank
. . . the memories of Primavera. If he'd decided to,
sure, but . . .

But maybe he was getting old.

The Facilities Inspection Committee—staff members, actually, for three of the most powerful senators in the Placidan legislature—waited for Jolober
with doubtful looks. Higgey and Wayne leaned
against the conference room window, watching Hoffritz's tank reverse sedately in the street. The woman,

Rodall, stood by the stairhead watching the port commandant's return.

"Why don't you have an elevator put in?" she asked. "Or at least a ramp?" Between phrases, Rodall's full features relaxed to the pout that was her normal expression.

Jolober paused beside her, noticing the whisper of air from beneath his plenum chamber was causing her to twist her feet away as if she had stepped into slime. "There aren't elevators everywhere, Mistress," he said. "Most places, there isn't even enough smooth surface to depend on ground effect alone to get you more than forty meters."

He smiled and gestured toward the conference room's window. Visible beyond the China Doll and the other buildings across the street was the reddish-brown expanse of the surrounding landscape: ropes of lava on which only lichen could grow, where a man had to hop and scramble from one ridge to another.

The Placidan government had located Paradise Port in a volcanic wasteland in order to isolate the mercenaries letting off steam between battles with Armstrong, the other power on the planet's sole continent. To a cripple in a chair which depended on wheels or unaided ground effect, the twisting lava would be as sure a barrier as sheer walls.

Jolober didn't say that so long as he could go anywhere other men went, he could pretend he was still a man. If the Placidan civilian could have understood that, she wouldn't have asked why he didn't have ramps put in.

"Well, what *was* that?" demanded Higgey—thin, intense, and already half bald in his early thirties. "Was anyone killed?"

"Nothing serious, Master Higgey," Jolober said as he slid back to the table and lowered himself to his "seated" height. "And no, no one was killed or even injured."

Thank the Lord for his mercy.

"It *looked* serious, Commandant," said the third committee member—Wayne, half again Jolober's age and a retired colonel of the Placidan regular army. "I'm surprised you permit things like that to happen."

Higgey and Rodall were seating themselves. Jolober gestured toward the third chair on the curve of the round table opposite him and said, "Colonel, your, ah—opposite numbers in Armstrong tried to stop those tanks last week with a battalion of armored infantry. They got their butts kicked until they didn't *have* butts any more."

Wayne wasn't sitting down. His face flushed and his short white moustache bristled sharply against his upper lip.

Jolober shrugged and went on in a more conciliatory tone, "Look, sir, units aren't rotated back here unless they've had a hell of a rough time in the line. I've got fifty-six patrolmen with stunners to keep order . . . which we *do*, well enough for the people using Paradise Port. We aren't here to start a major battle **of** our own. Placida needs these mercenaries and needs them in fighting trim."

"That's a matter of opinion," said the retired officer with his lips pressed together, but at last he sat down.

The direction of sunrise is also a matter of opinion, Jolober thought. It's about as likely to change as Placida is to survive without the mercenaries who had undertaken the war her regular army was losing.

"I requested this meeting—" requested it with the

senators themselves, but he hadn't expected them to agree "—in order to discuss just that, the fighting trim of the troops who undergo rest and refit here. So that Placida gets the most value for her, ah, payment."

The committee staff would do, if Jolober could get them to understand. Paradise Port was, after all, a wasteland with a village populated by soldiers who had spent all the recent past killing and watching their friends die. It wasn't the sort of place you'd pick for a senatorial junket.

Higgey leaned forward, clasping his hands on the table top, and said, "Commandant, I'm sure that those—" he waggled a finger disdainfully toward the window "—men out there would be in better physical condition after a week of milk and religious lectures than they will after the regime they choose for themselves. There are elements—"

Wayne nodded in stern agreement, his eyes on Mistress Rodall, whose set face refused to acknowledge either of her fellows while the subject was being discussed.

"—in the electorate and government who would like to try that method, but fortunately reality has kept the idea from being attempted."

Higgey paused, pleased with his forceful delivery and the way his eyes dominated those of the much bigger man across the table. "If you've suddenly got religion, Commandant Jolober," he concluded, "I suggest you resign your current position and join the ministry."

Jolober suppressed his smile. Higgey reminded him of a lap dog, too nervous to remain either still or silent, and too small to be other than ridiculous in its posturing. "My initial message was unclear, madam, gentlemen," he explained, looking around the table. "I'm not suggesting that Placida close the brothels that are part of the recreational facilities here."

His pause was not for effect, but because his mouth had suddenly gone very dry. But it was his duty to—

"I'm recommending that the Dolls be withdrawn from Paradise Port and that the facilities be staffed with human, ah, females."

Colonel Wayne stiffened and paled.

Wayne's anger was now mirrored in the expression on Rodall's face. "Whores," she said. "So that these—*soldiers*—can disgrace and dehumanize real women for their fun."

"And kill them, one assumes," added Higgey with a touch of amusement. "I checked the records, Commandant. There've been seventeen Dolls killed during the months Paradise Port's been in operation. As it is, that's a simple damage assessment, but if they'd been human prostitutes—each one would have meant a manslaughter charge or even murder. People don't cease to have rights when they choose to sell their bodies, you know."

"When they're forced to sell their bodies, you mean," snapped Rodall. She glared at Higgey, who didn't mean anything of the sort.

"Scarcely to the benefit of your precious mercenaries," said Wayne in a distant voice. "Quite apart from the political difficulties it would cause for any senator who recommended the change."

"As a matter of fact," said Higgey, whose natural caution had tightened his visage again, "I thought you were going to use the record of violence here at Paradise Port as a reason for closing the facility.

Though I'll admit that I couldn't imagine anybody selfless enough to do away with his own job."

No, you couldn't, you little weasel, thought Horace Jolober. But politicians have different responsibilities than soldiers, and politicians' flunkies have yet another set of needs and duties.

And none of them are saints. Surely no soldier who does his job is a saint.

"Master Higgey, you've precisely located the problem," Jolober said with a nod of approval. "The violence isn't a result of the soldiers, it's because of the Dolls. It isn't accidental, it's planned. And it's time to stop it."

"It's time for us to leave, you mean," said Higgey as he shoved his chair back. "Resigning still appears to be your best course, Commandant. Though I don't suppose the ministry is the right choice for a new career, after all."

"Master Higgey," Jolober said in the voice he would have used in an argument with a fellow officer, "I know very well that no one is irreplaceable—but *you* know that I am doing as good a job here as anybody you could hire to run Paradise Port. I'm asking you to listen for a few minutes to a proposal that will make the troops you pay incrementally better able to fight for you."

"We've come this far," said Rodall.

"There are no listening devices in my quarters," Jolober explained, unasked. "I doubt that any real-time commo link out of Paradise Port is free of interception."

He didn't add that time he spent away from *his* duties was more of a risk to Placida than pulling these three out of their offices and expensive lunches could be. The tanks roaring down the street should have proved *that* even to the committee staffers.

Jolober paused, pressing his fingertips to his eyebrows in a habitual trick to help him marshal his thoughts while the others stared at him. "Mistress, masters," he said calmly after a moment, "the intention was that Paradise Port and similar facilities be staffed by independent contractors from off-planet."

"Which is where they'll return as soon as the war's over," agreed Colonel Wayne with satisfaction. "Or as soon as they put a toe wrong, any one of them."

"The war's bad enough as it is," said Rodall. "Building up Placida's stock of *that* sort of person would make peace hideous as well."

"Yes, ma'am, I understand," said the port commandant. There were a lot of "that sort of person" in Placida just now, including all the mercenaries in the line—and Horace Jolober back here. "But what you have in Paradise Port isn't a group of entrepreneurs, it's a corporation—a monarchy, almost—subservient to an alien called Red Ike."

"Nonsense," said Wayne.

"We don't permit that," said Rodall.

"Red Ike owns a single unit here," said Higgey. "The China Doll. Which is all he *can* own by law, to prevent just the sort of situation you're describing."

"Red Ike provides all the Dolls," Jolober stated flatly. "Whoever owns them on paper, they're his. And *everything* here is his because he controls the Dolls."

"Well . . ." said Rodall. She was beginning to blush.

"There's no actual proof," Colonel Wayne said, shifting his eyes toward a corner of walls and ceiling. "Though I suppose the physical traits are indicative . . ."

"The government has decided it isn't in the best interests of Placida to pierce the corporate veil in this instance," said Higgey in a thin voice. "The androids in question are shipped here from a variety of off-planet suppliers."

The balding Placidan paused and added, with a tone of absolute finality, "If the question were mine to decide—which it isn't—I would recommend searching for a new port commandant rather than trying to prove the falsity of a state of affairs beneficial to us, to Placida."

"I think that really must be the final word on the subject, Commandant Jolober," Rodall agreed.

Jolober thought she sounded regretful, but the emotion was too faint for him to be sure. The three Placidans were getting up, and he had failed.

He'd failed even before the staff members arrived, because it was now quite obvious that they'd decided their course of action before the meeting. They—and their elected superiors—would rather have dismissed Jolober's arguments.

But if the arguments proved to be well founded, they would dismiss the port commandant, if necessary to end the discussion.

"I suppose I should be flattered," Jolober said as hydraulics lifted him in the saddle and pressure of his stump on the throttle let him rotate his chair away from the table. "That you came all this way to silence me instead of refusing me a meeting."

"You might recall," said Higgey, pausing at the doorway. His look was meant to be threatening, but the port commandant's bulk and dour anger cooled the Placidan's face as soon as their eyes met. "That is, we're in the middle of a war, and the definition of treason can be a little loose in such times. While you're not technically a Placidan citizen, Commandant, you—would be well advised to avoid activities which oppose the conduct of war as the government has determined to conduct it."

He stepped out of the conference room. Rodall had left ahead of him.

"Don't take it too hard, young man," said Colonel Wayne when he and Jolober were alone. "You mercenaries, you can do a lot of things the quick and easy way. It's different when you represent a government and need to consider political implications."

"I'd never understood there were negative implications, Colonel," Jolober said with the slow, careful enunciation which proved he was controlling himself rigidly, "in treating your employees fairly. Even the mercenary soldiers whom you employ."

Wayne's jaw lifted. "I beg your pardon, Commandant," he snapped. "I don't see anyone holding guns to the heads of poor innocents, forcing them to whore and gamble."

He strode to the door, his back parade-ground straight. At the door he turned precisely and delivered the broadside he had held to that point. "Besides, Commandant—if the Dolls are as dangerous to health and welfare as you say, why are you living with one yourself?"

Wayne didn't expect an answer, but what he saw in Horace Jolober's eyes suggested that his words might bring a physical reaction that he hadn't counted on. He skipped into the hall with a startled sound, banging the door behind him.

The door connecting the conference room to the

port commandant's personal suite opened softly. Jolober did not look around.

Vicki put her long, slim arms around him from behind. Jolober spun, then cut power to his fans and settled his chair firmly onto the floor. He and Vicki clung to one another, legless man and Doll whose ruddy skin and beauty marked her as inhuman.

They were both crying.

Someone from Jolober's staff would poke his head into the conference room shortly to ask if the meeting was over and if the commandant wanted non-emergency calls routed through again.

The meeting was certainly over . . . but Horace Jolober had an emergency of his own. He swallowed, keyed his implant, and said brusquely, "I'm out of action till I tell you different. Unless it's another Class A flap."

The kid at the commo desk stuttered a "Yessir" that was a syllable longer than Jolober wanted to hear. Vicki straightened, wearing a bright smile beneath the tear streaks, but the big human gathered her to his chest again and brought up the power of his fans.

Together, like a man carrying a moderate-sized woman, the couple slid around the conference table to the door of the private suite. The chair's drive units were overbuilt because men are overbuilt, capable of putting out huge bursts of hysterical strength.

Drive fans and power packs don't have hormones, so Jolober had specified—and paid for—components that would handle double the hundred kilos of his own mass, the hundred kilos left after the tribarrel had chewed him. The only problem with carrying

Vicki to bed was one of balance, and the Doll remained still in his arms.

Perfectly still, as she was perfect in all the things she did.

"I'm not trying to get rid of you, darling," Jolober said as he grounded his chair.

"It's all right," Vicki whispered. "I'll go now if you like. It's all right."

She placed her fingertips on Jolober's shoulders and lifted herself by those fulcrums off his lap and onto the bed, her toes curled beneath her buttocks. A human gymnast could have done as well—but no better.

"What I *want*," Jolober said forcefully as he lifted himself out of the saddle, using the chair's handgrips, "is to do my job. And when I've done it, I'll buy you from Red Ike for whatever price he chooses to ask."

He swung himself to the bed. His arms had always been long—and strong. Now he knew that he must look like a gorilla when he got on or off his chair . . . and when the third woman he was with after the amputation giggled at him, he began to consider suicide as an alternative to sex.

Then he took the job on Placida and met Vicki.

Her tears had dried, so both of them could pretend they hadn't poured out moments before. She smiled shyly and touched the high collar of her dress, drawing her fingertip down a centimeter and opening the garment by that amount.

Vicki wasn't Jolober's ideal of beauty—wasn't what he'd *thought* his ideal was, at any rate. Big blondes, he would have said. A woman as tall as he was, with hair the color of bleached straw hanging to the middle of her back.

Vicki scarcely came up to the top of Jolober's breastbone when he was standing—at standing height in his chair—and her hair was a black fluff that was as short as a soldier would cut it to fit comfortably under a helmet. She looked buxom, but her breasts were fairly flat against her broad, powerfully muscled chest.

Jolober put his index finger against hers on the collar and slid down the touch-sensitive strip that opened the fabric. Vicki's body was without blemish or pubic hair. She was so firm that nothing sagged or flattened when her dress and the supports of memory plastic woven into it dropped away.

She shrugged her arms out of the straps and let the garment spill as a pool of sparkling shadow on the counterpane as she reached toward her lover.

Jolober, lying on his side, touched the collar of his uniform jacket.

"No need," Vicki said blocking his hand with one of hers and opening his trouser fly with the other. "Come," she added, rolling onto her back and drawing him toward her.

"But the—" Jolober murmured in surprise, leaning forward in obedience to her touch and demand. The metallic braid and medals on his stiff-fronted tunic had sharp corners to prod the Doll beneath him whether he wished or not.

"Come," she repeated. "This time."

Horace Jolober wasn't introspective enough to understand why his mistress wanted the rough punishment of his uniform. He simply obeyed.

Vicki toyed with his garments after they had finished and lay on the bed, their arms crossing. She had a trick of folding back her lower legs so that they vanished whenever she sat or reclined in the port commandant's presence.

Her fingers tweaked the back of Jolober's waistband and emerged with the hidden knife, the only weapon he carried.

"I'm at your mercy," he said, smiling. He mimed as much of a hands-up posture as he could with his right elbow supporting his torso on the mattress. "Have your way with me."

In Vicki's hand, the knife was a harmless cylinder of plastic—a weapon only to the extent that the butt of the short tube could harden a punch. The knife was of memory plastic whose normal state was a harmless block. No one who took it away from Jolober in a struggle would find it of any use as a weapon.

Only when squeezed after being cued by the pore Pattern of Horace Jolober's right hand would it—

The plastic cylinder shrank in Vicki's hand, sprouting a double-edged 15-CM blade.

"*Via!*" swore Jolober. Reflex betrayed him into thinking that he had legs. He jerked upright and started to topple off the bed because the weight of his calves and feet wasn't there to balance the motion.

Vicki caught him with both arms and drew him to her. The blade collapsed into the handle when she dropped it, so that it bounced as a harmless cylinder on the counterpane between them.

"My love, I'm *sorry,*" the Doll blurted fearfully. "I didn't mean—"

"No, no," Jolober said, settled now on his thighs and buttocks so that he could hug Vicki fiercely. His eyes peered secretively over her shoulders, searching for the knife that had startled him so badly. "I was surprised that it . . . How *did* you get the blade to open, dearest? It's fine, it's nothing you did wrong, but I didn't expect that, is all."

They swung apart. The mattress was a firm one, but still a bad surface for this kind of conversation. The bedclothes rumpled beneath Jolober's heavy body and almost concealed the knife in a fold of cloth. He found it, raised it with his fingertips, and handed it to Vicki. "Please do that again," he said calmly. "Extend the blade."

Sweat was evaporating from the base of Jolober's spine, where the impermeable knife usually covered the skin.

Vicki took the weapon. She was so doubtful that her face showed no expression at all. Her fingers, short but perfectly formed, gripped the baton as if it were a knife hilt—and it became one. The blade formed with avalanche swiftness, darkly translucent and patterned with veins of stress. The plastic would not take a wire edge, but it could carve a roast or, with Jolober's strength behind it, ram twenty millimeters deep into hardwood.

"Like this?" Vicki said softly. "Just squeeze it and . . . ?"

Jolober put his hand over the Doll's and lifted the knife away between thumb and forefinger. When she loosed the hilt, the knife collapsed again into a short baton.

He squeezed—extended the blade—released it again—and slipped the knife back into its concealed sheath.

"You see, darling," Jolober said, "the plastic's been keyed to *my* body. Nobody else should be able to get the blade to form."

"I'd never use it against you," Vicki said. Her face

was calm, and there was no defensiveness in her simple response.

Jolober smiled. "Of course, dearest; but there was a manufacturing flaw or you wouldn't be able to do that."

Vicki leaned over and kissed the port commandant's lips, then bent liquidly and kissed him again. "I told you," she said as she straightened with a grin. "I'm a part of you."

"And believe me," said Jolober, rolling onto his back to cinch up his short-legged trousers. "You're not a part of me I intend to lose."

He rocked upright and gripped the handles of his chair.

Vicki slipped off the bed and braced the little vehicle with a hand on the saddle and the edge of one foot on the skirt. The help wasn't necessary—the chair's weight anchored it satisfactorily, so long as Jolober mounted swiftly and smoothly. But it *was* helpful, and it was the sort of personal attention that was as important as sex in convincing Horace Jolober that someone really cared—*could* care—for him.

"You'll do your duty, though," Vicki said. "And I wouldn't want you not to."

Jolober laughed as he settled himself and switched on his fans. He felt enormous relief now that he had proved beyond doubt—he was sure of that—how much he loved Vicki. He'd calmed her down, and that meant he was calm again, too.

"Sure I'll do my job," he said as he smiled at the Doll. "That doesn't mean you and *me*'ll have a problem. Wait and see."

Vicki smiled also, but she shook her head in what Jolober thought was amused resignation. Her hairless body was too perfect to be flesh, and the skin's red pigment gave the Doll the look of a statue in blushing marble.

"Via, but you're lovely," Jolober murmured as the realization struck him anew.

"Come back soon," she said easily.

"Soon as I can," the commandant agreed as he lifted his chair and turned toward the door. "But like you say, I've got a job to do."

If the government of Placida wouldn't give him the support he needed, by the Lord! he'd work through the mercenaries themselves.

Though his belly went cold and his stumps tingled as he realized he would again be approaching the tanks which had crippled him.

The street had the sharp edge which invariably marked it immediately after a unit rotated to Paradise Port out of combat. The troops weren't looking for sex or intoxicants—though most of them would have claimed they were.

They were looking for life. Paradise Port offered them things they thought equaled life, and the contrast between reality and hope led to anger and black despair. Only after a few days of stunning themselves with the offered pleasures did the soldiers on leave recognize another contrast: Paradise Port might not be all they'd hoped, but it was a lot better than the muck and ravening hell of combat.

Jolober slid down the street at a walking pace. Some of the soldiers on the pavement with him offered ragged salutes to the commandant's glittering uniform. He returned them sharply, a habit he had ingrained in himself after he took charge here.

Mercenary units didn't put much emphasis on saluting and similar rear-echelon forms of discipline.

An officer with the reputation of being a tight-assed martinet in bivouac was likely to get hit from behind the next time he led his troops into combat.

There were regular armies on most planets—Colonel Wayne was an example—to whom actual fighting was an aberration. Economics or a simple desire for action led many planetary soldiers into mercenary units . . . where the old habits of saluting and snapping to attention surfaced when the men were drunk and depressed.

Hampton's Legion hadn't been any more interested in saluting than the Slammers were. Jolober had sharpened his technique here because it helped a few of the men he served feel more at home—when they were very far from home.

A patrol jeep passed, idling slowly through the pedestrians. Sergeant Stecher waved, somewhat uncertainly.

Jolober waved back, smiling toward his subordinate but angry at himself. He keyed his implant and said "Central, I'm back in business now, but I'm headed for the Refit Area to see Captain van Zuyle. Let anything wait that can till I'm back."

He should have cleared with his switchboard as soon as he'd . . . calmed Vicki down. Here there'd been a crisis, and as soon as it was over he'd disappeared. Must've made his patrolmen very cursed nervous, and it was sheer sloppiness that he'd let the situation go on beyond what it had to. It was his job to make things simple for the people in Paradise Port, both his staff and the port's clientele.

Maybe even for the owners of the brothel: but it was going to have to be simple on Horace Jolober's terms.

At the gate, a tank was helping the crew repairing

damage. The men wore khaki coveralls—Slammers rushed from the Refit Area as soon as van Zuyle, the officer in charge there, heard what had happened. The faster you hid the evidence of a problem, the easier it was to claim the problem had never existed.

And it was to everybody's advantage that problems never exist.

Paradise Port was surrounded with a high barrier of woven plastic to keep soldiers who were drunk out of their minds from crawling into the volcanic wasteland and hurting themselves. The fence was tougher than it looked—it looked as insubstantial as moonbeams—but it had never been intended to stop vehicles.

The gate to the bivouac areas outside Paradise Port had a sturdy framework and hung between posts of solid steel. The lead tank had been wide enough to snap both gateposts off at the ground. The gate, framework and webbing, was strewn in fragments for a hundred meters along the course it had been dragged between the pavement and the tank's skirt.

As Jolober approached, he felt his self-image shrink by comparison to surroundings which included a hundred and seventy tonne fighting vehicle. The tank was backed against one edge of the gateway.

With a huge *clang!* the vehicle set another steel post, blasting it home with the apparatus used in combat to punch explosive charges into deep bunkers. The ram vaporized osmium wire with a jolt of high voltage, transmitting the shock waves to the piston head through a column of fluid. It banged home the replacement post without difficulty, even though the "ground" was a sheet of volcanic rock.

The pavement rippled beneath Jolober, and the undamped harmonics of the quivering post were a scream that could be heard for kilometers. Jolober pretended it didn't affect him as he moved past the tank. He was praying that the driver was watching his side screens—or listening to a ground guide— as the tank trembled away from the task it had completed.

One of the Slammers' non-coms gestured reassuringly toward Jolober. His lips moved as he talked into his commo helmet. The port commandant could hear nothing over the howl of the drive fans and prolonged grace notes from the vibrating post, but the tank halted where it was until he had moved past it.

A glance over his shoulder showed Jolober the tank backing into position to set the other post. It looked like a great tortoise, ancient and implacable, maneuvering to lay a clutch of eggs.

Paradise Port was for pleasure only. The barracks housing the soldiers and the sheds to store and repair their equipment were located outside the fenced perimeter. The buildings were pre-fabs extruded from a dun plastic less colorful than the ruddy lava fields on which they were set.

The bivouac site occupied by Hammer's line companies in rotation was unusual in that the large leveled area contained only four barracks buildings and a pair of broad repair sheds. Parked vehicles filled the remainder of the space.

At the entrance to the bivouac area waited a guard shack. The soldier who stepped from it wore body armor over her khakis. Her sub-machine gun was slung, but her tone was businesslike as she said,

"Commandant Jolober? Captain van Zuyle's on his way to meet you right now."

*Hold right here till you're invited in*, Jolober translated mentally with a frown.

But he couldn't blame the Slammers' officer for wanting to assert his authority *here* over that of Horace Jolober, whose writ ran only to the perimeter of Paradise Port. Van Zuyle just wanted to prove that his troopers would be punished only with his assent—or by agreement reached with authorities higher than the port commandant.

There was a flagpole attached to a gable of one of the barracks. A tall officer strode from the door at that end and hopped into the driver's seat of the jeep parked there. Another khaki-clad soldier stuck her head out the door and called something, but the officer pretended not to hear. He spun his vehicle in an angry circle, rubbing its low-side skirts, and gunned it toward the entrance.

Jolober had met van Zuyle only once. The most memorable thing about the Slammers officer was his anger—caused by fate, but directed at whatever was nearest to hand. He'd been heading a company of combat cars when the blower ahead of his took a direct hit.

If van Zuyle'd had his face shield down—but he hadn't, because the shield made him, made most troopers, feel as though they'd stuck their head in a bucket. That dissociation, mental rather than sensory, could get you killed in combat.

The shield would have darkened instantly to block the sleet of actinics from the exploding combat car. Without its protection . . . well, the surgeons could rebuild his face, with only a slight stiffness to betray the injuries. Van Zuyle could even see—by daylight or under strong illumination.

There just wasn't any way he'd ever be fit to lead a line unit again—and he was very angry about it.

Commandant Horace Jolober could understand how van Zuyle felt—better, perhaps, than anyone else on the planet could. It didn't make his own job easier, though.

"A pleasure to see you again, Commandant," van Zuyle lied brusquely as he skidded the jeep to a halt, passenger seat beside Jolober. "If you—"

Jolober smiled grimly as the Slammers officer saw—and remembered—that the port commandant was legless and couldn't seat himself in a jeep on his air-cushion chair.

"No problem," said Jolober, gripping the jeep's side and the seat back. He lifted himself aboard the larger vehicle with an athletic twist that settled him facing front.

Of course, the maneuver was easier than it would have been if his legs were there to get in the way.

"Ah, your—" van Zuyle said, pointing toward the chair. Close up, Jolober could see a line of demarcation in his scalp. The implanted hair at the front had aged less than the gray-speckled portion which hadn't been replaced.

"No problem, Captain," Jolober repeated. He anchored his left arm around the driver's seat, gripped one of his chair's handles with the right hand, and jerked the chair into the bench seat in the rear of the open vehicle.

The jeep lurched: the air-cushion chair weighed almost as much as Jolober did without it, and he was a big man. "You learn tricks when you have to," he said evenly as he met the eyes of the Slammers officer.

And your arms get very strong when they do a lot of the work your legs used to—but he didn't say that.

"My office?" van Zuyle asked sharply.

"Is that as busy as it looks?" Jolober replied, nodding toward the door where a soldier still waited impatiently for van Zuyle to return.

"Commandant, I've had a tank company come in shot to *hell*," van Zuyle said in a voice that built toward fury. "Three vehicles are combat lossed and have to be stripped—*and* the other vehicles need more than routine maintenance—*and* half the personnel are on medic's release. Or dead. I'm trying to run a refit area with what's left, my staff of twenty-three, and the trainee replacements Central sent over who haven't *ridden* in a panzer, much less pulled maintenance on one. And you ask if I've got time to waste on you?"

"No, Captain, I didn't ask that," Jolober said with the threatening lack of emotion which came naturally to a man who had all his life been bigger and stronger than most of those around him. "Find a spot where we won't be disturbed, and we'll park there."

When the Slammers officer frowned, Jolober added, "I'm not here about Captain Hoffritz, Captain."

"Yeah," sighed van Zuyle as he lifted the jeep and steered it sedately toward a niche formed between the iridium carcasses of a pair of tanks. "We're repairing things right now—" he thumbed in the direction of the gate "—and any other costs'll go on the damage chit; but I guess I owe you an apology besides."

"Life's a dangerous place," Jolober said easily. Van

Zuyle wasn't stupid. He'd modified his behavior as
soon as he was reminded of the incident an hour
before—and the leverage it gave the port commandant if he wanted to push it.

Van Zuyle halted them in the gray shade that
brought sweat to Jolober's forehead. The tanks
smelled of hot metal because some of their vaporized
armor had settled back onto the hulls as fine dust.
Slight breezes shifted it to the nostrils of the men
nearby, a memory of the blasts in which it had
formed.

Plastics had burned also, leaving varied pungenc-
ies which could not conceal the odor of cooked
human flesh.

The other smells of destruction were unpleasant.
That last brought Jolober memories of his legs
exploding in brilliant coruscance. His body tingled
and sweated, and his mouth said to the Slammers
officer, "Your men are being cheated and misused
every time they come to Paradise Port, Captain. For
political reasons, my superiors won't let me make
the necessary changes. If the mercenary units ser-
viced by Paradise Port unite and demand the
changes, the government will be forced into the
proper decision."

"Seems to me," said van Zuyle with his perfectly
curved eyebrows narrowing, "that somebody could
claim you were acting against your employers just
now."

"Placida hired me to run a liberty port," said
Jolober evenly. He was being accused of the worst
crime a mercenary could commit: conduct that
would allow his employers to forfeit his unit's bond
and brand them forever as unemployable contract-
breakers.

Jolober no longer *was* a mercenary in that sense; but he understood van Zuyle's idiom, and it was in that idiom that he continued, "Placida wants and needs the troops she hires to be sent back into action in the best shape possible. Her *survival* depends on it. If I let Red Ike run this place to his benefit and not to Placida's, then I'm not doing my job."

"All right," said van Zuyle. "What's Ike got on?"

A truck, swaying with its load of cheering troopers, pulled past on its way to the gate of Paradise Port. The man in the passenger's seat of the cab was Tad Hoffritz, his face a knife-edge of expectation.

"Sure, they need refit as bad as the hardware does," muttered van Zuyle as he watched the soldiers on leave with longing eyes. "Three days straight leave, half days after that when they've pulled their duty. But Via! I could use 'em here, especially with the tanks that're such a bitch if you're not used to crawling around in 'em."

His face hardened again. "Go on," he said, angry that Jolober knew how much he wanted to be one of the men on that truck instead of having to run a rear-echelon installation.

"Red Ike owns the Dolls like so many shots of liquor," Jolober said. He never wanted a combat job again—the thought terrified him, the noise and flash and the smell of his body burning. "He's using them to strip your men, everybody's men, in the shortest possible time," he continued in a voice out of a universe distant from his mind. "The games are honest— that's my job—but the men play when they're stoned, and they play with a Doll on their arm begging them to go on until they've got nothing left. How many of those boys—" he gestured to where the truck, now long past, had been "—are going to last three days?"

"We give 'em advances when they're tapped out," said van Zuyle with a different kind of frown. "Enough to last their half days—*if* they're getting their jobs done here. Works out pretty good.

"As a matter of fact," he went on, "the whole business works out pretty good. I never saw a soldier's dive without shills and B-girls. Don't guess you ever did either, Commandant. Maybe they're better at it, the Dolls, but all that means is that I get my labor force back quicker—and Hammer gets his tanks back in line with that much fewer problems."

"The Dolls—" Jolober began.

"The Dolls are clean," shouted van Zuyle in a voice like edged steel. "They give full value for what you pay 'em. And I've never had a Doll knife one of my guys—which is a curst sight better'n anyplace I been staffed with human whores!"

"No," said Jolober, his strength a bulwark against the Slammer's anger. "But you've had your men knife or strangle Dolls, haven't you? All the units here've had incidents of that sort. Do you think it's chance?"

Van Zuyle blinked. "I think it's a cost of doing business," he said, speaking mildly because the question had surprised him.

"No," Jolober retorted. "It's a major profit center for Red Ike. The Dolls don't just drop soldiers when they've stripped them. They humiliate the men, taunt them . . . and when one of these kids breaks and chokes the life out of the bitch who's goading him, Red Ike pockets the damage assessment. And it comes out of money Placida would otherwise have paid Hammer's Slammers."

The Slammers officer began to laugh. It was Jolober's turn to blink in surprise.

"Sure," van Zuyle said, "androids like that cost a lot more'n gateposts or a few meters of fencing, you bet."

"He's the only source," said Jolober tautly. "Nobody knows where the Dolls come from—or where Ike does."

"Then nobody can argue the price isn't fair, can they?" van Zuyle gibed. "And you know what, Commandant? Take a look at this tank right here."

He pointed to one of the vehicles beside them. It was a command tank, probably the one in which Hoffritz's predecessor had ridden before it was hit by powerguns heavy enough to pierce its armor.

The first round, centered on the hull's broadside, had put the unit out of action and killed everyone aboard. The jet of energy had ignited everything flammable within the fighting compartment in an explosion which blew the hatches open. The enemy had hit the iridium carcase at least three times more, cratering the turret and holing the engine compartment.

"We couldn't replace this for the cost of twenty Dolls," van Zuyle continued. "And we're going to have to, you know, because she's a total loss. All I can do is strip her for salvage . . . and clean up as best I can for the crew, so we can say we had something to bury."

His too-pale, too-angry eyes glared at Jolober. "Don't talk to me about the cost of Dolls, Commandant. They're cheap at the price. I'll drive you back to the gate."

"You may not care about the dollar cost," said Jolober in a voice that thundered over the jeep's drive fans. "But what about the men you're sending back into the line thinking they've killed somebody they loved—or that they *should've* killed her?"

"Commandant, that's one I can't quantify," the Slammers officer said. The fans' keening lowered as the blades bit the air at a steeper angle and began to thrust the vehicle out of the bivouac area. "First time a trooper kills a human here, that I *can* quantify: we lose him. If there's a bigger problem and the Bonding Authority decides to call it mutiny, then we lost a lot more than that.

"And I tell you, buddy," van Zuyle added with a one-armed gesture toward the wrecked vehicles now behind them. "We've lost too fucking much already on this contract."

The jeep howled past the guard at the bivouac entrance. Wind noise formed a deliberate damper on Jolober's attempts to continue the discussion. "Will you forward my request to speak to Colonel Hammer?" he shouted. "I can't get through to him myself."

The tank had left the gate area. Men in khaki, watched by Jolober's staff in white uniforms, had almost completed their task of restringing the perimeter fence. Van Zuyle throttled back, permitting the jeep to glide to a graceful halt three meters short of the workmen.

"The Colonel's busy, Commandant," he said flatly. "And from now on, I hope you'll remember that *I* am, too."

Jolober lifted his chair from the back seat. "I'm going to win this, Captain," he said. "I'm going to do my job whether or not I get any support."

The smile he gave van Zuyle rekindled the respect in the tanker's pale eyes.

*        *        *

There were elements of four other mercenary units bivouacked outside Paradise Port at the moment. Jolober could have visited them in turn—to be received with more or less civility, and certainly no more support than the Slammers officer had offered.

A demand for change by the mercenaries in Placidan service had to be just that: a demand by *all* the mercenaries. Hammer's Slammers were the highest-paid troops here, and by that standard—any other criterion would start a brawl—the premier unit. If the Slammers refused Jolober, none of the others would back him.

The trouble with reform is that in the short run, it causes more problems than continuing along the bad old ways. Troops in a combat zone, who know that each next instant may be their last, are more to be forgiven for short-term thinking than, say, politicians; but the pattern is part of the human condition.

Besides, nobody but Horace Jolober seemed to think there was anything to reform.

Jolober moved in a waking dream while his mind shuttled through causes and options. His data were interspersed with memories of Vicki smiling up at him from the bed and of his own severed leg toppling in blue-green silhouette. He shook his head violently to clear the images and found himself on the street outside the Port offices.

His stump throttled back the fans reflexively; but when Jolober's conscious mind made its decision, he turned away from the office building and headed for the garish façade of the China Doll across the way.

Rainbow pastels lifted slowly over the front of the building, the gradation so subtle that close up it was impossible to tell where one band ended and the next began. At random intervals of from thirty seconds to a minute, the gentle hues were replaced by glaring, supersaturated colors separated by dazzling blue-white lines.

None of the brothels in Paradise Port were sedately decorated, but the China Doll stood out against the competition.

As Jolober approached, a soldier was leaving and three more—one a woman—were in the queue to enter. A conveyor carried those wishing to exit, separated from one another by solid panels. The panels withdrew sideways into the wall as each client reached the street—but there was always another panel in place behind to prevent anyone from bolting into the building without being searched at the proper entrance.

All of the buildings in Paradise Port were designed the same way, with security as unobtrusive as it could be while remaining uncompromised. The entryways were three-meter funnels narrowing in a series of gaudy corbelled arches. Attendants—humans everywhere but in the China Doll—waited at the narrow end. They smiled as the customers passed—but anyone whom the detection devices in the archway said was armed was stopped right there.

The first two soldiers ahead of Jolober went through without incident. The third was a short man wearing lieutenant's pips and the uniform of Division Legere. His broad shoulders and chest narrowed to his waist as abruptly as those of a bulldog, and it was with a bulldog's fierce intransigence that he braced himself against the two attendants who had confronted him.

"I am Lieutenant Alexis Condorcet!" he announced as though he were saying "major general." "What do you mean by hindering me?"

The attendants in the China Doll were Droids, figures with smoothly masculine features and the same blushing complexion which set Red Ike and the Dolls apart from the humans with whom they mingled.

They were not male—Jolober had seen the total sexlessness of an android whose tights had ripped as he quelled a brawl. Their bodies and voices were indistinguishable from one to another, and there could be no doubt that they were androids, artificial constructions whose existence proved that the Dolls could be artificial, too.

Though in his heart, Horace Jolober had never been willing to believe the Dolls were not truly alive. Not since Red Ike had introduced him to Vicki.

"Could you check the right-hand pocket of your blouse, Lieutenant Condorcet?" one of the Droids said.

"I'm not carrying a weapon!" Condorcet snapped. His hand hesitated, but it dived into the indicated pocket when an attendant started to reach toward it.

Jolober was ready to react, either by grabbing Condorcet's wrist from behind or by knocking him down with the chair. He didn't have time for any emotion, not even fear.

It was the same set of instincts that had thrown him to his feet for the last time, to wave off the attacking tanks.

Condorcet's hand came out with a roll of coins between two fingers. In a voice that slipped between injured and minatory he said, "Can't a man bring money into the Doll, then? Will you have me take my business elsewhere, then?"

"Your money's very welcome, sir," said the atten-

dant who was reaching forward. His thumb and
three fingers shifted in a sleight of hand; they reap-
peared holding a gold-striped China Doll chip worth
easily twice the value of the rolled coins. "But let us
hold these till you return. We'll be glad to give them
back then without exchange."

The motion which left Condorcet holding the chip
and transferred the roll to the attendant was also
magically smooth.

The close-coupled soldier tensed for a moment as
if he'd make an issue of it; but the Droids were
as strong as they were polished, and there was no
percentage in being humiliated.

"We'll see about that," said Condorcet loudly. He
strutted past the attendants who parted for him like
water before the blunt prow of a barge.

"Good afternoon, Port Commandant Jolober," said
one of the Droids as they both bowed. "A pleasure
to serve you again."

"A pleasure to feel wanted," said Jolober with an
ironic nod of his own. He glided into the main hall
of the China Doll.

The room's high ceiling was suffused with clear
light which mimicked daytime outside. The hall
buzzed with excited sounds even when the floor carried only a handful of customers. Jolober hadn't
decided whether the space was designed to give
multiple echo effects or if instead Red Ike augmented the hum with concealed sonic transponders.

Whatever it was, the technique made the blood
of even the port commandant quicken when he
stepped into the China Doll.

There were a score of gaming stations in the main
hall, but they provided an almost infinite variety of
ways to lose money. A roulette station could be col-

lapsed into a skat table in less than a minute if a squad of drunken Frieslanders demanded it. The displaced roulette players could be accommodated at the next station over, where until then a Droid had been dealing desultory hands of fan-tan.

Whatever the game was, it was fair. Every hand, every throw, every pot was recorded and processed in the office of the port commandant. None of the facility owners doubted that a skewed result would be noticed at once by the computers, or that a result skewed in favor of the house would mean that Horace Jolober would weld their doors shut and ship all their staff off-planet.

Besides, they knew as Jolober did that honest games would get them most of the available money anyhow, so long as the Dolls were there to caress the winners to greater risks.

At the end of Paradise Port farthest from the gate were two establishments which specialized in the leftovers. They were staffed human males, and their atmosphere was as brightly efficient as men could make it.

But no one whose psyche allowed a choice picked a human companion over a Doll.

The main hall was busy with drab uniforms, Droids neatly garbed in blue and white, and the stunningly gorgeous outfits of the Dolls. There was a regular movement of Dolls and uniforms toward the door on a room-width landing three steps up at the back of the hall. Generally the rooms beyond were occupied by couples, but much larger gatherings were possible if a soldier had money and the perceived need.

The curved doors of the elevator beside the front entrance opened even as Jolober turned to look at

them. Red Ike stepped out with a smile and a Doll
on either arm.

"Always a pleasure to see you, Commandant," Red
Ike said in a tone as sincere as the Dolls were
human. "Shana," he added to the red-haired Doll.
"Susan—" he nodded toward the blond. "Meet Commandant Jolober, the man who keeps us all safe."

The redhead giggled and slipped from Ike's arm
to Jolober's. The slim blond gave him a smile that
would have a been demure except for the fabric of
her tank-top. It acted as a polarizing filter, so that
when she swayed her bare torso flashed toward the
port commandant.

"But come on upstairs, Commandant," Red Ike
continued, stepping backwards into the elevator and
motioning Jolober to follow him. "Unless your business is here—or in back?" He cocked an almost-
human eyebrow toward the door in the rear while
his face waited with a look of amused tolerance.

"We can go upstairs," said Jolober grimly. "It
won't take long." His air cushion slid him forward.
Spilling air tickled Shana's feet as she pranced along
beside him; she giggled again.

There must be men who found that sort of girlish
idiocy erotic or Red Ike wouldn't keep the Doll in
his stock.

The elevator shaft was opaque and looked it from
outside the car. The car's interior was a visiscreen
fed by receptors on the shaft's exterior. On one side
of the slowly rising car, Jolober could watch the
games in the main hall as clearly as if he were hanging in the air. On the other, they lifted above the
street with a perfect view of its traffic and the port
offices—even though a concrete wall and the shaft's
iridium armor blocked the view in fact.

The elevator switch was a small plate which hung in the "air" that was really the side of the car. Red Ike had toggled it up. Down would have taken the car—probably much faster—to the tunnel beneath the street, the escape route which Jolober had suspected even before the smiling alien had used it this afternoon.

But there was a second unobtrusive control beside the first. The blond Doll leaned past Jolober with a smile and touched it.

The view of the street disappeared. Those in the car had a crystalline view of the activities in back of the China Doll as if no walls or ceilings separated the bedrooms. Jolober met—or thought he met—the eyes of Tad Hoffritz, straining upward beneath a black-haired Doll.

"*Via!*" Jolober swore and slapped the toggle hard enough to feel the solidity of the elevator car.

"Susan, Susan," Red Ike chided with a grin. "She will have her little joke, you see, Commandant."

The blond made a moue, then winked at Jolober.

Above the main hall was Red Ike's office, furnished in minimalist luxury. Jolober found nothing attractive in the sight of chair seats and a broad onyx desk top hanging in the air, but the decor did show off the view. Like the elevator, the office walls and ceiling were covered by pass-through visiscreens.

The russet wasteland, blotched but not relieved by patterns of lichen, looked even more dismal from twenty meters up than it did from Jolober's living quarters.

Though the view appeared to be panorama, there was no sign of where the owner himself lived. The back of the office was an interior wall, and the vista over the worms and pillows of lava was transmitted through not only the wall but the complex of rooms that was Red Ike's home.

On the roof beside the elevator tower was an air-car sheltered behind the concrete coping. Like the owners of all the other facilities comprising Paradise Port, Red Ike wanted the option of getting out *fast*, even if the elevator to his tunnel bolthole was blocked.

Horace Jolober had fantasies in which he watched the stocky humanoid scramble into his vehicle and accelerate away, vanishing forever as a fleck against the milky sky.

"I've been meaning to call on you for some time, Commandant," Red Ike said as he walked with quick little steps to his desk. "I thought perhaps you might like a replacement for Vicki. As you know, any little way in which I can make your task easier . . . ?"

Shana giggled. Susan smiled slowly and, turning at a precisely-calculated angle, bared breasts that were much fuller than they appeared beneath her loose garment.

Jolober felt momentary desire, then fierce anger in reaction. His hands clenched on the chair handles, restraining his violent urge to hurl both Dolls into the invisible walls.

Red Ike sat behind the desk top. The thin shell of his chair rocked on invisible gimbals, tilting him to a comfortable angle that was not quite disrespectful of his visitor.

"Commandant," he said with none of the earlier hinted mockery, "you and I really ought to cooperate, you know. We need each other, and Placida needs us both."

"And the soldiers we're here for?" Jolober asked softly. "Do they need you, Ike?"

The Dolls had become as still as painted statues.

"You're an honorable man, Commandant," said the alien. "It disturbs you that the men don't find what they need in Paradise Port."

The chair eased more nearly upright. The intensity of Red Ike's stare reminded Jolober that he'd never seen the alien blink.

"But men like that—all of them now, and most of them for as long as they live . . . all they really need, Commandant, is a chance to die. I don't offer them that, it isn't my place. But I sell them everything they pay for, because I too am honorable."

"You don't know what honor is!" Jolober shouted, horrified at the thought—the nagging possibility—that what Red Ike said was true.

"I know what it is to keep my word, Commandant Jolober," the alien said as he rose from behind his desk with quiet dignity. "I promise you that if you cooperate with me, Paradise Port will continue to run to the full satisfaction of your employers.

"And I also promise," Red Ike went on unblinkingly, "that if you continue your mad vendetta, it will be the worse for you."

"Leave here," Jolober said. His mind achieved not calm, but a dynamic balance in which he understood everything—so long as he focused only on the result, not the reasons. "Leave Placida, leave human space, Ike. You push too hard. So far you've been lucky—it's only me pushing back, and I play by the official rules."

He leaned forward in his saddle, no longer angry. The desktop between them was a flawless black mirror. "But the mercs out there, they play by their own rules, and they're not going to like it when they figure out the game you're running on them. Get out while you can."

"Ladies," Red Ike said. "Please escort the commandant to the main hall. He no longer has any business here."

Jolober spent the next six hours on the street, visiting each of the establishments of Paradise Port. He drank little and spoke less, exchanging salutes when soldiers offered them and, with the same formality, the greetings of owners.

He didn't say much to Vicki later that night, when he returned by the alley staircase which led directly to his living quarters.

But he held her very close.

The sky was dark when Jolober snapped awake, though his bedroom window was painted by all the enticing colors of the façades across the street. He was fully alert and already into the short-legged trousers laid on the mobile chair beside the bed when Vicki stirred and asked, "Horace? What's the matter?"

"I don't—" Jolober began, and then the alarms sounded: the radio implanted in his mastoid, and the siren on the roof of the China Doll.

"Go ahead," he said to Central, thrusting his arms into the uniform tunic.

Vicki thumbed up the room lights but Jolober didn't need that, not to find the sleeves of a white garment with this much sky-glow. He'd stripped a jammed tribarrel once in pitch darkness, knowing that he and a dozen of his men were dead if he screwed up—and absolutely confident of the stream of cyan fire that ripped moments later from his gun muzzles.

"Somebody shot his way into the China Doll," said the voice. "He's holed up in the back."

The bone-conduction speaker hid the identity of the man on the other end of the radio link, but it wasn't the switchboard's artificial intelligence. Somebody on the street was cutting through directly, probably Stecher.

"Droids?" Jolober asked as he mounted his chair and powered up, breaking the charging circuit in which the vehicle rested overnight.

"Chief," said the mastoid, "we got a man down. Looks bad, and we can't get medics to him because the gun's covering the hallway. D'ye want me to—"

"*Wait!*" Jolober said as he bulled through the side door under power. Unlocking the main entrance— the entrance to the office of the port commandant— would take seconds that he knew he didn't have. "Hold what you got, I'm on the way."

The voice speaking through Jolober's jawbone was clearly audible despite wind noise and the scream of his chair as he leaped down the alley staircase in a single curving arc. "Ah, Chief? We're likely to have a, a crowd control problem if this don't get handled real quick."

"I'm on the way," Jolober repeated. He shot onto the street, still on direct thrust because ground effect wouldn't move him as fast as he needed to go.

The entrance of the China Doll was cordoned off, if four port patrolmen could be called a cordon. There were over a hundred soldiers in the street and more every moment that the siren—couldn't somebody cut it? Jolober didn't have time—continued to blare.

That wasn't what Stecher had meant by a "crowd control problem." The difficulty was in the way soldiers in the Division Legere's mottled uniforms were shouting—not so much as onlookers as a lynch mob.

Jolober dropped his chair onto its skirts—he needed the greater stability of ground effect. "Lemme through!" he snarled to the mass of uniformed backs which parted in a chorus of yelps when Jolober goosed his throttle. The skirt of his plenum chamber caught the soldiers just above the bootheels and toppled them to either side as the chair powered through.

One trooper spun with a raised fist and a curse in French. Jolober caught the man's wrist and flung him down almost absently. The men at the door relaxed visibly when their commandant appeared at their side.

Behind him, Jolober could hear off-duty patrolmen scrambling into the street from their barracks under the port offices. That would help, but—

"You, Major!" Jolober shouted, pointing at a Division Legere officer in the front of the crowd. The man was almost of a size with the commandant; fury had darkened his face several shades beyond swarthiness. "I'm deputizing you to keep order here until I've taken care of the problem inside."

He spun his chair again and drove through the doorway. The major was shouting to his back, "But the bastard's shot my—"

Two Droids were more or less where Jolober had expected them, one crumpled in the doorway and the other stretched full length a meter inside. The Droids were tough as well as strong. The second one had managed to grasp the man who shot him and be pulled a pace or two before another burst into the back of the Droid's skull had ended matters.

Stecher hadn't said the shooter had a sub-machine gun. That made the situation a little worse than it might have been, but it was so bad already that the increment was negligible.

Droids waited impassively at all the gaming stations, ready to do their jobs as soon as customers returned. They hadn't fled the way human croupiers would have—but neither did their programming say anything about dealing with armed intruders.

The Dolls had disappeared. It was the first time Jolober had been in the main hall when it was empty of their charming, enticing babble.

Stecher and two troopers in Slammers khaki, and a pair of technicians with a portable medicomp, stood on opposite sides of the archway leading into the back of the China Doll. A second patrolman was huddled behind the three room-wide steps leading up from the main hall.

*Man down*, Jolober thought, his guts ice.

The patrolman heard the chair and glanced back. *"Duck!"* he screamed as Sergeant Stecher cried, *"Watch—"*

Jolober throttled up, bouncing to the left as a three-shot burst snapped from the archway. It missed him by little enough that his hair rose in response to the ionized track.

There *was* a man down, in the corridor leading back from the archway. There was another man firing from a room at the corridor's opposite end, and he'd just proved his willingness to add the port commandant to the night's bag.

Jolober's chair leaped the steps to the broad landing where Stecher crouched, but it was his massive arms that braked his momentum against the wall. His tunic flapped and he noticed for the first time that he hadn't sealed it before he left his quarters.

"Report," he said bluntly to his sergeant while running his thumb up the uniform's seam to close it.

"Their officer's in there," Stecher said, bobbing his chin to indicate the two Slammers kneeling beside him. The male trooper was holding the female and trying to comfort her as she blubbered.

To Jolober's surprise, he recognized both of them—the commo tech and the driver of the tank which'd nearly run him down that afternoon.

"He nutted, shot his way in to find a Doll," Stecher said quickly. His eyes flicked from the commandant to the archway, but he didn't shift far enough to look down the corridor. Congealed notches in the arch's plastic sheath indicated that he'd been lucky once already.

"Found her, found the guy she was with and put a burst into him as he tried to get away." Stecher thumbed toward the body invisible behind the shielding wall. "Guy from the Legere, an El-Tee named Condorcet."

"The bitch made him do it!" said the tank driver in a scream strangled by her own laced fingers.

"She's sedated," said the commo tech who held her.

In the perfect tones of Central's artificial intelligence, Jolober's implant said, "Major de Vigny of the Division Legere requests to see you. He is offering threats."

Letting de Vigny through would either take the pressure off the team outside or be the crack that made the dam fail. From the way Central put it, the dam wasn't going to hold much longer anyhow.

"Tell the cordon to pass him. But tell him keep his head down or he's that much more t'clean up t'morrow," Jolober replied with his mike keyed, making the best decision he could when none of 'em looked good.

"Tried knock-out gas but he's got filters," said Stecher. "Fast, too." He tapped the scarred jamb. "All the skin absorbtives're lethal, and I don't guess we'd get cleared t' use 'em anyhow?"

"Not while I'm in the chain of command," Jolober agreed grimly.

"She was with this pongo from the Legere," the driver was saying through her laced fingers. "Tad, he wanted her so much, so fucking *much*, like she was human or something . . ."

"The, ah, you know. Beth, the one he was planning to see," said the commo tech rapidly as he stroked the back of the driver—Corporal Days—Daisy. . . . "He tried to, you know, buy 'er from the frog, but he wouldn't play. She got 'em, Beth did, to put all their leave allowance on a coin flip. She'd take all the money and go with the winner."

"The bitch," Daisy wailed. "The bitch the bitch the bitch . . ."

The Legere didn't promote amateurs to battalion command. The powerful major Jolober had seen outside rolled through the doorway, sized up the situation, and sprinted to the landing out of the shooter's line of sight.

Line of fire.

"Hoffritz, can you hear me?" Jolober called. "I'm the port commandant, remember?"

A single bolt from the sub-machine gun spattered plastic from the jamb and filled the air with fresher stenches.

The man sprawling in the corridor moaned.

"I've ordered up an assault team," said Major de Vigny with flat assurance as he stood up beside

Jolober. "It was unexpected, but they should be here in a few minutes."

Everyone else in the room was crouching. There wasn't any need so long as you weren't in front of the corridor, but it was the instinctive response to knowing somebody was trying to shoot you.

"Cancel the order," said Jolober, locking eyes with the other officer.

"You aren't in charge when one of my men—" began the major, his face flushing almost black.

"The gate closes when the alarm goes off!" Jolober said in a voice that could have been heard over a tank's fans. "And I've ordered the air defense batteries," he lied, "to fire on anybody trying to crash through now. If you want to lead a mutiny against your employers, Major, now's the time to do it."

The two big men glared at one another without blinking. Then de Vigny said, "Blue Six to Blue Three," keying his epaulet mike with the code words. "Hold Team Alpha until further orders. Repeat, hold Alpha. Out."

"Hold Alpha," repeated the speaker woven into the epaulet's fabric.

"If Condorcet dies," de Vigny added calmly to the port commandant, "I will kill you myself, sir."

"Do you have cratering charges warehoused here?" Jolober asked with no emotion save the slight lilt of interrogation.

"What?" said de Vigny. "Yes, yes."

Jolober crooked his left ring finger so that Central would hear and relay his next words. "Tell the gate to pass two men from the Legere with a jeep and a cratering charge. Give them a patrol guide, and download the prints of the China Doll into his commo link so they can place the charge on the wall outside the room at the T of the back corridor."

De Vigny nodded crisply to indicate that he too understood the order. He began relaying it into his epaulet while Stecher drew and reholstered his needle stunner and Corporal Days mumbled.

"Has she tried?" Jolober asked, waving to the driver and praying that he wouldn't have to . . .

"He shot at 'er," the commo tech said, nodding sadly. "That's when she really lost it and medics had to calm her down."

No surprises there. Certainly no good ones.

"Captain Hoffritz, it's the port commandant again," Jolober called.

A bolt spat down the axis of the corridor.

"That's right, you bastard, *shoot!*" Jolober roared. "You blew my legs off on Primavera. Now finish the job and *prove* you're a fuck-up who's only good for killing his friends. Come on, I'll make it easy. I'll come out and let you take your time!"

"Chief—" said Stecher.

Jolober slid away from the shelter of the wall.

The corridor was the stem of a T, ten meters long. Halfway between Jolober and the cross corridor at the other end, capping the T, lay the wounded man. Lieutenant Condorcet was a tough little man to still be alive with the back of his tunic smoldering around the holes punched in him by three powergun bolts. The roll of coins he'd carried to add weight to his fist wouldn't have helped; but then, nothing much helped when the other guy had the only gun in the equation.

Like now.

The door of the room facing the corridor and Horace Jolober was ajar. Beyond the opening was darkness and a bubble of dull red: the iridium muzzle of Hoffritz's sub-machine gun, glowing with the heat of the destruction it had spit at others.

De Vigny cursed; Stecher was pleading or even calling an order. All Jolober could hear was the roar of the tank bearing down on him, so loud that the slapping bolts streaming toward him from its cupola were inaudible.

Jolober's chair slid him down the hall. His arms were twitching in physical memory of the time they'd waved a scrap of white cloth to halt the oncoming armor.

The door facing him opened. Tad Hoffritz's face was as hard and yellow as fresh bone. He leaned over the sight of his sub-machine gun. Jolober slowed, because if he kept on at a walking pace he would collide with Condorcet, and if he curved around the wounded man it might look as if he were dodging what couldn't be dodged.

He didn't want to look like a fool and a coward when he died.

Hoffritz threw down the weapon.

Jolober bounced to him, wrapping the Slammers officer in both arms like a son. Stecher was shouting. "Medics!" but the team with the medicomp had been in motion as soon as the powergun hit the floor. Behind all the battle was Major de Vigny's voice, remembering to stop the crew with the charge that might otherwise be set—and fired—even though the need was over.

"I *loved* her," Hoffritz said to Jolober's big shoulder, begging someone to understand what he didn't understand himself. "I, I'd been drinking and I came back . . ."

With a sub-machine gun that shouldn't have made

it into Paradise Port . . . but the detection loops hadn't been replaced in the hours since the tanks ripped them away; and anyhow, Hoffritz was an officer, a company commander.

He was also a young man having a bad time with what he thought was a woman. Older, calmer fellows than Hoffritz had killed because of that.

Jolober carried Hoffritz with him into the room where he'd been holed up. "Lights," the commandant ordered, and the room brightened.

Condorcet wasn't dead, not yet; but Beth, the Doll behind the trouble, surely was.

The couch was large and round. Though drumhead-thin, its structure could be varied to any degree of firmness the paying half of the couple desired. Beth lay in the center of it in a tangle of long black hair. Her tongue protruded from a blood-darkened face, and the prints of the grip that had strangled her were livid on her throat.

"She told me she loved *him*," Hoffritz mumbled. The commandant's embrace supported him, but it also kept Hoffritz from doing something silly, like trying to run.

"After what I'd done," the boy was saying, "she tells me she doesn't love me after all. She says I'm no good to her in bed, that I never gave her any pleasure at all. . . ."

"Just trying to maximize the claim for damages, son," Jolober said grimly. "It didn't mean anything real, just more dollars in Red Ike's pocket."

But Red Ike hadn't counted on Hoffritz shooting another merc. Too bad for Condorcet, too bad for the kid who shot him—

And just what Jolober needed to finish Red Ike on Placida.

"Let's go," Jolober said, guiding Hoffritz out of the room stinking of death and the emotions that led to death. "We'll get you to a medic."

And a cell.

Condorcet had been removed from the corridor, leaving behind only a slime of vomit. Thank the Lord he'd fallen face down.

Stecher and his partner took the unresisting Hoffritz and wrapped him in motion restraints. The prisoner could walk and move normally, so long as he did it slowly. At a sudden movement, the gossamer webs would clamp him as tightly as a fly in a spiderweb.

The main hall was crowded, but the incipient violence facing the cordon outside had melted away. Judging from Major de Vigny's brusque, bellowed orders, the victim was in the hands of his medics and being shifted to the medicomp in Division Legere's bivouac area.

That was probably the best choice. Paradise Port had excellent medical facilities, but medics in combat units got to know their jobs and their disagnostic/healing computers better than anybody in the rear echelons.

"Commandant Jolober," said van Zuyle, the Slammers' bivouac commander, "I'm worried about my man here. Can I—"

"He's not your man any more, Captain," Jolober said with the weary chill of an avalanche starting to topple. "He's mine and the Placidan courts'—until I tell you different. We'll get him sedated and keep him from hurting himself, no problem."

Van Zuyle's face wore the expression of a man whipping himself to find a deity who doesn't respond. "Sir," he said, "I'm sorry if I—"

"You did the job they paid you t'do," Jolober said, shrugging away from the other man. He hadn't felt so weary since he'd awakened in the Legion's main hospital on Primavera: alive and utterly unwilling to believe that he could be after what happened.

"Outa the man's way," snarled one of the patrolmen, trying to wave a path through the crowd with her white-sleeved arms. "Let the commandant by!"

She yelped a curse at the big man who brushed through her gestures. "A moment, little one," he said—de Vigny, the Legere major.

"You kept the lid on good," Jolober said while part of his dazed mind wondered whose voice he was hearing. "Tomorrow I'll want to talk to you about what happened and how to keep from a repeat."

Anger darkened de Vigny's face. "I heard what happened," he said. "Condorcet was not the only human victim, it would seem."

"We'll talk," Jolober said. His chair was driving him toward the door, pushing aside anyone who didn't get out of the way. He didn't see them any more than he saw the air.

The street was a carnival of uniformed soldiers who suddenly had something to focus on that wasn't a memory of death—or a way to forget. There was dark undercurrents to the chatter, but the crowd was no longer a mob.

Jolober's uniform drew eyes, but the port commandant was too aloof and forbidding to be asked for details of what had really happened in the China Doll. In the center of the street, though—

"Good evening, Commandant," said Red Ike, strolling back toward the establishment he owned. "Without your courage, tonight's incident would have been even more unfortunate."

Human faces changed in the play of light washing them from the brothel fronts. Red Ike's did not. Colors overlay his features, but the lines did not modify as one shadow or highlight replaced another.

"It couldn't be more unfortunate for you, Ike," Jolober said to the bland alien while uniforms milled around them. "They'll pay you money, the mercs will. But they won't have you killing their men."

"I understand that the injured party is expected to pull through," Red Ike said emotionlessly. Jolober had the feeling that the alien's eyes were focused on his soul.

"I'm glad Condorcet'll live," Jolober said, too tired for triumph or subtlety. "But you're dead on Placida, Ike. It's just a matter of how long it takes me to wrap it up."

He broke past Red Ike, gliding toward the port offices and the light glowing from his room on the upper floor.

Red Ike didn't turn around, but Jolober thought he could feel the alien watching him nonetheless.

Even so, all Jolober cared about now was bed and a chance to reassure Vicki that everything was all right.

The alley between the office building and the Blue Parrot next door wasn't directly illuminated, but enough light spilled from the street to show Jolober the stairs.

He didn't see the two men waiting there until a third had closed the mouth of the alley behind him. Indonesian music began to blare from the China Doll.

*Music on the exterior's a violation*, thought the part of Jolober's mind that ran Paradise Port, but reflexes from his years as a combat officer noted the man behind him held a metal bar and that knives gleamed in the hands of the two by the stairs.

It made a hell of a fast trip back from the nightmare memories that had ruled Jolober's brain since he wakened.

Jolober's left stump urged the throttle as his torso shifted toward the alley mouth. The electronics reacted instantly but the mechanical links took a moment. Fans spun up, plenum chamber collapsed into a nozzle—

The attackers moved in on Jolober like the three wedges of a drill chuck. His chair launched him into the one with the club, a meter off the ground and rising with a hundred and eighty kilos of mass behind the impact.

At the last instant the attacker tried to duck away instead of swinging at Jolober, but he misjudged the speed of his intended victim. The center of the chair's frame, between the skirt and the saddle, batted the attacker's head toward the wall, dragging the fellow's body with it.

Jolober had a clear path to the street. The pair of knifemen thought he was headed that way and sprinted in a desperate attempt to catch a victim who moved faster than unaided humans could run.

They were in midstride, thinking of failure rather than defense, when Jolober pogoed at the alley mouth and came back at them like a cannonball.

But bigger and heavier.

One attacker stabbed at Jolober's chest and skidded the point off the battery compartment instead when the chair hopped. The frame slammed knife and man into the concrete wall from which they ricochetted to the ground, separate and equally motionless.

The third man ran away.

"Get 'em, boys!" Jolober bellowed as if he were launching his battalion instead of just himself in pursuit. The running man glanced over his shoulder and collided with the metal staircase. The noise was loud and unpleasant, even in comparison to the oriental music blaring from the China Doll.

Jolober bounced, cut his fan speed, and flared his output nozzle into a plenum chamber again. The chair twitched, then settled into ground effect.

Jolober's mind told him that he was seeing with a clarity and richness of color he couldn't have equalled by daylight, but he knew that if he really focused on an object it would blur into shadow. It was just his brain's way of letting him know that he was still alive.

Alive like he hadn't been in years.

Crooking his ring finger, Jolober said, "I need a pick-up on three men in the alley between us and the Blue Parrot."

"Three men in the alley between HQ and the Blue Parrot," the artificial intelligence paraphrased.

"They'll need a medic." One might need burial. "And I want them sweated under a psycomp—who sent 'em after me, the works."

Light flooded the alley as a team of patrolmen arrived. The point man extended a surface-luminescent area light powered from a backpack. The shadows thrown by the meter-diameter convexity were soft, but the illumination was the blaze of noon compared to that of moments before.

"Chief!" bellowed Stecher. "You all right? Chief!" He wasn't part of the team Central vectored to the alley, but word of mouth had brought him to the scene of the incident.

Jolober throttled up, clamped his skirts, and boosted himself to the fourth step where everyone could see him. The man who'd run into the stairs moaned as the sidedraft spat grit from the treads into his face.

"No problem," Jolober said. No problem they wouldn't be able to cure in a week or two. "I doubt these three know any more than that they got a call from outside Port to, ah, handle me . . . but get what they have, maybe we can cross-reference with some outgoing traffic."

From the China Doll; or just maybe from the Blue Parrot, where Ike fled when the shooting started. But probably not. Three thugs, non-descripts from off-planet who could've been working for any establishment in Paradise Port *except* the China Doll.

"Sir—" came Stecher's voice.

"It'll keep, Sergeant," Jolober interrupted. "Just now I've got a heavy date with a bed."


Vicki greeted him with a smile so bright that both of them could pretend there were no tears beneath it. The air was steamy with the bath she'd drawn for him.

He used to prefer showers, back when he'd had feet on which to stand. He could remember dancing on Quitly's Planet as the afternoon monsoon battered the gun carriages his platoon was guarding and washed the soap from his body.

But he didn't have Vicki then, either.

"Yeah," he said, hugging the Doll. "Good idea, a bath."

Instead of heading for the bathroom, he slid his

chair to the cabinet within arm's reach of the bed and cut his fans. Bending over, he unlatched the battery compartment—the knifepoint hadn't even penetrated the casing—and removed the powerpack.

"I can—" Vicki offered hesitantly.

"S'okay, dearest," Jolober replied as he slid a fresh pack from the cabinet into place. His stump touched the throttle, spinning the fans to prove that he had good contact, then lifted the original pack into the cabinet and its charging harness.

"Just gave 'em a workout tonight and don't want t' be down on power tomorrow," he explained as he straightened. Vicki could have handled the weight of the batteries, he realized, though his mind kept telling him it was ludicrous to imagine the little woman shifting thirty-kilo packages with ease.

But she wasn't a woman.

"I worry when it's so dangerous," she said as she walked with him to the bathroom, their arms around one another's waist.

"Look, for Paradise Port, it was dangerous," Jolober said in a light appearance of candor as he handed Vicki his garments. "Compared to downtown in any capital city I've seen, it was pretty mild."

He lowered himself into the water, using the bars laid over the tub like a horizontal ladder. Vicki began to knead the great muscles of his shoulders, and Lord! but it felt good to relax after so long. . . .

"I'd miss you," she said.

"Not unless I went away," Jolober answered, leaning forward so that her fingers could work down his spine while the water lapped at them. "Which isn't going to happen any time soon."

He paused. The water's warmth unlocked more than his body. "Look," he said quietly, his chin touching the surface of the bath and his eyes still closed. "Red Ike's had it. He knows it, I know it. But I'm in a position to make things either easy or hard, and he knows that, too. We'll come to terms, he and I. And you're the—"

"Urgent from the gate," said Jolober's mastoid implant.

He crooked his finger, raising his head. "Put him through," he said.

*Her* through. "Sir," said Feldman's attenuated voice, "a courier's just landed with two men. They say they've got an oral message from Colonel Hammer, and they want me to alert you that they're coming. Over."

"I'll open the front door," Jolober said, lifting himself abruptly from the water, careful not to mis-key the implant while his hands performed other tasks.

He wouldn't rouse the human staff. No need—and if the message came by courier, it wasn't intended for other ears.

"Ah, sir," Feldman added unexpectedly. "One of them insists on keeping his sidearms. Over."

"Then he can insist on staying outside my perimeter!" Jolober snarled. Vicki had laid a towel on the saddle before he mounted and was now using another to silently dry his body. "You can detach two guards to escort 'em if they need their hands held, but *nobody* brings powerguns into Paradise Port."

"Roger, I'll tell them," Feldman agreed doubtfully. "Over and out."

"I have a fresh uniform out," said Vicki, stepping back so that Jolober could follow her into the bedroom, where the air was drier.

"That's three, today," Jolober said, grinning. "Well,

I've done a lot more than I've managed any three other days.

"Via," he added more seriously. "It's more headway than I've made since they appointed me commandant."

Vicki smiled, but her eyes were so tired that Jolober's body trembled in response. His flesh remembered how much he had already been through today and yearned for the sleep to which the hot bath had disposed it.

Jolober lifted himself on his hands so that Vicki could raise and cinch his trousers. He could do it himself, but he was in a hurry, and . . . besides, just as she'd said, Vicki was a part of him in a real way.

"Cheer up, love," he said as he closed his tunic. "It isn't done yet, but it's sure getting that way."

"Goodby, Horace," the Doll said as she kissed him.

"Keep the bed warm," Jolober called as he slid toward the door and the inner staircase. His head was tumbling with memories and images. For a change, they were all pleasant ones.

The port offices were easily identified at night because they *weren't* garishly illuminated like every other building in Paradise Port. Jolober had a small staff, and he didn't choose to waste it at desks. Outside of ordinary business hours, Central's artificial intelligence handled everything—by putting non-emergency requests on hold till morning, and by vectoring a uniformed patrol to the real business.

Anybody who insisted on personal service could get it by hammering at the Patrol entrance on the west side, opposite Jolober's private staircase. A patrolman would find the noisemaker a personal holding cell for the remainder of the night.

The front entrance was built like a vault door, not so much to prevent intrusion as to keep drunks from destroying the panel for reasons they'd be unable to remember sober. Jolober palmed the release for the separate bolting systems and had just begun to swing the door open in invitation when the two men in khaki uniforms, neither of them tall, strode up to the building.

"Blood and Martyrs!" Jolober said as he continued to back, not entirely because the door required it.

"You run a tight base here, Commandant," said Colonel Alois Hammer as he stepped into the waiting room. "Do you know my aide, Major Steuben?"

"By reputation only," said Jolober, nodding to Joachim Steuben with the formal correctness which that reputation enjoined. "Ah—with a little more information, I might have relaxed the prohibition on weapons."

Steuben closed the door behind them, moving the heavy panel with a control which belied the boyish delicacy of his face and frame. "If the colonel's satisfied with his security," Joachim said mildly, "then of course I am, too."

The eyes above his smile would willingly have watched Jolober drawn and quartered.

"You've had some problems with troops of mine today," said Hammer, seating himself on one of the chairs and rising again, almost as quickly as if he had continued to walk. His eyes touched Jolober and moved on in short hops that covered everything in the room like an animal checking a new environment.

"Only reported problems occurred," said Jolober, keeping the promise he'd made earlier in the day.

He lighted the hologram projection tank on the counter to let it warm up. "There was an incident a few hours ago, yes."

The promise didn't matter to Tad Hoffritz, not after the shootings; but it mattered more than life to Horace Jolober that he keep the bargains he'd made.

"According to Captain van Zuyle's report," Hammer said as his eyes flickered over furniture and recesses dim under the partial lighting, "you're of the opinion the boy was set up."

"What you do with a gun," said Joachim Steuben softly from the door against which he leaned, "is your own responsibility."

"As Joachim says," Hammer went on with a nod and no facial expression, "that doesn't affect how we'll deal with Captain Hoffritz when he's released from local custody. But it does affect how we act to prevent recurrences, doesn't it?"

"Load file Ike One into the downstairs holo," said Jolober to Central.

He looked at Hammer, paused till their eyes met. "Sure, he was set up, just like half a dozen others in the past three months—only they were money assessments, no real problem.

"And the data prove," Jolober continued coolly, claiming what his data suggested but could *not* prove, "that it's going to get a lot worse than what happened tonight if Red Ike and his Dolls aren't shipped out fast."

The holotank sprang to life in a three-dimensional cross-hatching of orange lines. As abruptly, the lines shrank into words and columns of figures. "Red Ike and his Dolls—they were all his openly, then—first show up on Sparrowhome a little over five years

standard ago, according to Bonding Authority records.
Then—"

Jolober pointed toward the figures. Colonel Hammer put his smaller, equally firm, hand over the commandant's and said, "Wait. Just give me your assessment."

"Dolls have been imported as recreational support in seven conflicts," said Jolober as calmly as if his mind had not just shifted gears. He'd been a good combat commander for the same reason, for dealing with the situation that occurred rather than the one he'd planned for. "There's been rear-echelon trouble each time, and the riot on Ketelby caused the Bonding Authority to order the disbandment of a battalion of Guardforce O'Higgins."

"There was trouble over a woman," said Steuben unemotionally, reeling out the data he gathered because he *was* Hammer's adjutant as well as his bodyguard. "A fight between a ranger and an artilleryman led to a riot in which half the nearest town was burned."

"Not a woman," corrected Jolober. "A Doll."

He tapped the surface of the holotank. "It's all here, downloaded from Bonding Authority archives. You just have to see what's happening so you know the questions to ask."

"You can get me a line to the capital?" Hammer asked as if he were discussing the weather. "I was in a hurry, and I didn't bring along my usual commo."

Jolober lifted the visiplate folded into the surface of the counter beside the tank and rotated it toward Hammer.

"I've always preferred non-humans for recreation areas," Hammer said idly as his finger played over the plate's keypad. "Oh, the troops complain, but

I've never seen *that* hurt combat efficiency. Whereas real women gave all sorts of problems."

"And real men," said Joachim Steuben, with a deadpan expression that could have meant anything.

The visiplate beeped. "Main Switch," said a voice, tart but not sleepy. "Go ahead."

"You have my authorization code," Hammer said to the human operator on the other end of the connection. From Jolober's flat angle to the plate, he couldn't make out the operator's features—only that he sat in a brightly-illuminated white cubicle. "Patch me through to the chairman of the Facilities Inspection Committee."

"Senator Dieter?" said the operator, professionally able to keep the question short of being amazement.

"If he's the chairman," Hammer said. The words had the angry undertone of a dynamite fuse burning.

"Yessir, she is," replied the operator with studied neutrality. "One moment please."

"I've been dealing with her chief aide," said Jolober in a hasty whisper. "Guy named Higgey. His pager's loaded—"

"Got you a long ways, didn't it, Commandant?" Hammer said with a gun-turret click of his head toward Jolober.

"Your pardon, sir," said Jolober, bracing reflexively to attention. He wasn't Hammer's subordinate, but they both served the same ideal—getting the job done. The ball was in Hammer's court just now, and he'd ask for support if he thought he needed it.

From across the waiting room, Joachim Steuben smiled at Jolober. *That* one had the same ideal, perhaps; but his terms of reference were something else again.

"The senator isn't at any of her registered work stations," the operator reported coolly.

"Son," said Hammer, leaning toward the visiplate, "you have a unique opportunity to lose the war for Placida. All you have to do is *not* get me through to the chairman."

"Yes, Colonel Hammer," the operator replied with an aplomb that made it clear why he held the job he did. "I've processed your authorization, and I'm running it through again on War Emergency Ord—"

The last syllable was clipped. The bright rectangle of screen dimmed gray. Jolober slid his chair in a short arc so that he could see the visiplate clearly past Hammer's shoulder.

"What is it?" demanded the woman in the dim light beyond. She was stocky, middle-aged, and rather attractive because of the force of personality she radiated even sleepless in a dressing gown.

"This is Colonel Alois Hammer," Hammer said. "Are you recording?"

"On *this* circuit?" the senator replied with a frosty smile. "Of course I am. So are at least three other agencies, whether I will or no."

Hammer blinked, startled to find himself on the wrong end of a silly question for a change.

"Senator," he went on without the hectoring edge that had been present since his arrival. "A contractor engaged by your government to provide services at Paradise Port has been causing problems. One of the Legere's down, in critical, and I'm short a company commander over the same incident."

"You've reported to the port commandant?" Senator Dieter said, her eyes unblinking as they passed over Jolober.

"The commandant reported to me because your

staff stonewalled him," Hammer said flatly while Jolober felt his skin grow cold, even the tips of the toes he no longer had. "I want the contractor, a non-human called Red Ike, off-planet in seventy-two hours with all his chattels. That specifically includes his Dolls. We'll work—"

"That's too soon," said Dieter, her fingers tugging a lock of hair over one ear while her mind worked. "Even if—"

"Forty-*eight* hours, Senator," Hammer interrupted. "This is a violation of your bond. And I promise you, I'll have the support of all the other commanders of units contracted to Placidan service. Forty-eight hours, or we'll withdraw from combat and you won't have a front line."

"You *can't*—" Dieter began. Then all muscles froze, tongue and fingers among them, as her mind considered the implications of what the colonel had just told her.

"I have no concern over being able to win my case at the Bonding Authority hearing on Earth," Hammer continued softly. "But I'm quite certain that the present Placidan government won't be there to contest it."

Dieter smiled without humor. "Seventy-two hours," she said as if repeating the figure.

"I've shifted the Regiment across continents in less time, Senator," Hammer said.

"Yes," said Dieter calmly. "Well, there are political consequences to any action, and I'd rather explain myself to my constituents than to an army of occupation. I'll take care of it."

She broke the circuit.

"I wouldn't mind getting to know that lady," said

*David Drake*

Hammer, mostly to himself, as he folded the visiplate back into the counter.

"That takes care of your concerns, then?" he added sharply, looking up at Jolober.

"Yes, sir, it does," said Jolober, who had the feeling he had drifted into a plane where dreams could be happy.

"Ah, about Captain Hoffritz . . ." Hammer said. His eyes slipped, but he snapped them back to meet Jolober's despite the embarrassment of being about to ask a favor.

"He's not combat-fit right now, Colonel," Jolober said, warming as authority flooded back to fill his mind. "He'll do as well in our care for the next few days as he would in yours. After that, and assuming that no one wants to press charges—"

"Understood," said Hammer, nodding. "I'll deal with the victim and General Claire."

"—then some accommodation can probably be arranged with the courts."

"It's been a pleasure dealing with a professional of your caliber, Commandant," Hammer said as he shook Jolober's hand. He spoke without emphasis, but nobody meeting his cool blue eyes could have imagined that Hammer would have bothered to lie about it.

"It's started to rain," observed Major Steuben as he muscled the door open.

"It's permitted to," Hammer said. "We've been wet be—"

"A jeep to the front of the building," Jolober ordered with his ring finger crooked. He straightened and said, "Ah, Colonel? Unless you'd like to be picked up by one of your own vehicles?"

"Nobody knows I'm here," said Hammer from the

doorway. "I don't want van Zuyle to think I'm sec-ond-guessing him—I'm not, I'm just handling the part that's mine to handle."

He paused before adding with an ironic smile, "In any case, we're four hours from exploiting the salient Hoffritz's company, formed when they took the junction at Kettering."

A jeep with two patrolmen, stunners ready, scraped to a halt outside. The team was primed for a situation like the one in the alley less than an hour before.

"Taxi service only, boys," Jolober called to the patrolmen. "Carry these gentlemen to their courier ship, please."

The jeep was spinning away in the drizzle before Jolober had closed and locked the door again. It didn't occur to him that it mattered whether or not the troops bivouacked around Paradise Port knew immediately what Hammer had just arranged.

And it didn't occur to him, as he bounced his chair up the stairs calling, "Vicki! We've won!" that he should feel any emotion except joy.

"Vicki!" he repeated as he opened the bedroom door. They'd have to leave Placida unless he could get Vicki released from the blanket order on Dolls—but he hadn't expected to keep his job anyway, not after he went over the head of the whole Placidan government.

"Vi—"

She'd left a light on, one of the point sources in the ceiling. It was a shock, but not nearly as bad a shock as Jolober would have gotten if he'd slid onto the bed in the dark.

"Who?" his tongue asked while his mind couldn't think of anything to say, could only move his chair to the bedside and palm the hydraulics to lower him into a sitting position.

Her right hand and forearm were undamaged. She flexed her fingers and the keen plastic blade shot from her fist, then collapsed again into a baton. She let it roll onto the bedclothes.

"He couldn't force me to kill you," Vicki said. "He was very surprised, very. . . ."

Jolober thought she might be smiling, but he couldn't be sure since she no longer had lips. The plastic edges of the knife Vicki took as she dressed him were not sharp enough for finesse, but she had not attempted surgical delicacy.

Vicki had destroyed herself from toes to her once-perfect face. All she had left was one eye with which to watch Jolober, and the parts of her body which she couldn't reach unaided. She had six ribs to a side, broader and flatter than those of a human's skeleton. After she laid open the ribs, she had dissected the skin and flesh of the left side further.

Jolober had always assumed—when he let himself think about it—that her breasts were sponge implants. He'd been wrong. On the bedspread lay a wad of yellowish fat steaked with blood vessels. He didn't have a background that would tell him whether or not it was human normal, but it certainly was biological.

It was a tribute to Vicki's toughness that she had remained alive as long as she had.

Instinct turned Jolober's head to the side so that he vomited away from the bed. He clasped Vicki's right hand with both of his, keeping his eyes closed so that he could imagine that everything was as it had been minutes before when he was triumphantly happy. His left wrist brushed the knife that should have remained an inert baton in any hands but his. He snatched up the weapon, feeling the blade flow out—

As it had when Vicki held it, turned it on herself.

"We are one, my Horace," she whispered, her hand squeezing his.

It was the last time she spoke, but Jolober couldn't be sure of that because his mind had shifted out of the present into a cosmos limited to the sense of touch: body-warm plastic in his left hand, and flesh cooling slowly in his right.

He sat in his separate cosmos for almost an hour, until the emergency call on his mastoid implant threw him back into an existence where his life had purpose.

"All units!" cried a voice on the panic push. "The—"

The blast of static which drowned the voice lasted only a fraction of a second before the implant's logic circuits shut the unit down to keep the white noise from driving Jolober mad. The implant would be disabled as long as the jamming continued—but jamming of this intensity would block even the most sophisticated equipment in the Slammers' tanks.

Which were probably carrying out the jamming.

Jolober's hand slipped the knife away without thinking—with fiery determination not to think—as his stump kicked the chair into life and he glided toward the alley stairs. He was still dressed, still mounted in his saddle, and that was as much as he was willing to know about his immediate surroundings.

The stairs rang. The thrust of his fans was a fitful gust on the metal treads each time he bounced on his way to the ground.

The voice could have been Feldman at the gate;

she was the most likely source anyway. At the moment, Jolober had an emergency.

In a matter of minutes, it could be a disaster instead.

It was raining, a nasty drizzle which distorted the invitations capering on the building fronts. The street was empty except for a pair of patrol jeeps, bubbles in the night beneath canopies that would stop most of the droplets.

Even this weather shouldn't have kept soldiers from scurrying from one establishment to another, hoping to change their luck when they changed location. Overhanging façades ought to have been crowded with morose troopers, waiting for a lull—or someone drunk or angry enough to lead an exodus toward another empty destination.

The emptiness would have worried Jolober if he didn't have much better reasons for concern. The vehicles sliding down the street from the gate were unlighted, but there was no mistaking the roar of a tank.

Someone in the China Doll heard and understood the sound also, because the armored door squealed down across the archway even as Jolober's chair lifted him in that direction at high thrust.

He braked in a spray. The water-slicked pavement didn't affect his control, since the chair depended on thrust rather than friction—but being able to stop didn't give him any ideas about how he should proceed.

One of the patrol jeeps swung in front of the tank with a courage and panache which made Jolober proud of his men. The patrolman on the passenger side had ripped the canopy away to stand, waving a yellow light-wand with furious determination.

The tank did not slow. It shifted direction just enough to strike the jeep a glancing blow instead of center-punching it. That didn't spare the vehicle; its light frame crumpled like tissue before it resisted enough to spin across the pavement at twice the velocity of the slowly-advancing tank. The slight adjustment in angle did save the patrolmen, who were thrown clear instead of being ground between concrete and the steel skirts.

The tank's scarred turret made it identifiable in the light of the building fronts. Jolober crooked his finger and shouted, "Commandant to Corporal Days. For the *Lord's* sake, trooper, don't get your unit disbanded for mutiny! Colonel Hammer's already gotten Red Ike ordered off-planet!"

There was no burp from his mastoid as Central retransmitted the message a microsecond behind the original. Only then did Jolober recall that the Slammers had jammed his communications.

Not the Slammers alone. The two vehicles behind the tank were squat armored personnel carriers, each capable of hauling an infantry section with all its equipment. Nobody had bothered to paint out the fender markings of the Division Legere.

Rain stung Jolober's eyes as he hopped the last five meters to the sealed façade of the China Doll. Anything could be covered, could be settled, except murder—and killing Red Ike would be a murder of which the Bonding Authority would have to take cognizance.

"Let me in!" Jolober shouted to the door. The armor was so thick that it didn't ring when he pounded it. "Let me—"

Normally the sound of a mortar firing was audible for a kilometer, a hollow *shoomp!* like a firecracker going off in an oil drum. Jolober hadn't heard the launch from beyond the perimeter because of the nearby roar of drive fans.

When the round went off on the roof of the China Doll, the charge streamed tendrils of white fire down as far as the pavement, where they pocked the concrete. The snake-pit coruscance of blue sparks lighting the roof a moment later was the battery pack of Red Ike's aircar shorting through the new paths the mortar shell had burned in the car's circuitry.

The mercs were playing for keeps. They hadn't come to destroy the China Doll and leave its owner to rebuild somewhere else.

The lead tank swung in the street with the cautious delicacy of an elephant wearing a hoopskirt. Its driving lights blazed on, silhouetting the port commandant against the steel door. Jolober held out his palm in prohibition, knowing that if he could delay events even a minute, Red Ike would escape through his tunnel.

Everything else within the China Doll was a chattel which could be compensated with money.

There was a red flash and a roar from the stern of the tank, then an explosion muffled by a meter of concrete and volcanic rock. Buildings shuddered like sails in a squall; the front of the port offices cracked as its fabric was placed under a flexing strain that concrete was never meant to resist.

The rocket-assisted penetrators carried by the Slammers' tanks were intended to shatter bunkers of any thickness imaginable in the field. Red Ike's bolt-hole was now a long cavity filled with chunks and dust of the material intended to protect it.

The tanks had very good detection equipment, and combat troops live to become veterans by observing their surroundings. Quite clearly, the tunnel had not escaped notice when Tad Hoffritz led his company down the street to hoo-rah Paradise Port.

"Wait!" Jolober shouted, because there's always a chance until there's no chance at all.

"Get out of the way, Commandant!" boomed the tank's public address system, loudly enough to seem an echo of the penetrator's earth-shock.

"Colonel Hammer has—" Jolober shouted.

"We'd as soon not hurt you," the speakers roared as the turret squealed ten degrees on its gimbals. The main gun's bore was a twenty-CM tube aligned perfectly with Jolober's eyes.

They couldn't hear him; they wouldn't listen if they could; and anyway, the troopers involved in this weren't interested in contract law. They wanted justice, and to them that didn't mean a ticket off-planet for Red Ike.

The tribarrel in the tank's cupola fired a single shot. The bolt of directed energy struck the descending arch just in front of Jolober and gouged the plastic away in fire and black smoke. Bits of the covering continued to burn, and the underlying concrete added an odor of hot lime to the plastic and the ozone of the bolt's track through the air.

Jolober's miniature vehicle thrust him away in a flat arc, out of the door alcove and sideways in the street as a powergun fired from a port concealed in the China Doll's façade. The tank's main gun demolished the front wall with a single round.

The street echoed with the thunderclap of cold air filling the track seared through it by the energy bolt. The pistol shot an instant earlier could almost have been a proleptic reflection, confused in memory with the sun-bright cyan glare of the tank cannon—and, by being confused, forgotten.

Horace Jolober understood the situation too well to mistake its events. The shot meant Red Ike was still in the China Doll, trapped there and desperate enough to issue his Droids lethal weapons that must have been difficult even for *him* to smuggle into Paradise Port.

Desperate and foolish, because the pistol bolt had only flicked dust from the tank's iridium turret. Jolober had warned Red Ike that combat troops played by a different rulebook. The message just hadn't been received until it was too late. . . .

Jolober swung into the three-meter alley beside the China Doll. There was neither an opening here nor ornamentation, just the blank concrete wall of a fortress.

Which wouldn't hold for thirty seconds if the combat team out front chose to assault it.

The tank had fired at the building front, not the door. The main gun could have blasted a hole in the armor, but that wouldn't have been a large enough entrance for the infantry now deploying behind the armored flanks of the APCs.

The concrete wall shattered like a bomb when it tried to absorb the point-blank energy of the twenty-CM gun. The cavity the shot left was big enough to pass a jeep with a careful driver. Infantrymen in battle armor, hunched over their weapons, dived into the China Doll. The interior lit with cyan flashes as they shot everything that moved.

The exterior lighting had gone out, but flames clawed their way up the thermoplastic façade. The fire threw a red light onto the street in which shadows of smoke capered like demons. Drips traced blazing lines through the air as they fell to spatter troops waiting their turn for a chance to kill.

The assault didn't require a full infantry platoon, but few operations have failed because the attackers had too many troops.

Jolober had seen the equivalent too often to doubt how it was going to go this time. He didn't have long; very possibly he didn't have long enough.

Standing parallel to the sheer sidewall, Jolober ran his fans up full power, then clamped the plenum chamber into a tight nozzle and lifted. His left hand paddled against the wall three times. That gave him balance and the suggestion of added thrust to help his screaming fans carry out a task for which they hadn't been designed.

When his palm touched the coping, Jolober used the contact to center him, and rotated onto the flat roof of the China Doll.

Sparks spat peevishly from the corpse of the aircar. The vehicle's frame was a twisted wire sculpture from which most of the sheathing material had burned away, but occasionally the breeze brought oxygen to a scrap that was still combustible.

The penthouse that held Ike's office and living quarters was a squat box beyond the aircar. The mortar shell had detonated just as the alien started to run for his vehicle. He'd gotten back inside as the incendiary compound sprayed the roof, but bouncing fragments left black trails across the plush blue floor of the office.

The door was a section of wall broad enough to have passed the aircar. Red Ike hadn't bothered to close it when he fled to his elevator and the tunnel exit. Jolober, skimming again on ground effect, slid into the office shouting, "Ike! This—"

Red Ike burst from the elevator cage as the door rotated open. He had a pistol and eyes as wide as a madman's as he swung the weapon toward the hulking figure in his office.

Jolober reacted as the adrenaline pumping through his body had primed him to do. The arm with which he swatted at the pistol was long enough that his fingers touched the barrel, strong enough that the touch hurled the gun across the room despite Red Ike's deathgrip on the butt.

Red Ike screamed.

An explosion in the elevator shaft wedged the elevator doors as they began to close and burped orange flame against the far wall.

Jolober didn't know how the assault team proposed to get to the roof, but neither did he intend to wait around to learn. He wrapped both arms around the stocky alien and shouted, "Shut up and hold *still* if you want to get out of here alive!"

Red Ike froze, either because he understood the warning—or because at last he recognized Horace Jolober and panicked to realize that the port commandant had already disarmed him.

Jolober lifted the alien and turned his chair. It glided toward the door at gathering speed, logy with the double burden.

There was another blast from the office. The assault team had cleared the elevator shaft with a cratering charge whose directed blast sprayed the room with the bits and vapors that remained of the cage. Grenades would be next, then grappling hooks and more grenades just before—

Jolober kicked his throttle as he rounded the aircar. The fans snarled and the ride, still on ground effect, became greasy as the skirts lifted undesirably.

The office rocked in a series of dense white flashes. The room lights went out and a large piece of shrapnel, the fuze housing of a grenade, powdered a fist-sized mass of the concrete coping beside Jolober.

His chair's throttle had a gate. With the fans already at normal maximum, he sphinctered his skirts into a nozzle and kicked again at the throttle. He could smell the chair's circuits frying under the overload as it lifted Jolober and Red Ike to the coping—

But it did lift them, and after a meter's run along the narrow track to build speed, it launched them across the black, empty air of the alley.

Red Ike wailed. The only sound Horace Jolober made was in his mind. He saw not a roof but the looming bow of a tank, and his fears shouted the word they hadn't been able to get out on Primavera either: *"No!"*

They cleared the coping of the other roof with a click, not a crash, and bounced as Jolober spilled air and cut thrust back to normal levels.

An explosion behind them lit the night red and blew chunks of Red Ike's office a hundred meters in the air.

Instead of trying to winkle out their quarry with gunfire, the assault team had lobbed a bunker-buster up the elevator shaft. The blast walloped Jolober even though distance and the pair of meter-high concrete copings protected his hunching form from dangerous fragments.

Nothing in the penthouse of the China Doll could have survived. It wasn't neat, but it saved lives where they counted—in the attacking force—and veteran soldiers have never put a high premium on finesse.

"You saved me," Red Ike said.

Jolober's ears were numb from the final explosion, but he could watch Red Ike's lips move in the flames lifting even higher from the front of the China Doll.

"I had to," Jolober said, marvelling at how fully human the alien seemed. "Those men, they're line soldiers. They think that because there were so many of them involved, nobody can be punished."

Hatches rang shut on the armored personnel carriers. A non-com snarled an order to stragglers that could be heard even over the drive fans.

Red Ike started toward the undamaged aircar parked beside them on this roof. Jolober's left hand still held the alien's wrist. Ike paused as if to pretend his movement had never taken place. His face was emotionless.

"Numbers made it a mutiny," Jolober continued. Part of him wondered whether Red Ike could hear the words he was speaking in a soft voice, but he was unwilling to shout.

It would have been disrespectful.

Fierce wind rocked the flames as the armored vehicles, tank in the lead as before, lifted and began to howl their way out of Paradise Port.

"I'll take care of you," Red Ike said. "You'll have Vicki back in three weeks, I promise. Tailored to *you*, just like the other. You won't be able to tell the difference."

"There's no me to take care of any more," said Horace Jolober with no more emotion than a man tossing his uniform into a laundry hamper.

"You see," he added as he reached behind him, "if they'd killed you tonight, the Bonding Authority

would have disbanded both units *whatever* the Placidans wanted. But me? Anything I do is my responsibility."

Red Ike began to scream in a voice that became
progressively less human as the sound continued.

Horace Jolober was strong enough that he wouldn't
have needed the knife despite the way his victim
struggled.

But it seemed like a fitting monument for Vicki.

# JOHN DALMAS

## He's done it all!

*John Dalmas has just about done it all—parachute infantryman, army medic, stevedore, merchant seaman, logger, smokejumper, administrative forester, farm worker, creamery worker, technical writer, free-lance editor—and his experience is reflected in his writing. His marvelous sense of nature and wilderness combined with his high-tech world view involves the reader with his very real characters. For lovers of fast-paced action-adventures!*

## THE REGIMENT
The planet Tyss is so poor that it has only one resource: its fighting men. Each year three regiments are sent forth into the galaxy. And once a regiment is constituted, it never recruits again: as casualties mount the regiment becomes a battalion . . . a company . . . a platoon . . . a squad . . . and then there are none. But after the last man of *this* regiment has flung himself into battle, the Federation of Worlds will never be the same!

## THE WHITE REGIMENT
All the Confederation of Worlds wanted was a little peace. So they applied their personnel selection technology to war and picked the greatest potential warriors out of their planets-wide database of psych profiles. And they hired the finest mercenaries in the galaxy to train the first test regiment—they hired the legendary black warriors of Tyss to create the first ever White Regiment.

## THE KALIF'S WAR
The White Regiment had driven back the soldiers of the Kharganik empire, but the Kalif was certain that

he could succeed in bringing the true faith of the Prophet of Kargh to the Confederation—even if he had to bombard the infidels' planets with nuclear weapons to do it! But first he would have to thwart a conspiracy in his own ranks that was planning to replace him with a more tractable figurehead . . .

## FANGLITH
Fanglith was a near-mythical world to which criminals and misfits had exiled long ago. The planet becomes all too real to Larn and Deneen when they track their parents there, and find themselves in the middle of the Age of Chivalry on a world that will one day be known as Earth.

## RETURN TO FANGLITH
The oppressive Empire of Human Worlds, temporarily filed in *Fanglith*, has struck back and resubjugated its colony planets. Larn and Deneen must again flee their home. Their final object is to reach a rebel base—but the first stop is Fanglith!

## THE LIZARD WAR
A thousand years after World War III and Earth lies supine beneath the heel of a gang of alien sociopaths who like to torture whole populations for sport. But while the 16th century level of technology the aliens found was relatively easy to squelch, the mystic warrior sects that had evolved in the meantime weren't. . . .

## THE LANTERN OF GOD
They were pleasure droids, designed for maximum esthetic sensibility and appeal, abandoned on a deserted planet after catastrophic systems failure on their transport ship. After 2000 years undisturbed, "real" humans arrive on the scene—and 2000 thousand years of droid freedom is about to come to a sharp and bloody end.

## THE REALITY MATRIX
Is the existence we call life on Earth for real, or is it a game? Might Earth be an artificial construct designed by a group of higher beings? Is everything an illusion? Everything is—except the Reality Matrix. And what if self-appointed "Lords of Chaos" place a chaos generator in the matrix, just to see what will happen? Answer: The slow destruction of our world.

## THE GENERAL'S PRESIDENT
The stock market crash of 1994 makes Black Monday of 1929 look like a minor market adjustment—and the fabric of society is torn beyond repair. The Vice President resigns under a cloud of scandal—and when the military hints that they may let the lynch mobs through anyway, the President resigns as well. So the Generals get to pick a President. But the man they choose turns out to be more of a leader than they bargained for....

# Trouble in a Tutti-Frutti Hat

It was half past my hangover and a quarter to the hair of the dog when *she* ankled into my life. I could smell trouble clinging to her like cheap perfume, but a man in my racket learns when to follow his nose and when to plug it. She was brunette, bouncy, beautiful. Also fruity. Also dead.

I watched her size up my cabin with brown eyes big as dinner plates, motioned her into the only other chair in the room. Her hips redefined the structure of DNA en route to a soft landing on the tatty cushion. Then they went right through the cushion. Like I said, dead. A crossover sister, which means my crack about smelling trouble was just figurative. You never get the scent-input off of what you civvies'd call a ghost. Never thought I'd meet one in the figurative flesh. Not on Space Station Three. Even the dead have taste.

*What was Carmen Miranda doing on board Space Station Three?*

CARMEN MIRANDA'S GHOST IS HAUNTING SPACE STATION THREE, edited by Don Sakers Featuring stories by Anne McCaffrey, C.J. Cherryh, Esther Friesner, Melissa Scott & Lisa Barnett and many more. Inspired by the song by Leslie Fish. 69864-8 * $3.95

# FRED SABERHAGEN

Fred Saberhagen needs very little introduction these days. His most famous creations—the awesome Berserkers—are known to SF readers around the world. He's reached the bestseller lists several times, most recently with his "Book of Swords" series, and his novels span the territory from hard science fiction to high fantasy. Quite understandably, Saberhagen's been labeled one of the best writers in the business.

These fine volumes by Saberhagen are available from Baen Books:

## PYRAMIDS
A fascinating new twist on the time-travel novel, introducing a great new series hero: Pilgrim, the Flying Dutchman of Time, whose only hope for returning home lies in subtly altering the history of our own timeline to more closely reflect his own. Learn why the curse of the Pharaoh Khufu (builder of the Great Pyramid) had a special reality, in *Pyramids*. "Saberhagen's light, imaginative and enjoyable adventures speed along twisting paths to a climax that is even more surprising than the rest of the book."

—*Publishers Weekly*

## AFTER THE FACT
This is the second novel featuring the great new series hero, Pilgrim—the Lost Traveller adrift in time and dimensionality. His current project: to rescue Abraham Lincoln from assassination, AFTER THE FACT!

## THE FRANKENSTEIN PAPERS

At last—the truth about a sinister Dr. Frankenstein and his monster with a heart of gold, based on a history written by the monster himself! Find out what happened when the mad Doctor brought his creation to life, and why the monster has no scars.

## THE EMPIRE OF THE EAST

A masterful blend of high technology and high sorcery; a world where magic rules—and science struggles to live again! "Ranks favorably with Tolkien. Exceptional in sheer unbridled zest and imaginative sweep!—*School Library Journal* "*Empire of the East* is one of the best science fiction fantasy epics—Saberhagen can be justly proud. Highly recommended."
—*Science Fiction Chronicle*

## THE BLACK THRONE with Roger Zelazny

Two masters of SF collaborate on a masterpiece of fantasy: As children they met and built sand castles on a beach out of space and time: Edgar Perry, little Annie, and Edgar Allan Poe. . . . Fifteen years later Edgar Perry has grown to manhood—and as the result of a trip through a maelstrom, he's leading a much more active life. Perry will learn to thrive in the dark, romantic world he's landed in, where lead can be transmuted to gold, ravens can speak, orangutans can commit murder, and beautiful women are easy to come by. But his alter ego, Edgar Allan, is stranded in a strange and unfriendly world where he can only write about the wonderful and mysterious reality he has lost forever. . . .

## THE GOLDEN PEOPLE

Genetically perfect, super-human children are created by a dedicated scientist for the betterment of Mankind. As the children mature, however, they begin to wonder if Man *should* survive. . . .

## LOVE CONQUERS ALL

In a future where childbirth is outlawed and promiscuity required, one woman dares fight the system for the right to bear children.

## OCTAGON

Players scattered across the continent are engaged in a game called "Starweb." Each player has certain attributes, and can ally with or attack any of the others. But one player seems to have confused the reality of the world: a player with the attributes of machinelike precision and mechanical ruthlessness. His name is Octagon, and he's out for blood.

# AN OFFER HE COULDN'T REFUSE

They were functional fangs, not just decorative, set in a protruding jaw, with long lips and a wide mouth; yet the total effect was lupine rather than simian. Hair a dark matted mess. And yes, fully eight feet tall, a rangy, tense-muscled body.

She clawed her wild hair away from her face and stared at him with renewed fierceness. Her eyes were a strange light hazel, adding to the wolfish effect. "What are you *really* doing here?"

"I came for you. I'd heard of you. I'm ... recruiting. Or I was. Things went wrong and now I'm escaping. But if you came with me, you could join the Dendarii Mercenaries. A top outfit—always looking for a few good men, or whatever. I have this master-sergeant who ... who *needs* a recruit like you." Sgt. Dyeb was infamous for his sour attitude about women soldiers, insisting that they were too soft ...

"Very funny," she said coldly. "But I'm not even human. Or hadn't you heard?"

"Human is as human does." He forced himself to reach out and touch her damp cheek. "Animals don't weep."

She jerked, as from an electric shock. "Animals don't lie. Humans do. All the time."

"Not *all* the time."

"Prove it." She tilted her head as she sat cross-legged. "Take off your clothes."

". . . what?"

"Take off your clothes and lie down with me as *humans* do. Men and women." Her hand reached out to touch his throat.

The pressing claws made little wells in his flesh. "Blrp?" choked Miles. His eyes felt wide as saucers. A little more pressure, and those wells would spring forth red fountains. *I am about to die. . . .*

*I can't believe this. Trapped on Jackson's Whole with a sex-starved teenage werewolf. There was nothing about this in any of my Imperial Academy training manuals. . . .*

**BORDERS OF INFINITY by LOIS McMASTER BUJOLD**
**69841-9 • $3.95**